FOUR THREE TWO ONE

Also by Courtney Stevens
Faking Normal
The Lies About Truth
Dress Codes for Small Towns

COURTNEY STEVENS

FOUR THREE TWO ONE

HARPER TEEN
An Imprint of HarperCollinsPublishers

HarperTeen is an imprint of HarperCollins Publishers.

Four Three Two One
Copyright © 2018 by Courtney Stevens
All rights reserved. Printed in the United States of America. No part of this
book may be used or reproduced in any manner whatsoever without written
permission except in the case of brief quotations embodied in critical articles
and reviews. For information address HarperCollins Children's Books, a
division of HarperCollins Publishers, 195 Broadway, New York, NY 10007.
www.epicreads.com

Library of Congress Control Number: 2017057322
ISBN 978-0-06-239854-3

Typography by Torborg Davern
This book is set in 12-point Dante

18 19 20 21 22   CG/LSCH   10 9 8 7 6 5 4 3 2 1

First Edition

I object to violence because when it appears to do good, the good is only temporary; the evil it does is permanent.
—Mahatma Gandhi

The attempt and not the deed confounds us.
—William Shakespeare, *Macbeth*

For Joan Ledbetter, who said, "You got the softball and
writing from me," and Heath High School
Ruth 1:16

0.

BOOM.

It's a bus.

BOOM.

It's a New York City sidewalk. Brilliant fists of light punch and punch and keep punching. They grind me into the concrete like I am sirloin beneath a chef's hammer. My jaw is throbbing, the bone displaced. My blood pools in the perfect shape of a kidney bean. I am seven hundred miles from home.

BOOM.

It's a color that's not color at all; a color there's not a word for. Red? No, that's not right. Orange-yellow-red-blue. A near-rainbow. The shade of burning metal. The toxic stench of accelerant.

BOOM.

It's ash-black, hell-black wisps heading up, up, up into the sun. Aluminum confetti framed against the patina belfry of New Wesley Church. Raining metal. Raining body parts. A severed leg lands; a purple shoestring slaps my nose. The rest of that person (who is no longer a person; who is a torso wearing a once-red now-singed American Eagle tank top) lands on Chandler's back. Chan gasps, the breath beaten out of him. He is alive. I watch his chest rise and fall, rise and fall, to be certain.

BOOM.

It's the almost-car-crash smell. Friction. Heated rubber. Traffic grinding to a halt. There are screaming bystanders I can't hear because the nerves in my ear are damaged. The thin membranes ripped and bleeding. Phones upload initial videos. #busexplosion. The first dulled wail of a siren. Blue. White. Blue. White. "Kid! Kid! Are you all right?"

BOOM.

It's Rudy on the ground. The laughter on his pink lips replaced with blood. Trickling like crimson paint spilled on the wall of his cheek. Trickling. Down his chin. Onto his neck. Into the collar of his shirt. Twelve hours ago, he smelled of lemons and cheap IPA. His mouth is open, closed, open again. He's screaming. My ears hear the void, the suction. They hear fear.

BOOM.

It's four survivors. I think I am one of them.

1. **Measure twice, cut once.**

$0

The first secret Chan kept from me was our eleventh birthday party.

We were paired, even back then. Our birthdays fell days apart, and all three parents were pleased with one *Happy Birthday, Golden and Chandler* cake, one gathering, one table of gifts. I assumed we'd dodged the pizza-and-ice-cream-for-twenty bullet when the two dates arrived and passed with zero fanfare, but no. The following Saturday came, and with it, adults ducked frantically behind too-small recliners and overstuffed couches, and kids yelled "Surprise!" in the pale afternoon light of Gran's living room. I soldiered through merrily enough, until Chan let slip our surprise party didn't surprise him. His

4

dad warned him the day before so Chan could *plan an appropriate attitude*. His father's words were altogether fair; Chan was absolute shit at handling surprises. As I was not absolute shit at handling surprises, I was not told. Chan reasoned the secret was for my own good, to which I said (and rather indignantly), "*Chan*, it's supposed to be us against the world."

"Are you serious about that?"

"As a heart attack," I said. (That phrase felt like a ten-pointer at the time.)

Chan tucked his fingers into his armpits and stretched the University of Kentucky basketball jersey to bursting. Back before his growth spurt, he was the boy who slammed home runs in PE, and none of the girls wanted to sit with him at lunch. He released his right hand from his armpit and spit in his palm. The lines and creases filled with blue cakey spittle. "Chandler and Golden versus the world?"

Our saliva mixed. "Chandler and Golden versus the world," I repeated.

The promise was legit. Six years later, Chan and I were still running hard, side by side. He was significantly more fetching than he'd been at eleven and still allergic to sudden changes. I was me. That is to say, a relatively resilient soul who worked well with the Chans of the world. (I hadn't grown much prettier though, so the exchange rate was fairly even.)

He was nursing another secret tonight, sipping it slow, making me watch.

He wasn't exactly gloating—he wasn't the type—but he

was intensely pleased with whatever trap he planned to spring. I spotted this thing, whatever it was, the moment we got home from school. Chan didn't usually commandeer our kitchen. Chan didn't usually invite the Hive, the entire Hive, to dinner at my place. The expense alone was cringeworthy. And Chan didn't usually plan celebrations when there was nothing to celebrate. For ten months we'd been devoid of events that required crystal goblets and place settings for twenty-seven, and then out of the blue, wham, "I'm throwing a party and you have to be there."

I really should have changed out of my ripped jeans.

Then again, Chan wore festive pot holders he'd sewn himself, printed with bright yellow rubber ducks. There was flour on his cheek and a handsome amount of steam on his glasses from opening the oven door. The hat he always wore when he wasn't at school, a rock-star cowboy job, was on the counter. "Chan, you look forty," I said, even though he didn't. He looked happy—and not the manufactured expression he donned to keep people from asking him what was wrong either. I prodded him with a spatula. "Don'tcha want to tell me what all this fuss is about?"

"What fuss?"

"All this." I waved at the entirety of the kitchen.

"Can't a guy do something nice for his girlfriend?"

"Uh, no," I said, dutifully frowning.

"Too bad. You'll just have to wait," he said, and then tickled me until I curled like a Cheeto on the kitchen hardwood.

Maybe I shouldn't have, but I side-eyed his playfulness, tried to examine what this happy streak might mean. Chan was not a tickler. He was a "measure twice, cut once" woodworker, the sort of person who said "Teamwork makes the dream work" with a straight face. He even used microfiche at the library *for pleasure*. Back before we went to New York, he memorized the entire subway system. "In case our phones die," he had said. *Because he is him*, I thought, knowing subway maps would be posted on the walls. I'd even gotten on the plane without my cell phone cord, which wasn't a problem, because he'd packed a spare.

"Golden," Mom said, "be kind to this boy. Your father has trouble boiling water."

I'd forgotten she was here, even though she was standing in the kitchen, stirring the gravy.

"Yeah, be kind to the boy making Hipponite delight," Chan chided.

Mom groaned. "I wish you wouldn't use that term."

"Right?" I echoed Mom's disgust. "He says *Hipponite* and I check the pantry for Kool-Aid and cyanide."

"Hive Delight doesn't have a pleasing rhythm," he said.

Chan claimed *Hipponite* was a tidy expression for us on-Hive folks, as we were a bit of hippie idealism without the rock music and drugs, and a bob of Mennonite without the horses and religion. I'd explained repeatedly that his description didn't make sense. If you casually said *commune*, you would be correct, even though Gran preferred the term *social*

experiment. We were the pound, if the pound were for stray people instead of dogs. Except we didn't put anyone down if no one came to claim them.

At any given time, we had twenty to forty regulars living on-property. Everyone worked. Everyone shared. And because of this, everyone had enough, when in other scenarios, they hadn't. Folks around Braxton Springs, Kentucky, found our living arrangement intriguing or they thought we were nuts. Say what you will, the Hive was a helluva place to live. Among our current motley crew, we had two midwives, three homesteaders, and a family I'd swear on a stack of Bibles was in witness protection. The kitchen where we stood was once the fellowship hall of a Methodist chapel built in 1923. If you held normalcy in one hand and character in the other, I could promise you which one filled up faster.

Chan washed his hands at the island, reached across the counter to where I was messing with my camera, and tugged on a ringlet of my hair. The blond strands rebounded with the vigor of an overfilled basketball. "Did you know," Chan said, "it takes three hundred and fifty ears of wheat to make a loaf of bread?"

"Did you know you're a weirdo?"

"But I'm your weirdo, right?"

I pulled my toes under my knees and straightened my spine, exhaled for show. It should have been easy to tell him yes. Or . . . for him to avoid asking the question. But he'd been seeking my constant reassurance since June, and I was tempted

to tell him he was eight gallons of crazy in a five-gallon bucket for not trusting me. Steering a conversation was like steering a horse. Words, the bit. Our inflection, the reins. The mood turned whenever we gave the leathers a hard yank to the left.

I gave the conversation a significant tug. "You know the answer to that, Chan."

Chan stuck his head in the oven and peeled back the aluminum foil from the roast, basting the kitchen in smells of onions and salted meat. "Fifteen more minutes," he said, his voice husky and frustrated. He slammed the oven door a little too hard, plopped on the stool, and crossed his long legs at the ankles. Everything on him looked crossed. He'd developed a habit of lacing his arms like a pretzel when he was stressed, and he was doing that now.

I walked over, kissed his knuckles firmly, and said, "Thank you for fixing me dinner."

Chan untangled his arms and returned to his rolling pin and dough.

This meal would be perfect. Chan had seen to that with his meticulous grocery lists and charts of what must come out of the oven at 6:05 and reenter by 6:07 with a brushing of butter. But I longed to retreat to my room and let the party go on without me. *Accelerant Orange*, an online video series about the bombing of Bus #21, was dropping a new episode at eight. The show host had hinted at a big announcement for tonight, but . . . I couldn't exactly excuse myself from a party at *my* house with *my* family and friends that *my* boyfriend was throwing. So

we followed Chan's extensive charts. Mom dimmed the lights to a romantic setting. Dad filled plastic goblets with sparkling grape. I lit tea candles in the old church windowsills, bathing the room in shadows that made missing the episode slightly more palatable. As the Hive arrived, everyone chatted loosely like they'd had wine. We ate off chargers and real china. Freshly polished silver. Holiday treatment on a Monday evening in April. It was quite lovely, this thing Chan had planned.

Eight o'clock came and went.

When only cake crumbs dressed the plates, Chandler scooted his chair away from the table. The claw feet screeched against the hardwood and the Hive turned in our direction. People giggled nervously when Chan crashed into the low-hanging lamp with his forehead and displaced his glasses. Mom gave him a discreet thumbs-up—which he couldn't see at the time with his 20/600 vision, but I did. He righted the frames and clinked his fork against my water glass. The room responded with silence.

"Everyone." I inched my fingers closer to Chan's on the table, knowing that would steady him. "Go and I were lucky last June."

My eyes rocketed to Chan's, startled. My inside thoughts making their way outside. He gave me a half wink. A very casual *It's okay, I promise.*

One of the smaller kids whispered loudly, "What happened in June?" and another slightly older child said, "You know," and mimicked an explosion.

Chan pumped my arm. "It has been ten months—"

"Right," I said, sending him strength.

"And . . . I really don't want to talk about it or think about it ever again. I want to focus all my energy on a new plan. Start the process of moving on." He clasped his sweat-drenched hands around mine. "That means making you a promise, Go."

Chan and I had made plenty of promises to each other over the years. Not to cheat. Not to lie. Not to watch episodes of *Supergirl* without each other. None of those required four-course meals.

"Around here"—Chan's eyes swept to Gran and then drifted to a stained glass window where an old Methodist cross was still mounted—"when a promise is especially important we make it official. Gran?"

I bit through the nail on my index finger so loudly my teeth clicked together. I usually liked Hive rituals. Promises made here were harder to break, and there was something special invoked by formality and history. But creeds were markedly better when they didn't involve Chan or me.

Gran hunched when she stood, her paisley button-up shirt exposing fine wrinkles around her collarbone. She was still so regal, so glorious, with her watery blue eyes and silky white hair pulled into a loose bun. One hand raised to the ceiling, she spoke with complete authority. "A community like ours would never last without public accountability and trust. Early on, we established ceremonial rhetoric for big life events: moving on or off Hive, weddings, funerals, business decisions, etcetera.

We did this to honor and respect each person who abides here. By invoking Hive language, Chandler, you're making a promise before your family and friends. Are you certain you are ready to give your word?"

Chan straightened his back. "I am."

There were more required words for Chan to repeat. For the community too. As the formality finished, Chan removed a blue felt box from his pocket and lifted the lid. The ring inside was an antique or a copy of an antique. Two yellow-gold interlinking hearts studded with a speck diamond. Probably a quarter of a quarter of a carat.

"What do you say, Go?" he asked shyly. "Someday, would you want to make a good thing a sure thing?"

My cousin had asked his girlfriend to marry him in a very similar fashion two years ago, but they were in their twenties and had real jobs. This wasn't an engagement—there was a different creed for that—but it was certainly a preengagement-shaped thing, and Chan, asking right now—before we graduated or voted—felt way off in left field. Totally flattering in a *my boyfriend really loves me* way, but also quite strange.

"I . . ."

There was our age. There was the shift in our chemistry since last June. And there was the fact that three days ago, I'd been worried he was ending things between us.

"I . . ."

I had very little time to screw my face into something resembling a smile. Stalling, I said, "Uh, well . . . you really

are forty tonight." And then I swatted him with my napkin to buy myself a private thought. The napkin batting made everyone chuckle and one of the kids chanted, "Chan and Golden sitting in a tree," and my mother said something to the effect of, "Who here had their forever sweetheart locked in by eighteen? Let's see a show of hands." She was proud, luminescent as the bug zapper on the back porch. Dad, who rarely spoke unless it was to yell at the television during a University of Kentucky basketball game or to read poetry to his cows (not a joke), raised my camera, a used Canon, and snapped a picture of Chan lifting the box to my hand. That could have been at Mom's instruction, but maybe not—the guy read Wendell Berry to his bull.

Only Gran looked twitchy and unimpressed.

I leaned close to Chan's ear, planted a kiss against his lips, and said, so only he could hear, "I wish you'd told me," and he said, so only I could hear, "I tried three days ago." This close, his anxiety beat against me like a hammer. He reached back in time and found a phrase. "Chan and Golden versus the world?"

I nodded. I owed him that and much more.

The world, it turned out, was a fairly large opponent.

2. In a perfect universe

$0

After the dishes were washed and the silver was polished and returned to the sideboard, I walked Chan home. The night air was a towel taken out of the dryer too soon. Warm and damp. We were quiet, neither of us broaching the blazing-hot topic of the evening. I was soaking in thoughts and pruny from the effort. We were nearly to his door, and I came right out with my question. "Why in the world would you do that?"

"Because I love you."

"And?"

"No and."

Despite being one great big bounding teenaged love story with all the bells and whistles and firsts, loving me wasn't

the only reason he'd asked. I was certain. Sometimes a voice was like a deep, deep cave. Most parts, you've explored and mapped, but there are always uncharted sections. I knew what Chan sounded like when he was excited, happy, angry, hurt, worried, delighted; he was none of those now. He was something else entirely, and I had no idea what.

He laughed uneasily, the whole thing so very backward that I felt outside of myself. "I guess you're stuck with me now, Golden Jennings," he said, fiddling with a button.

"Guess so."

And we stared at each other oddly, and he went inside and I walked home. No kiss. No conversation. No text to say, *Sorry that was strange as hell.* We didn't even exchange our nightly *I love yous.* I certainly didn't think we'd stopped loving each other, but understanding each other . . . that appeared to be a problem.

At home, I placed my sparkling new ring in the bathroom soap dish and collapsed resentfully at my desk. I was so out of it I didn't hear Gran climbing the steps. She leaned halfway into my room. "Are we watching or do you need a break after that meal?"

She avoided the word *engagement.* I was grateful she let the whole thing breathe and waved her inside. Gran shut the door and I opened tonight's episode of *Accelerant Orange.* Sitting shoulder to shoulder with her, connected by a shared pair of earbuds, I felt better than I had all evening. Mom thinks we're watching Miyazaki films, because sometimes we do, but really

we're obsessed with this inexplicable event in my life that is so bizarre, we, along with millions of other followers, can view its footage from any Wi-Fi connection in the world. Actors must feel similarly when they watch a movie they've starred in. Viewing the experience on the same thirteen-inch screen where I watched Netflix and cat videos built mental distance, but it also presented the delusion that Bus #21 wasn't about *my* life. But it was. It really, really was.

I hovered over the Play button. "You ready?"

"Are you?"

"What do you think the announcement is?"

She twirled a diamond stud in her ear, which made me think of the diamond ring in my soap dish. "You never know with Carter."

Carter Stockton was one of those men with an Evinrude boat and a John Deere Gator in his garage. He had a Southern accent that pleased instead of grated, and a mouth buried under a mustache built for two. Gran thought he looked like a young Lionel Richie, and when I googled the singer, I saw what she meant.

I pressed Play. The opening screen read: Accelerant Orange *is one New York City medic's attempt to craft the remnants of Charter Bus #21 into a life-size art installment.*

This was episode 45. The title flashed: "Opening Day."

I clutched the center of my T-shirt. Beside me, Gran gripped the laminate edge of the desk. "He's done. He's finished it," she said.

The camera zoomed in on a street sign outside the Green-Conwell Hotel and then back to Carter. "Hey, y'all," he said. "For you out-of-towners, or those who missed episode two, I'm standing in front of the Green-Conwell Hotel with a big announcement. Before I get to that, thank you, folks, for following this difficult journey." Carter took a sip from his Venti cup and sighed in a way that made the world sigh along. "In a perfect universe, you wouldn't know me and this series wouldn't have a half-million followers, but here we are. Doing our best to honor the families of Charter Bus Number Twenty-one."

Gran squeezed my hand. I squeezed right back. There was always a lot of hand squeezing that went on during these things. Plus, she had a little crush on Carter, and I can't say I blamed her.

"People ask why I've spent so much time and money working on this project. I gotta tell you, I didn't know myself at first. I saw rubble and ruin licking my streets last June and thought, *Carter, somebody needs to do something.* And you know how it is. Something became *Accelerant Orange*, and somebody became me. Every now and then stories climb inside you and start telling themselves."

Someone bumped into Carter and the image jarred. There was no "Sorry, sir." New York bustled by on her way somewhere else. The camera caught the shuffle of air and an Alabama medic smoothing his mustache.

"I hope you've enjoyed my interviews with the families. It's

been a while since I showed you progress on the bus itself, and I'm hoping that means people will attend opening day. Which brings me to my big announcement. The mayor of New York and the manager of the Green-Conwell have asked me to move the installment." Carter panned down the street. "To here."

I was transported in an instant.

I am on my back. The city rises around me. The sky is warm gray haze. The sun is the color of buttercream icing. I try to place where I am. Buildings: 1920s architecture. Art deco arches with polished ivory pastiche. The Green-Conwell. Thousands of interlaced clay bricks forming dulled red walls. The muted patina trim racing along its elegant rooflines. New Wesley Church. Bicycles bumping and thumping over metal plates in the street. The closest street cart: falafel platter, half chicken, half lamb over rice, for $7.99. Starbucks coffee sleeves, trash bags piled in heaps, pedestrians crossing streets before the sign changes. Dogs on leashes.

Everything pauses like a movie. Everything except the blood.

I am not at home. I am in New York City. There was an explosion.

Gran twisted a lock of my hair around her finger and I leaped back to the present, where Carter was still speaking through my computer. "We're gonna block off the street and sell tickets.

You'll be able to walk through the bus and see what each family has donated to remember these precious kids. All the ticket sales will benefit them.

"Speaking of money. From your emails, I'm aware many of you can't make the opening in person and you're champing to do something good. As you know, there are four survivors of Bus Twenty-one. They're teenagers who should be thinking about what movie to see on Friday night instead of how to recover from an explosion. I got to know one of them through this process, and he's a remarkable young man. In fact, this display wouldn't be possible without his help."

"Not Chan," Gran said.

Not Chan. The survivor helping Carter would need the spine of a sea urchin or a hedgehog. When it came to Bus #21, Chan had the exoskeleton of a cicada, crunchy and firm, and easily pulverized. "Must be Rudy."

Carter kept talking. "This community can do something special for him, for all four of them. I asked myself, what did I need at that age? The answer was simple. Money for college. So, I'm starting a donation fund between now and the opening—the web address is on your screen—and I'll make sure every dollar is split evenly among all four survivors. I believe the people who are watching *Accelerant Orange* can invest in these young people and remind them we believe their future is more powerful than their past."

I paused the show. My emotions usually hung from

shipshape shelves like a freshly stocked vending machine, and now, they were . . . not shipshape. In fact, they bore the disheveled look of a thing that would never be shipshape again. Like a dump. Or preschoolers working forty puzzles on a brightly carpeted rug.

Gran and I faced each other. Her eyes were soupy with tears. "People are going to give," she said.

"No," I said. *Accelerant Orange* was like rubbernecking an accident on the highway; everyone turned to see, hardly anyone cared enough to pull over and help.

"I'll start." Gran seized control of my keyboard, opened a separate screen, and typed the address Carter listed. She put *one hundred dollars* into the account—the account that had already climbed to four thousand dollars in seconds—while I watched. I usually got twenty dollars in cash for my birthday. But a hundred dollars? That was steep love.

"You didn't have to do that."

"I did." She clicked back to the show.

Carter was wrapping up his spiel. "I'm humbly asking you to join me on this Sunday afternoon, April fifteenth, in front of the Green-Conwell to see *Accelerant Orange* in person."

This Sunday.

Bus #21. Back on the street.

"I'm gonna close the way I always do, with one addition. To the four survivors, I'm here. If you want to talk or you need to discuss this project or you'd like to be involved, email me

at busmedic421@wipturn.net. I'd love for you to be here to receive the college fund in person. If you can't, we here at *Accelerant Orange* love you and believe in you. Thanks, y'all, and I hope to see everyone this Sunday."

Cut to black.

3. Leave the FAFSA unmailed.

$4,128.00

Gran wiped her earbud clean with the inside of her shirt. "Do you want to go?" she asked.

"To college, or to the opening?"

"Yes and yes."

"I don't know." I did know about college—yes—but the opening? She might as well have asked me if I'd considered living on Mars.

There were noises in the hallway. Gran lowered her voice conspiratorially. "Think about your real answer. I'll talk to your wardens." She giggled at calling my parents wardens, and I did too. They weren't strict, per se, but they'd grown particular about me adventuring too far from the nest.

Mom knocked, and before I said "Come in," she poked her head through the door wearing that same light, breezy happiness she'd had since dinner. "You two have fun watching TV?" she asked, to which Gran said, "I believe that was my favorite so far."

Slowly, Gran uncoiled the Tums roll she carried in her pants pocket, popped a chalky tablet into her mouth, and added, "Something at dinner gave me indigestion." She disappeared into the hallway, and I steadied my face into an expression that wouldn't make Mom think we were up to something. But Gran was always scheming. She'd started a commune, for God's sake. And now she wanted me to consider college or New York, and I . . . I wanted my mother to leave so my brain could be alone.

She was after a second viewing of Chan's ring.

"In the bathroom," I told her.

She disappeared, and the faucet ran—a dull white noise followed by a spritzing sound. Comet. She was cleaning scum from the soap dish. "You'll have to be careful with the gold," she yelled.

"Gold doesn't tarnish," I yelled back.

"Won't tarnish, but it dulls."

I drummed my fingers on the desk. "Noted."

Mom was supposed to be sitting on the edge of my bed saying things like "Now, baby, are you sure about this thing with Chan?" Or "Don't make Kentucky or the Hive a stereotype." Or "You've got your whole life ahead of you. No rushing."

Instead, she returned to my room moony, twirling her own wedding ring around her finger.

"He picked something classy."

I leaned toward my computer, hoping I looked uninterested. "Yep."

"A promise isn't a marriage."

"No, it's not."

"But I . . ." She *tsk*ed. She was the queen of *tsks*.

"What, Mom?"

"I can't help but think stability would be good for you. After everything that's happened."

"Stability like early marriage?"

"Your father and I got married when we were your age. Gran and Granddad too. It's not that strange for you to be thinking long-term when you're surrounded by people who have done it successfully."

"So you're for this? Balls to the wall; go get married."

"That's not what I said, honey."

"What did you say?" I was aware I had acquired a slight growl, and given the circumstances, it didn't seem disrespectful.

"Don't put words in my mouth," she said. "I was simply stating that your relationship with Chan has always been solid, and I want solid things for your life. That doesn't have to be marriage, early or late, with Chan or without, but never underestimate a good man to love and a great place to live." There were no windows in my room, no way to point to a specific

location, but she gestured widely with her arms, and I understood she meant the Hive.

She wanted to keep me here. No big surprise. Kids raised in the Hive often stayed in the Hive. They learned a trade or an art form and they invested in the neighborly family who had invested in them. There were no repercussions for those who didn't follow suit; we weren't a dangerous, insidious cult or anything, but there was pressure to leave the FAFSA unmailed, on the kitchen table, for a very long time.

"What about a career? College?"

"You could commute. Take online classes? I think we could help you swing the cost of PCC, maybe. Your art is already very good, honey. You could open a shop and sell prints like gangbusters."

Did people still sell things like gangbusters? I didn't think so, and certainly not from a commune in the middle of nowhere, Kentucky. I jumped right to the heart of the matter. "Maybe the world's not so bad out there, Mom."

"Oh, sweetie." She gave a soft, haughty laugh and flattened the wide cuff of her capri pants until it rested against her calf. "You of all people know how bad it can be."

I chose not to answer, and she chose to smooth my comforter, which was already military straight. After which, she moved on to my headboard, searching for something to do that would keep her wisdom and influence in my domain for another few moments. Atop the right wooden post was a stack of red beanies. She wove her fingers into the loose fabric of the

topmost beanie as if testing its moral fiber. "What you guys have, what you nearly lost"—she suppressed a sigh that always came when a reference to New York was made—"what we all nearly lost . . . is it wrong for me to want you to spend the rest of your life feeling safe and loved?"

As had always been true, agreeing with my mother was the only way to get rid of her. "You're right, Mom. Now, I really need to finish this paper." I angled my computer screen toward the opposite wall and nodded toward the door, since she seemed to have grown roots.

"Don't stay up too late," she said.

I was finally alone. Not totally alone. Gran's voice was still there. *Do you want to go? Do you want to go? Do you want to go?* What if I did?

I opened an email window. Forty-four times Carter Stockton had invited me to reach out, and forty-four times I'd ignored him.

Dear Mr. Stockton,
My name is Golden Jennings and I survived Bus #21.
I've been following *Accelerant Orange,* and I'd like to talk.

CAROLINE

I was eating takeout from Taco Bell when bombs surfaced in their conversation the first time. Someone, maybe Johnny, maybe Dozer, had seen fifteen minutes of *The Hurt Locker* on TNT and wouldn't shut up about it. There was some discussion of whether you had to be batshit or just not give a damn if you worked with bombs. I took another bite of a chicken quesadilla that needed more sauce and wished my homework would finish itself.

Simon said, "Bombs are unpredictable."

And because I was testing my boundaries or nauseously tired I said, "Bombs are pure science."

Pure science is the wrong phrase to describe what I meant, but that's what I said, so I can't change it now. I meant bombs are systemic. Reliable. At least, that's what my chemistry

teacher drilled into our brains during a section on chemical reactions. Therefore, one could be perfectly sane, care about the dignity of life, and be a bomb maker. The army employed bros like that all the time.

"Normal people make bombs. Crazy people set them off," I told the guys.

Simon paused the game and looked away from the screen. "Okay, little Miss *Pure Science*, tell us how to make a bomb."

"Potassium and sugar."

"That's a heavy-ass redneck bomb. What if it needs to be portable?"

"Google homemade C-Four and start from there."

"Really?"

"No, asshole. I'm pretty sure you have to buy C-Four, and the government doesn't take too kindly to purchasers."

I shouldn't have called Simon an asshole. Not then. Not ever. Such brazen behavior led to "corrections" makeup couldn't easily cover. As such, I didn't ask why three dude-bros wanted portable bombs. I pretended I was bored with the conversation and buried my nose in Conrad's *Heart of Darkness*. Surprisingly enough, they went back to their game and Doritos.

They crunched chips. Between the pages, I crunched ideas for ridding my life of Simon and came up empty. He had me over a never-ending barrel. Kids like us were mostly left among the housekeepers to raise ourselves, but two weeks ago, our fathers—*the Westwoods and Ascotts go back three generations*—informed us we would be attending the University of Rochester

together and we would be sharing a house.

"It's an investment," his father said of the half-million-dollar property we were to consider a dorm.

My father had chuckled and said, "It's a tax break." How very convenient.

There's a disconnect that happens when you know your parents love money and wine more than they love you. It keeps you from saying, "Daddy, I'd rather not live with a psychopath."

Simon and the boys ate another bag of Doritos and chased it with pints of ice cream. I read the same page of my book over and over. Eventually, Dozer ran to the Hornell GameStop for some update and Johnny left to score from his brother. The second their footfalls disappeared down the steps, the atmosphere in the boathouse attic shifted. A chill tiptoed along my arms and crawled all the way to my ear canals. The game paused, some *Fallout* character lunged mid-screen, and I knew what would happen when I turned my head.

Simon stood statue-like at my side, waiting on me to give him attention. There was a foot-long PVC plumbing pipe in his hand.

When I think of Simon, I think of hard edges and razor corners, but he was very visually soft. He had a round Angus Macfadyen face and a stomach that bulged between the buttons when he sat. Oddly enough, he'd collected me with those unassuming looks—the guy you swore couldn't be controlling because he wasn't beautiful and shiny. I was in too deep by

the time I realized he'd charmed my parents and memorized all our security codes. Sometimes he would touch my hair or stroke my wrist or say he loved me, and then the threats would come. Not coldly, not cruelly, never like a villain. Just statements. "You betray me, and I can be in and out of here before your last shit begins to smell." I nearly told my mom, but she launched into a soliloquy of why the Westwoods were vital to Ascotts in the wine world and how she grew up dirt-poor and couldn't ever go back, so I never did.

He dug his fingernails into the skin around my elbow. His breath cannoned into his cheek, each word precise and laced with delight. "Hey, Pure Science."

"Yes."

I braced for a blow.

"I bet you can't make a bomb."

"There's a big difference between can't and won't," I said.

"Didn't your mom ever tell you *can't* and *won't* never did anything?"

4. The Upper Organ Pipe Chamber

$12,345.30

When we moved into the chapel there was a mounted plaque beside what would become my bedroom door: Upper Organ Pipe Chamber. I decided to leave the wall of exposed pipes jutting through the floor—the Swell Division is the formal name—and I mounted the finicky brass plate to the door. With a renovation like ours—the slow, one-room-as-we-can-afford-it kind—I could have picked a boring square Sunday school room with more space, but here, I was surrounded by a deluge of old music and tradition. The organ could not be "played" anymore, but the honk that emitted was an all-encompassing, out-of-tune blast of air that dusted my room with the grit of God, Jesus, and the Holy Spirit. Dad occasionally struck the

keys to be funny when Chan and I were alone in my room.

Living with Bus #21 was like rooming inside the Upper Organ Pipe Chamber.

Most of the time the brute stayed dormant, but you never knew when it would sound off and scare the bejesus out of you.

The time ticked from 4:00 to 4:01.

Were Rudy Guthrie or Caroline Ascott awake at that very minute? I prayed for the families of the other victims, questioning if grief moved among them like the creeping minute hand of a clock. 4:01 to 4:02. Was a mother in New Jersey lying on pink-and-purple-striped sheets, squeezing a Pillow Pet named Zippity Zebra, wishing she could bring herself to wash her daughter's smell from the tear-soaked stuffed animal? 4:02 to 4:03. Did some father in New York trace the angles of a dry-cleaned suit, recalling that the last time he wore his black-and-gray tie was to his son's funeral? 4:04. Down the lane, was Chandler Clayton lying stock-still, interrogating God?

Did they know about *Accelerant Orange*?

Did they know $12,345.30 was in Carter Stockton's college fund?

Did they think about me thinking about them?

4:05 a.m.

I got up.

In ten minutes, I worked all the necessary maintenance to myself and crossed our yard to Gran's. She wouldn't be awake yet, but she wouldn't mind if I accidentally woke her. After Granddad died, she put a twin bed on the sunporch, which

meant I could visit her previous bedroom with minimal footfall. The house was familiarly warm and smelled of Bengay, cedar, and an orange-scented cleaning product. In every room there was a clock that ticked and a piece of art that had started its life as an ox yoke or a horseshoe or a watering can. Useful things on their second run of usefulness. I couldn't stomach the clutter in such a small house, but I also couldn't imagine her place any other way.

The space to the right of Gran's closet was covered wall-to-wall in photos. The run-of-the-mill wedding, baby, life montage hung in the living room, but this wall was my grandparents' semisecret stash. Them pretending to be Ginger Rogers and Fred Astaire. There are dozens of famous couplings. Bonnie and Clyde. Scarlett and Rhett. Ilsa and Rick from *Casablanca*. (A classic I've seen rather than pretended I've seen, like people sometimes do.) Gran sewed the costumes and, believe it or not, Granddad did their makeup. The photos traveled through time. The crow's-feet grew long and deep.

The last photo wasn't framed. The snapshot got shoved into the edge of the dresser mirror. The edges were dented and dinged, as if Gran held it frequently.

Their relationship was written in grainy black-and-white squares with cheap, dusty frames. I'd fallen in love with falling in love in this room. Gran said their obsession started when *the family camera*—that's what she called the No. 3 Autographic Kodak, because families didn't own multiple cameras—was damaged in 1968. All the prints contained a strange ghostly

shape in the corner. Granddad didn't have the money to replace or repair the camera, so he consoled his young bride with promises to make art instead of memories. They'd made both.

This enigmatic display became who they were and how they spent their spare time. Now, many years later, beside every photo of Gran and Granddad, there was another photo taped to the frame. Those were the images I'd wanted to see this morning. They were of Chan and me. We'd replicated each of their replications. All with the family No. 3 Kodak.

Well, all but one.

The picture Gran and Granddad made in New York at Ellis Island.

The picture Chan and I were hoping to re-create the day the world blew up.

"You could take him with you," Gran said from the doorway. "Get the last photo. Finish the project."

The No. 3 was lost in the explosion. "We wouldn't have your camera."

"So use yours."

"Who says I'm going back?"

"Me."

"Like I have the money."

"Use your greenhouse money." I grew plants in our greenhouse and sold them at the farmers' market from spring to fall. It wasn't lucrative, but there was a small nest egg in my checking account.

She left my retort alone and shot a hair rubber band at my

chest. "Let me put on my boulder holder and grab some coffee. We'll go take photos better than these."

Fifteen minutes later Gran and I were at the pond shore armed with my Canon, a straightened wire coat hanger, and some steel wool. The shot was for vanity. One I'd seen in a magazine. I'd exhausted things around here to shoot. Hawks and eagles. Moles and squirrels. Beavers. Butterflies. Dew drops. Spiderwebs. Old dilapidated buildings. Barns. I'd shot them all.

I explained that she needed to twirl like a ballerina for a thirty-second exposure shot. She explained she'd have to douse herself in an aspirin bath later, but I was worth it.

"When I say go, light the steel wool and spin the hanger in a circle."

"Dizzy before daylight. That's how I like things."

Rings of sparks sprayed the ground. I snapped and then just watched her dance. People are such a delight when they're fully alive. The image was a whirl of bright orangey-yellow light trails and umbrella-shaped flickers landing on the beaten grass. It resembled the long-exposure photos I'd seen of amusement park rides.

Gran fanned her sleeping gown like royalty. "How was I, darling?"

"Oh, like always, you were on fire."

"Good to know I still have it."

In spades.

Not long ago, Dad and I were on our way to a Saturday-

morning swap meet and he dialed down Green Day and told me he really thought I'd rebounded from the bombing better than he would have. And then he said, "You know, I think you get that from Mom." I've thought about that a lot. I don't feel rebounded, not in the slightest, but I do think having someone like Gran in my life makes it easier to keep living a full life with a damaged past rather than a damaged life.

In the still-dark, we packed my equipment and parted with her yelling, "Think about New York," and my yelling, "Mind your own business, young lady."

I slipped inside our kitchen door and stifled a yawn. Dad stood at the counter, making the same two peanut butter sandwiches he made every morning and placing them, along with two cans of Coke, in a lunch bag older than me. If he thought it strange I was awake, he kept his comments to himself. But then again, he kept most things to himself. I'd always liked that about him.

"Have a good one," I said, starting toward the steps.

And he nodded, which meant, *I will* and *You too.*

"You're gonna let me know if you want to replace the camera, yeah?"

This wasn't kismet; he asked nearly every time he saw me packing gear.

"You know it was irreplaceable."

"There are other working models."

I loved that he knew that, but he had an imperfect understanding of my doting affection for the No. 3 Kodak. I didn't

love old cameras because I loved old cameras. I loved *that* old camera because its leather and bellows and glass ran down through my family like DNA. It had crossed oceans—from New York to England in 1879 and then back again in 1907.

"Thanks for asking, Dad."

He poured the rest of his coffee into a thermos and left the kitchen with a grunt.

I decided the grunt was about last night. If I got my father alone and convinced him I'd never tell Mom what he really thought, he'd say, "Get married when you're sixty-five and not a day sooner." Truth was: he caved to Mom the way I caved to Chan. How many people in the world knew what *they* wanted apart from what people wanted for them? And of those who knew, how many were strong enough to fight the people they loved—people they never wanted to hurt—for the journey they desired?

Upstairs, I posted the best photo to my account, knowing it would get the attention it deserved. My photo project had done well. There were even a few likes from *Nat Geo*. Mostly because I'd thrown myself into the work and gone after shots that excited me. Now, I needed to throw myself at school, but instead, I pulled up my email, wondering if Carter Stockton had responded to my message.

There was a name I recognized in Facebook Messenger. Rudy Guthrie. 4:45 a.m. While I'd been playing with fire, another survivor had emailed me.

5. Important things happen in threes.

$17,592.00

According to press reports, Rudy Guthrie and Caroline Ascott were residents of Florida and New York, respectively. Months ago, I'd searched online, hoping to connect my fuzzy memories of who they'd been on June 15 with the tangible pieces of who they were now. I'd sent Facebook messages to every Rudy Guthrie under the age of twenty who lived in the United States and all the Carolines as well.

The message to the Rudys read: Are you the Rudy Guthrie who was on Charter Bus #21? I am the red beanie girl you nearly kissed in the bathroom of Down Yonder Bar. I've been looking for you.

That second sentence was like grabbing a rosebush; everything pricked. But the right Rudy probably needed proof I wasn't the media scamming him for a story. More often than not, the Rudys answered my messages. There were any number of responses ranging from crude—I'd (((kiss))) you in the bathroom—to sympathetic—I'm not your Rudy, but I watched coverage of Bus #21 on the news. So sorry. Some Good Samaritan Rudys even offered to help. Had I considered the White Pages? Or a Google image search?

I'd snapped a photo of him in that bathroom hallway of Down Yonder—half turned and grinning—and I'd spent hours obsessing over the lost picture. Sometimes that film had a blue-tinted exposure. And always, when I imagined him, he lived in black-and-white, midnight tones streaking his dark hair.

His message:

Golden,

You found me in January, but I didn't answer then because things are complicated. I'm reaching out now because of "Accelerant Orange." Carter messaged me early this morning and said you contacted him. (He's going to call you soon.) I never told him I had your info. It sounds like this thing is happening. I can't believe the college fund already has $17,592.00. Can you?

Also, how are you?

(When people ask me that, I say: I'm FINE, SUPER fine,

ALWAYS, always fine, couldn't be better. So I'll understand if you do the same, but you don't have to.)

    Peace—

    Rudy

Peace. That was a nice touch. My current condition ranged from jittery to more jittery to the jitteriest I'd been in months. I didn't know what to say.

In the end, I sent him this message:

Rudy,

I understand not writing back. No worries.

Thank you for letting me reach out to Carter on my own.

The college fund is . . . overwhelming, remarkable; I'm awed. I CAN'T believe strangers care so much. When I was showering this morning, I thought: a stranger took something precious from me, but half a million strangers are trying to give it back. What a wicked, crazy, wonderful world!

It is very nice to talk to you again.

HOW ARE YOU?

Peace—

Golden

I attached the photo of the steel wool, pressed Send. The floor swayed like I was balanced on tippy toes atop the Braxton Springs community pool high dive. Talking to Rudy had only

ever gotten me into trouble. It took me five minutes to realize I was shoving my right foot into my left shoe and I'd put my T-shirt on backward.

"Go! Shake a leg!" Based on Mom's volume and a wealth of experience, she was probably standing at the bottom of the steps. "Honey! Did you fall asleep?" One foot on the next step. Two feet.

She was coming for me.

"I'm almost ready," I called, even though I'd done nothing to my curls and I couldn't find my bobby pins. I hadn't even printed my homework. Despite being late, I hastily stapled my Orwell paper and googled *promise rings*. Because I had no idea where to wear that sucker. Google said: Some girls wear them on chains around their necks, but left-hand ring finger was the consensus. Noted. Becky Cable was going to have a million questions when I saw her in the hall. School. Jesus. I guessed I really did have to go.

I finished my makeup. My hair looked like swamp shrub, but I was out of time. When I climbed into Chan's truck, seventeen minutes late, Chan was drinking cola from a plastic cup and doodling in his sketchbook. He didn't comment on the time, because school wasn't a priority, but he'd been watching the clock.

He said, "You haven't posted a photo of your ring yet?"

"It's not nature."

"Neither is steel wool."

"Fire is."

"Diamonds and gold come from the earth. Can't get any more *nature* than that."

"Maybe it'll be tomorrow's image," I said, and then we rode to school in silence.

When Chan dropped me at the gym for first period he said, "I love you" and I said, "I love you," and I considered how the same words, the exact same words, could mean different things to different people. Like how Bob Dylan, Elvis Costello, and the Beatles all sang a song "I Want You," and *You* was most certainly a different *You* to each singer. What if *love* could be a different *love* to Chan and me? What if that's what I needed to say instead of the creed we'd said the night before?

There was an old adage that said *Important things happens in threes.* They ganged up on you like a wombful of triplets. And that's how I felt. Ganged up on by Chan's engagement and Carter's announcements and anxious that whatever was happening in the ether probably wasn't done happening.

I put the ring in my backpack and escaped to my locker, glad Chan started school on the other end of the building and never walked me to homeroom. Unfortunately, I'd never been good with combinations. After every school break, I found myself in the secretaries' office asking for the numbers as if I'd never known them. ATM cards and pins or codes to open my phone: I wasn't to be trusted. Yesterday, I entered the combination six times and could not remember it today for the life of

me. I walked toward the office, knowing a text to Chan would solve the problem.

The secretary leaned her freshly-dieted-I've-lost-twenty-pounds-and-gotten-Botoxed face through the round hole in the glass partition. "Let me see it."

"See what?" I assumed she'd guess why I was here, my being a regular customer and all.

"Your ring, Golden Jennings. Your ring."

"Oh."

I froze. "I'll trade you a peek for a locker combination," I said, buying myself enough time to dig the diamond from my bag.

She reeled the numbers off without checking a sheet. "Forty, twenty-five, seventeen. Now, show me that hand, missy." I pressed my fingers to the glass. Appropriate, audible sigh. "Fancy," she said, even though it wasn't. "What's the story?"

She probably already knew.

Mom, a teacher's aide here, must have flitted person to person, room to room, telling staff and teachers the "good news." Since New York, I'd noticed her treating me delicately. I pictured her saying, "Now, congratulate Golden on the ring, but let's remember, we don't relate it to last June, okay?"

"Your mom said he made a roast." The secretary said this as if making the roast were the same as summiting Everest.

"He did. It was amazing. What's that combination again?" I asked.

I fielded four additional "Oooooooo! Ahhhhhhhh!" requests to see the ring as I walked to my locker and dumped my extra bag. Several assholes asked me if we were having a boy or a girl. This looked to be a long day.

Now, in any given class at Braxton Springs High School, I might see a girl writing her first name with her significant other's last name on her folder. Trying on a surname was like trying on a prom dress: you checked if it fit before you arrived at an event decked out in peach taffeta and chiffon. That was normal enough. Also normal: ninety-nine times out of a hundred, those girls scratched through several last names or had to buy a new folder because they ditched relationships faster than favorite songs. Everyone played house, but no one wanted to buy a freaking house.

I decided it was better to leave the ring on over panicking every time someone asked to see the goods. I was in no state for class and went instead to a hidden cubicle in the library. Screw *1984*. I'd turn the paper in later.

There was a new message from Rudy.

Golden,

Good day today! Maybe that's because we're finally talking, or because my nephew just honked my nose and called me Wudy. It's the small things, you know?

As you provided me flaming steel wool—nice shot, btw—I have collected these fine facts for you:

If you put superglue on a cotton ball it will catch on fire.

Walt Disney World uses compressed air instead of gunpowder for their fireworks shows.

"Fahrenheit 451" got its name when Ray Bradbury asked a local fireman the temperature a book would burn at. The dude put Bradbury on hold, burned a book, and the rest is a classic.

I used to love fire. I hate it now.

Peace—

Wudy

I wrote him back: I dream of fire.

He must have been there, right on the other side of the internet.

He wrote: Me too.

I wrote: Tell me about Carter Stockton.

He wrote: He's exactly who you think he is.

I typed, Are you going to New York on Sunday? but the school alarm went off before I hit Send.

Between the screaming pulses, the secretary issued instructions over the loudspeaker: "Please exit the building now. This is not a drill. I repeat. Please exit the building now. This is not a drill."

6. Survivor of strange atrocities

$21,291.00

Teachers directed students out the gym doors. Several tennis girls waved me over as we exited the building, but only Becky Cable waited until I reached her. Becky and I were doubles partners and sometimes we traded biology notes and gossip. I wouldn't call us bosom buddies, but we knew each other's basics. Like I knew her parents were local dentists, who wanted her to be a dentist, and she happened to be terrible at science. Really, really terrible. I also knew she thought her voice was too masculine. Not true. Everywhere my voice was smooth and Southern, hers gripped the surface of words like eggshell paint mixed with sand. Husky and distinct. I was glad

she was the one who waited.

"Keep going!" a teacher said. "Farther. Farther."

Becky stood motionless, bored by the fluttering masses. "This seems a little extreme."

"I'm sure it's a drill," I said.

Braxton Springs wasn't large by high school standards—Class A in sports, four hundred students most years. Nearby, a mass of kids hovered in a lopsided lump near the teachers. A freshman volleyball girl, who was clearly not flummoxed by the announcement, asked about Becky's mascara (which was always A+, but today A++), and Becky somehow kept two conversations going at the same time. Becky was good at doubles tennis, and that held true across the board. I couldn't stay focused on her, let alone the crowd. I was thinking about how every time I spoke to Rudy Guthrie an alarm sounded.

A whistle blew. I felt the shrill in my chest.

"Keep going, toward the exterior lot."

"Faster. Orderly. Faster!"

"This is not a joke. Stop laughing."

I followed the herd. This would be over soon; the teachers were overreacting, as they'd been trained to do. We had a million drills. Natural disasters. Earthquakes. Tornados. Fires. Lockdowns. Worse-case scenario here: one of the lunch ladies burned a pan of broccoli, or the chemistry department dropped a Bunsen burner. Even that was doubtful. There was

no visible smoke. Per protocol, the fire trucks screamed into the circle drive. Our crowd reached the gravel lot where the buses perched during the day, and two teachers directed us to board.

"No," I said.

Becky peered at me and noted my discomfort with concern. "No what?"

"I'm not getting on a bus."

Becky Cable had a moment where she remembered I wasn't Golden Jennings her tennis bud, I was Golden Jennings, survivor of strange atrocities, and in solidarity said, "I'm not boarding either, bitches." But she kept the *bitches* part between us.

God bless Becky Cable.

The more docile students followed directions promptly. Teachers easily noted our rebellion, as we were the only students left in the parking lot. "On the bus!" they called, as if this were an easy task. It should have been.

"You go," I told Becky, but I tightened my grip on her arm.

Mr. Keller jogged over; he was practically spitting fire. "I need you to board. Now."

This might have felt truer if the windows of the yellow fellow weren't lowered and Dominik Dvorak wasn't hanging halfway out playing taps on his trumpet and Seth Fallman wasn't singing about the end of the world in a singsong off-key voice.

"We never get on buses for fire drills," I said.

"This isn't a fire drill!"

Half the bus heard Mr. Keller scream. Those who didn't hear his precise words heard his trepidation. Behind him, speculation began. Whispers. Conversations. Rumors. "Shooter!" someone suggested. No one argued.

"Girls, I'm not telling you again," Mr. Keller said. He was a white-hot ball of fury.

Becky pressed her lips into my ear. "Would it help if you put your face inside your shirt and I guided you?"

"No."

Logical solution. But whatever was out here, shooter, terrorist, kingdom come, I planned to watch it attack from the wide-open space. Hidden things—a backpack abandoned beneath a park bench; a bulky sweatshirt on a dumpy, angry boy; a suitcase idling at airport security—kept the most dangerous of secrets. Mr. Keller kept spitting his instructions, but he climbed the first step toward our classmates and abandoned us. Later, he would call this *protocol*. I would always label it fear, and fear I understood.

The whispers, taps, and our insubordination continued. I thought about Chan, who was on the opposite side of campus. Was someone making him board a bus too? I hoped they weren't. Becky took to Twitter, hoping to discover what was going on. Plenty of teachers' kids with the inside hookup lived online; there would be something if she searched the right

people. Her thumb stopped scrolling.

"What is it?" I asked.

"You don't want to know."

"Becky?"

"They're saying it's a bomb threat."

7. Out of oranges

$27,466.00

"I'm leaving."

Becky was already tugging me toward the senior lot. "I'll drive," she said, peeling off her sweater and stripping down to a bright yellow tank top like she meant business. I was busy tugging my own shirt to my nose, which was bleeding. I'd lost more than one T-shirt to spiked blood pressure, stress, and allergies.

Behind our backs Mr. Keller threatened suspension. Behind *his* back, Becky flipped him off like she was grinding birds into his face. Under different circumstances, I would have laughed. Under these, I was searching for Chan's truck among the sea of senior automobiles. It wasn't here.

"Keller is an unthinking asshole!" she said.

"Pretty much."

We arrived at Becky's electric-blue Mustang, a vehicle I admired. Every vehicle we owned except Dad's had duct tape somewhere. There was no duct tape to be found on the Mustang. The paint was always gleaming from a fresh wash. The car sat so low she probably had to change the tires to cross train tracks. Usually she and her closest girlfriends (all with pretty hair and pretty cardigans and pretty ankle boots) tore from the parking lot, horn honking, on their way to Cason's Market, where everyone hung out after school. I'd never asked to go along. And now I wasn't quite sure why. Maybe because I didn't have razor-sharp bangs or Warby Parker glasses.

Inside, the Mustang was a thing to behold. "Make space, Jennings," she told me. When I didn't respond swiftly, Becky raked her arm across the passenger seat and junk? stuff? all her worldly belongings? fell onto the floorboard. I wiggled into the remaining available space and made sure I didn't bleed on the fabric. She squealed from the lot, leaving fresh treads on Main Street.

"Grab that for me, will you?" She flung a hand in the general direction of my feet. I handed her four different items of various shapes and sizes before she said, "The lipstick, silly." I had to dig under the seat but was eventually successful. Mechanically, she flipped the sunshade, leveled her face with the mirror, and painted her lips brick red.

"You should try this color," she said, and passed the tube to me.

My hand was shaking too badly to try. I guess Becky was amped too, because she chewed the lipstick right off her lips.

By the stop sign at Cason's my nosebleed had settled down. Becky gave it a once-over and said, "So . . . you and Chan the Man?"

"I have no idea."

"You preggo, Jennings? Got Chan's little western sizzlin' in your belly? Because I'd rather not train a new tennis partner."

"No. I'm semi-promised." I fluttered my left hand where she could see the ring.

"Seems that you're semi-*unhappy*. That because of bomb drills or whatnot?"

"That's because—"

"Oh, just say it, Jennings. Chandler Clayton is a jalapeño pepper, but there's plenty more like him who have mastered the incredible art of . . . *smiling*."

"It's not so much Chan as it is the ring doesn't make sense."

"Because you don't love him? Or because you only high school love him and plan to bone some lawyer with a trust fund in college? Or do you mean you wanted white gold and a little more flicker?"

My cheeks were on fire as I thought of a proper way to respond. "I love Chan, but . . . *aaahhh*, this is the dumbest thing he's ever done." I growled and clutched the ceiling handle until

my arm muscles trembled with fatigue.

"You want to throw something?"

"Yes."

"There's an orange on the floorboard. That's biodegradable. Launch that bastard at a street sign."

I did. And unsurprisingly, I underestimated our speed, missed the sign by a yard, and didn't feel better. Becky noticed.

"I'm out of oranges, so you'd better just tell me everything."

I decided I would. The Mustang was blocking the city park for the third time—probably because I hadn't given her specific directions—when I unloaded. "We were fine, Becky. You know, couple of the year for like—"

"Ten years running."

"Six. But exactly. Then New York happened, and everything changed. Like literally everything. I get that trauma makes you crazy sometimes, but shouldn't it be the same type of trauma if we lived through the same event? It makes you ask weird questions. Like what if we were this way before and I can't remember. Whatever we were before Bus Twenty-One . . . I don't know what we are anymore."

The windows were down from my orange launching so she was forced to yell over the wind. "I know what you are. You're *semi-promised*."

I laced my hands around my skull and squeezed. "Do you know what I want?"

"What?"

"To get off the Hive. See who we are. See if we can get over who we've been." The phrases slipped out like someone greased my windpipe.

Becky beat a drumroll on the steering wheel. "Yep."

"But I clearly can't."

"Yep," she said again. "Preaching to the choir."

"At least we got away today," I said, hoping that sounded enough like *thank you*.

"Let's just keep driving," she said.

"Fine by me."

She stomped on the gas.

We weren't really leaving town, but the speed and the wind made everything better. We were nearing the interstate when Becky's phone rang.

"School?" she said, and answered.

Mine rang immediately after. We sat in a pull-off, fingers plugged in our opposite ears, listening to Principal Sanduskin in Becky's case and Mom in mine explain we'd been suspended for leaving campus during a bomb threat. Oh, also, some freshman boy called the threat in from his cell phone because he didn't want to take an algebra test. Mom didn't blame me, and based on her tone, Sanduskin had his work cut out for him.

Becky was equally unfazed. "What are we doing with our vacation? Don't say tennis. Don't say homework."

Strangely, the *we* worked. She was a quality person with a quality car and über-quality lipstick. That plus loyalty was enough to start. I could be a Becky person.

"You won't be in trouble?" I asked.

"I'm sure I will." She said this in a way that conjured no pity.

"Figure that out and we'll make a plan."

We turned around and Becky drove me home. Before she entered the outer Hive gate, she said, "Am I allowed in here, Jennings?"

My left eyebrow shot up. "Why wouldn't you be?"

"My first commune experience."

"Yeah, well, it's the first time in ten months I've ridden in a car I didn't check beneath."

"Guess we're both living on the edge."

8. The exclusive and privileged club

$31,087.00

Becky dropped me in the driveway and promised to call later. I left Chan a message that I was home and went inside for a long shower. The water was scorching, and I stayed until my skin was pink and raw.

That stupid, stupid freshman. Bomb threats weren't pranks.

There I stood, naked and angry and wet, thinking maybe I should drive to school and kick that douchebag kid in the crotch. And then I was suddenly and inexplicably angry with Chan. Where was he in all this? Why should I be the crotch kicker? He had two legs. He should kick that kid twice on our behalf. Or at least want to. But he'd be passive about this.

"Golden, let it go," he'd say. And then I'd be staring at his ass and the back of his shoulders as he walked away. Our next conversation would be about the latest Nolan movie or a new photo technique.

How was it that two of the four survivors of Bus #21 lived on the same property, and we never talked about what happened or how it kept affecting our lives? *How?* was the wrong question. *Why?* was better.

Gran knocked on the bathroom door and I told her to come in. She dropped the toilet seat lid and lowered herself slowly to a resting position. Still dripping, I tightened a threadbare towel around my chest, flung back the curtain, and took the tub ledge. We sighed together. Maybe from the steam, maybe from the day.

"Rough one?"

"I got suspended."

She grabbed a second towel from under the sink and flung it in my direction. "Did you do anything wrong?"

"No." I wrung my hair and twisted the towel into a turban.

"Will you miss anything that keeps you from graduating?"

"No." Thank God. I didn't think this would hurt my grades.

"Then take the vacation, kid."

"Did you check the fund?"

She eyeballed a tube of drugstore mascara, examining the color. "You bet I did. Three times today. Hit it like a joint." It occurred to me that Becky and Gran would be great friends. I gave an appropriately chastising expression. "What?" she said.

"Do kids not call them joints anymore? Also, the fund's almost to thirty-two thousand."

"Dang."

She looked a little nervous and confessed, "I put in another ten dollars. Couldn't help myself."

"Gran! Stop it."

"Don't tell your elders what to do with their money. It's insulting."

On the one hand, I imagined eight thousand dollars for college. On the other, I knew I didn't deserve those donors' hard-earned money. I shouldn't have been on that bus to begin with.

"Where would you go?" Gran asked.

"I don't know."

"Sure you do. Every kid has an answer to that question. You're just scared to say it out loud in case that makes it come true."

"College."

"Where?"

"There's a place in Boston."

"Maybe you should go to New York this weekend and swing by Boston on your way home."

"Gran!" She was being ridiculous.

"I'm just saying"—she eased her body off the seat, around the corner, and then poked her face back into the bathroom—"you've got the time."

"Yeah, right."

She put a hand on my forehead and the weight and coolness of her skin made me melt. "Golden," she said, "you can always come back if it doesn't work out. That should make it easier to leave. Not easier to stay."

I nodded to make her happy. I went straight to my computer and discovered Rudy Guthrie had left three messages in my absence.

Do you ever dream you're back on the bus?

I'm sorry. I shouldn't have asked.

I hope you're not mad.

He attached a photo—an excellent photo by a photographer I admire—of a mongoose sticking out its tongue.

I thought of Rudy, Caroline, Chan. Of the exclusive and privileged club we belonged to after last June. Of Carter Stockton's heart. Of the six thousand plus people who had already given to the fund.

I wrote him back.

I'm not mad at you. Are you ready for this? My morning got interrupted by a fake bomb threat at school. And believe it or not, that, plus everything else, is conspiring to make me . . . The cursor blinked. I finished the sentence. . . . want to attend the opening of "Accelerant Orange."

9. The person in the back isn't allowed to steer.

$35,611.00

Chan loved movies, often obscure movies, the way I loved photos. He was the one who initially suggested we re-create Gran's photo wall. "Think of it, Go. We'd be the next generation's past. We do this, and our lives are elastic." He'd said that right after his mom died, and looking back, it was an eleven-year-old figuring out death more than an eleven-year-old choosing a weird-ass hobby. But when a hobby is tied to your heart, part of you is hooked in that space forever.

He was also the one who demanded we watch films corresponding to the photos. That first summer we checked movies out of the Braxton Springs Library no one had checked out in decades. When word got out Chan and I were viewing films

starring Gregory Peck, Lauren Bacall, James Stewart, and Ingrid Bergman, to name a few, the Hive requested we project them on the barn wall and watch as a group. That was probably illegal, but we happily obliged. Sometimes *Casablanca*, for me, is the smell of wild onions and Chan's yellow Dial soap because I watched with my head on his shoulder in an itchy field.

On those nights, Gran prodded us with her cane when we reached the reenactment scenes she'd done with Granddad. Chan hit Pause, which always caused an uproar. "Hey, this is my favorite part!" someone would call, as if worried we might stop the movie early. I'd snap photos of the scene for Chan and then we'd settle down again. Him watching the movie, me watching him.

I wasn't a girl who ogled her boyfriend. Chan was nearly always concrete. A firm thing with solid edges. When he watched movies, he dreamed. And when he dreamed, he was a different version of himself. Maybe it's shallow, but I loved dream-him so much more. If I wanted Chan to drive to New York with me to *shoot the final picture in our series*, I needed to engage the dreamer.

Wherever he was, he would likely know about my school suspension. News traveled swiftly, carried on the whispers and social media accounts of Braxton Springs High students. He'd been eerily silent over text, so I jogged across the quad, petting the various stray animals and occasional toddlers as I went. His truck was parked by the woodshop. The hood, cold. He

didn't care about the bomb threat, because he wasn't there.

Inside his shop, sawdust coated the air. Sap flew. A heavy mist fell on my shirt like dandruff. The whole place smelled like Christmas. Chan had his head bent over a pine log. In his hands, the chain saw was a peeler and the tree a potato. Bark sloughed off in long elegant strips. I climbed atop a stack of ten-foot logs he'd felled before last September and watched him work. This was also Chan the dreamer, and I was in love all over again.

Eight-foot statues of Mary and Joseph, each feature carved with such precision and humanity that they might have birthed baby Jesus two minutes ago, were positioned around a crude crèche. No wonder churches kept hiring him to build these displays. I was tracing the lines in Mary's face when he turned around. Happy as he was at my surprise appearance, he checked his watch and called over the rumbling saw, "You sick?"

"You skipped?"

"I was taking a mental wealth day." He attempted a dance, chain saw in hand.

People didn't think someone as handsome as Chan could be a dork; they were wrong. "You'll cut off your leg," I said.

"For five thousand dollars, it might be worth it."

"Ha. Ha," I said, not amused.

Saw powered off, he walked over and arranged his body in my lap—220 pounds of grubby dude on 120 pounds of girl. I grunted like the weight was too much, and he buried his nose

in the hollow of my neck. "Ugh. You should not have come here freshly showered. Haven't I warned you about that, you vanilla witchwoman?"

"Indeed you have, but . . . I was suspended by our fine educational establishment and thought I'd mosey over here to persuade you, Mr. Clayton, to get creative with me."

He tossed his safety goggles and hat toward the workbench and gave me his full attention, his green eyes impossibly large and curious. "Seriously? What's up?"

I held his earlobe, which was also covered in sawdust; massaged it until he squirmed. Smug as anything, I said, "Told you. I was suspended."

"Okay, I'll play. Why?"

"I left school without asking."

"I do that all the time. They don't ask me to be gone longer."

"I had a good reason."

"Come on. Don't stall. You know I can check Facebook or something." Without saying a word, Chan swapped so I was seated on his lap. His voice was careful and kind. "Tell me, Golden."

His heartbeat idled stronger than a chain saw.

"Some idiot called in a fake bomb"—he flinched. Viciously. And then squeezed me harder—"threat. They tried to put us on a bus." Another shudder. "So Becky Cable and I left."

He pressed his forehead to my skull and breathed deep. "I'd like to kill that idiot."

"Trust me, I was fantasizing about that in the shower. But he's not the real problem."

"I beg to differ—"

"Chan, I looked at that school bus, which, by the way, was the precise one we rode to elementary school—Bus Nineteen—and it was . . . I don't know . . . like staring at my executioner."

"Your fear seems logical to me."

"Sure. Maybe. But that doesn't mean I like it."

"Of course you don't."

Chan had always had a certain sensibility regarding fear. *Face the necessary. Ignore the unnecessary.* And it wasn't that I didn't understand. The reason was fine for him, but fear was a slippery slope for me. I said, "I don't like thinking a single event changed something benign into cancer and now every bus is Bus Twenty-One. Every bus is New York—"

"Go."

"Do you think airplane crash survivors ever fly again? Do New Yorkers who were on the street during September Eleventh always flinch from low-flying planes? Do you—"

He covered my mouth with his dirty hand. I tasted pine on my lips.

"I don't know about them, but I promise you, for the rest of our lives, you will never have to get on another bus."

This was not dreamer Chan. This was the most-concrete-of-concrete Chans.

"I cannot avoid this."

"We're seven hundred miles away."

"No, we're not."

He took a dramatic look around the workshop. "I don't see any buses in here."

"So you're never going to a city again?"

He scrubbed a hand through his hair. Sawdust ground into his scalp like wooden glitter. "Why would I?"

I've never ridden a two-person bicycle, but I assume the person in the back isn't allowed to steer. That was what I felt like watching Chan sweep the workshop in a glance and decide that this teeny world was enough for him. That, if I wanted to be with him, we would only go places that didn't scare him. I twisted the ring on my finger all the way to the knuckle. "When we were young, I remember us talking about the Great Wall of China and how we'd climb to the top and dance."

"We were little, Go. And we were stupid."

I wiggled free and held his face with my hands. I had a dreamer face too, and I suspected Chan could spot mine the way I spotted his. I wore it loudly and said, "What if I wanted to go to New York and try that photo again? If you won't go for you, would you go for me?"

He turned away so I couldn't see him. He pointed to his chain saw. "I'll build you a set better than the real thing. We can make the shot here. Same as all the other shots we've made. Gran won't care."

She wouldn't, but I would. "That's a cheap imitation," I whispered. Gran and Granddad's photo from Ellis Island was the only photo not made on-Hive.

"Not to me."

"You're only half the equation."

"Hey." His voice lightened considerably, the way it always did when he wanted to exit the conversation without a fight. "I thought I was your favorite half."

I made a noise somewhere between a sigh and grunt.

"We don't have to travel to be happy, Golden. We were happy as larks for sixteen years and where were we? Right here. On good ol' Kentucky dirt. What more could we possibly need?"

Emerson College in Boston.

Diversity.

Joy.

Photos of the world.

Windmills in the Netherlands.

Namib desert after a dust storm.

The Pepto pink of Lake Retba.

Machu Picchu at sunset.

Mongooses with their tongues out.

Accelerant Orange.

Courage.

Everything.

10. Then there's the Chilean warlock.

$39,791.72

There was no fight. Chandler buried his mood under the brim of his lowered hat and returned to carving Jesus, and I called Becky Cable. She was on her way to the grocery store for a rotisserie chicken but assured me she had time to meet. All the time in the world. "Four days. Technically six because of the weekend." I gave her directions to the blue hole.

Blue holes occurred where underground rivers burrowed their way to the surface. A single droplet of water tunneling upward through soil and rock and gravity, desperate for sunlight. Pure magic, and I needed some of that.

I heard the Mustang coming. Through the tinted glass, I watched Becky reapply lipstick and check her teeth.

"Nice place!" she yelled through the window.

"You got that chicken?"

"Am I bringing it with me?"

I shrugged, because I wasn't going to force her, but I didn't have lunch. She put the chicken container and a loaf of bread under her arm like a football and made the climb. The teeny half-moon basin was nestled between two rises in the land not large enough to be hills and too large to be mounds. We crammed our bodies side by side on the narrow ledge and after a quick survey of me, Becky turned on music. Cat Stevens. Fleet Foxes. The Tallest Man on Earth. We let the songs speak as we pulled chicken off the bone and ate. Finally, Becky wiped her mouth with the back of her hand and said, "That's enough foreplay. You have to talk now."

"Which part?"

"The loudest part."

I shrugged first—a habit I'd gained from my father. "Shrugging makes people believe you don't care," Gran always said. I cared. Probably too much.

"When do you think a promise is for real?" I asked.

"When is a promise *not* for real?" she retorted, but then softened. "You still thinking about Chan the Man?"

I was. Usually, with me, a promise made was a promise kept. I liked people who did what they said. Chan always did what he said, but in this case, his commitment was the problem. He wasn't leaving the Hive, so who was I if I left? A promise breaker? An idiot? The last time I demanded something I'd put

us on a bus that blew up.

"We disagree about the future," I told Becky.

"You're not married."

"So you don't think it's wrong if, hypothetically, I go to New York without him?"

"*Chica*, I'm a feminist. I think it's wrong if you go to New York *with* him." She laughed and handed me another piece of bread.

"I feel responsible."

"For what?"

"Ruining his life."

There, I said it.

Becky tweaked the placement of two bobby pins around my ears. In a very even tone, she said, "Did you know there's supposed to be a cave in Chile where warlocks hid stolen babies and deformed them? Like . . . they made their heads turn around backward and cut off their right arm and sewed it elsewhere on the body."

"What's *that* have to do with Chan?"

"Oh, I just thought you needed a reminder of what ruining someone's life actually looked like. There's you, ruining Chan's life"—she used air quotes—"for not keeping some asinine promise you made, and then there's the Chilean warlock baby deformers."

"They're not real."

"Maybe not. Maybe so. But lucky for us, I have more

examples. There are plenty of life ruiners among politicians. Shall I make an alphabetical list starting with last or first names?"

"You don't understand."

"Help me. Because as far as I can see, Chandler Clayton is doing fine."

Could I take her into that terrible day and explain how I felt when I couldn't even make Chan understand? And he was with me. There's no way to Xerox a feeling. There was only telling someone the story and letting them apply their lens. Instead of trying, I told her about Carter Stockton rebuilding Bus #21 into an art installation. "The exhibit opens this Sunday."

"That's messed up. Amazingly messed up."

I nibbled on the bread. Thought about all those people who believed in me. I googled the current donation amount—$39,791.72—and showed her the generosity of strangers. She was properly astounded and impressed.

"So are you going?"

I stared at the blue hole and then the pines towering above us like stubbly overlords.

"Because if Becky Cable ran the world"—she looked as though this might be a solid plan—"Golden Jennings would climb aboard that fucking bus and show all those people she's alive and she's doing something phenomenal with her life."

"One problem."

There were a host of problems.

"This is Kentucky, and that's New York? Chan's a reluctant dick and you're a *Go*-getter?"

If only.

"I'm terrified of buses."

CAROLINE

There's something about three a.m. that makes you examine your life. I was parked at the Bath Dunkin' Donuts waiting on the drive-through lady to deliver two dozen doughnuts, three coffees, and an apple fritter. The smell of glazed icing made me want to lick the air; the smell inside the Beamer, well, we needed another cardboard pine tree to combat the contact high. Simon lounged in the passenger seat; Dozer and Johnny were in the back. They were all coming off something and demanded I drive them for decaf and pastries. So, it was three a.m. and I was thinking about suicide, really thinking about it, for the first time, and they had the munchies.

I'd never been a sad person. I'd never been the life of the party either.

But I used to have goals—college, write a book, watch

Game of Thrones—and now, I had Simon.

I'd tried to leave him. I didn't know whether my efforts were pathetic or his efforts were extraordinary. Maybe both. Simon told me once, "There's a moment in every caterpillar's life when he knows it's either him or the butterfly, and, honey, the butterfly always wins." He was the butterfly.

Sometimes, at three a.m., like now, I let myself wonder the most terrible things. Like if Simon was the reincarnation of H. H. Holmes, who built a murder hotel in Chicago in the 1800s. Holmes supposedly constructed halls and staircases that led to nowhere, bricked-in doors, trick locks that imprisoned guests. He tortured and killed them. That sounded hyperbolic, but Simon might as well have built a hotel around me brick by brick. Every time I found a way out, the exit led nowhere.

Death was the only sure exit that led somewhere else.

Dear Butterfly, suck it. Love, Caterpillar.

I wasn't sure how I would kill myself—if I followed through—but it should probably be somewhere significant. Somewhere out of Steuben County. Somewhere it would take a while to identify my body. Maybe even somewhere historic. Simon should have a few days to think, *She escaped*.

11. Sit down, Superman.

$44,591.00

I was online again.

Hidden away in my room after begging off Hamburger Helper and a rewatch of *Die Hard* with Chan. All in the name of a raging headache. (Which wasn't a lie.) *Accelerant Orange* episode 22—one of my favorites—played in the background. Facebook was also open. There was a new message from Rudy.

I'm not sure how I would handle a fake bomb threat. Sounds like you took it in stride. Amazing. Even more amazing, you're thinking about going to New York.

A surge of pride hit my gut. I was, wasn't I? Gran wanted me to go. Even Becky seemed to think I should. If the bombing of Bus #21 had happened just to me instead of Chan and me, this would be simpler. As it stood, his feelings were grafted to mine. Going to New York would scare Chan. Going to New York with Rudy—maybe even having this conversation with Rudy—would betray him.

Thud. Shuffle. Shuffle. Thud. Shuffle. Shuffle. I smiled, marveling at Gran, who always knew when to appear. She'd been watching some crime drama with my folks and was now tapping her cane on my bedroom door. The world righted a little.

"Just checking in," she said.

"Thanks."

"Any"—she lowered her voice dramatically—"New York news?"

Mom and Dad were bound to be on their way to bed, and if they—*they* was Mom—caught us mentioning the bombing of Bus #21, they'd overreact. *Because New York! Terrible things happened in New York!* Mom trended toward "You're our baby" in a tone that meant *You in pain tortures us* as an excuse to avoid the topic.

"Not really," I said.

"Is that episode twenty-two?"

I nodded. She took her chair and an earbud.

Carter Stockton was in his garage, reattaching a crushed mirror to the bus. The blowtorch was off, the protective shield

propped on his forehead. He rubbed the sweat off with the back of his hand, a dozen beads instantly replacing the ones he'd wiped away. He said, "Now, let me tell you about the bus driver. His name was Oscar Reyes. I spent a few hours with his widow last Saturday, so you'll get to meet her later in the episode. This amazing lady is writing a memoir about her husband called *Life on the Bus*."

The camera cut away to a photo of Mrs. Reyes seated at a computer desk, pen in hand.

"He wasn't supposed to be the driver on his last trip. Winston Alden, who was scheduled to work that trip, had a baby come two months early, and Oscar volunteered so Winston could stay with his wife at the hospital. All proceeds from *Life on the Bus* will go to the preemie's medical bills. You see, folks, these are people who need to be remembered. Every seat on that bus had a story, and I'm making it my job to tell them all."

"I love that man," Gran said.

"The first time we watched we thought he was crazy as a loon."

"He's the good kind of crazy."

He must be. This video had been downloaded 1.3 million times.

I traced a circle in the plywood desk where I'd left a glass of ice water sweating for too long. I made a third round, a fourth. Carter was still talking in the background. "Gran, I found one of the other survivors."

"Oh, Go, that's fabulous." She saw my face. "Is it not? Fabulous?"

"Do you think I'm betraying Chan by talking to him?"

Gran worked her glasses off her face, chewed the earpiece. "Well, dear, that depends on what you say to this boy." Gran patted my arm and stood. She bent toward me. "You know I love Chan, but I think he's betraying you by refusing to talk. And, dear, it bears some advice, there are no equilateral triangles when it comes to love. Do you understand?"

I nodded that I did, but it was quite a revolutionary thought. She left me thinking. *Thud. Shuffle. Shuffle. Thud. Shuffle. Shuffle.* All the way down the steps. Rudy didn't give me a chance to ignore him. He was there, complimenting me, and right or wrong, I caved to the conversation.

Rudy: I think you're brave. I have zero interest in being some broken dude.

Golden: Same.

Rudy: Do you know how to get past this?

Golden: Not exactly.

Rudy: Ride a bus again?

Golden: Have you tried?

Rudy: I bought a few tickets in town.

Golden: And?

Rudy: Chickened out so far. One of these days . . . I'll go cross-country.

Golden: Good for you.

Golden: I tried to ask Chan to take me to "Accelerant

Orange," but I chickened out.

Rudy: Chan, the other survivor? Your boyfriend?

Golden: Yeah. And yeah.

I rocked back in my chair, stretched for the ceiling, and rubbed my eyes.

Rudy: He won't go with you?

Golden: He won't talk about Bus #21.

Minutes passed. I took out my contacts, brushed my teeth, and washed my face. He didn't reply. I crawled under the covers and my phone lit with a message.

Rudy: I wrote something about Bus #21. I'm attaching, in case you want to read or write something too.

I opened the document.

a journal entry by Rudy Guthrie

I boarded the bus outside the Green-Conwell. Our tour group had 9/11 Memorial/Wall Street/Battery Park/Ellis Island on the agenda. Ellis Island was a curiosity for me. My great-grandfather came through on November 9, 1919. I was born November 9, 2001. I'm named after him, so I wanted to find a remnant of him there. That's a micro-moment.

That day was made of micro-moments and mega-moments.

Micro-moment:

I was listening to Ryan Adams cover Taylor Swift and drowning my hangover under a gallon of water. Someone in close proximity had his shoes off. I don't know who. Maybe Neil.

Mega-moment:

Simon Westwood rocketed down the aisle, his hips bumping against shoulders as he went.

"THERE'S A BOMB ON THIS BUS! ANYONE RECORDS ME AND I'LL BLOW THE BUS IN A HEARTBEAT." *He lifted his sweatshirt. There was the vest. Like something I'd seen on television.*

Micro-moment:

Someone shrieked.

Someone said, "Is this for real?"

Someone said, "Simon, calm down, dude."

How did no one notice he was wearing that sweatshirt in June? Except the bus had been cold the entire trip. It wasn't cold now. The first symptoms of pandemonium were interior. Hearts raced; blood thundered through veins; oxygen caught in throats. Words stopped. Everyone checked with one another. Is this really happening? *our expressions asked.*

The consensus: yes.

Two seats in front of me (three seats from the exit), the girl I met in the bathroom last night scanned the bus.

Mega-moment:

Simon yelling, "STAND UP, BABY."

Nothing happened.

Simon's iron grip squeezing Caroline's shoulder. I see the flesh turn pink, red. "I SAID, 'STAND UP, BABY!'"

She stood.

"HERE'S WHAT'S GOING TO HAPPEN. CAROLINE IS GOING TO TELL EVERYONE THAT SHE SCREWED JIM LAST NIGHT. AND THEN JIM IS GOING TO PUT ON THIS VEST."

Micro-moment:
Down Yonder bar last night. Jim Conner, who I don't really know, walks to the jukebox. Caroline walks by. She stretches her index and middle fingers out. They brush Jim's thigh. She disappears down the steps to the bathroom. Three seconds later, Jim has selected a song, and he's following her, looking over his shoulder to see if anyone noticed.

Mega-moment:
Simon wrestled another vest like his from a duffel bag.
"OH, JIM. CALLING JIM CONNER." His finger curled in a come-here motion.
"YOU'RE THE NEXT CONTESTANT ON 'NO ONE SCREWS MY GIRLFRIEND BUT ME.'"

Micro-moment:
I have to say something, do something. Who sits here and lets this happen? Simon is five feet away. I've side-tackled guys from much farther. None of them were in suicide vests.

Mega-moment:
"Easy, Simon," I said.
"Sit down, Superman. I don't need your help."
Simon sounded calmer when speaking to me.

Micro-moment:

The dude across the aisle from me, Neil Johnson, shrank to the floor. He was fourteen, and his rich grandma had bought him a ticket. A small puddle of urine spilled onto the floor.

Others were panicking. I examined the exits. Front door. Was there a back door? An emergency release window? Maybe a window in the bathroom?

Mega-moment:

Jim Conner walked bravely to the front.

Simon zipped the vest to his Adam's apple. Taunted Jim with a simple remote. Taunted us all with how easy it had been to rig the dynamite to a wireless fireworks control system.

"YOUR TURN, BABY DOLL. TELL THE BUS YOU SCREWED THIS LAME DICK."

Caroline was incapable of words. Or standing. Or breathing. I worried she might pass out.

Mega-moment:

I was not Superman.

The bus blew.

12. Have you ever heard film winding?

$47,977.00

The end of Rudy's journal entry.

I was not Superman.

The bus blew.

Raw. Unrelenting. Incomplete. I tossed the covers off, froze, pulled them over me again. I reread the end. *I was not Superman. The bus blew.* God, Rudy. There were a million mega-moments and micro-moments that happened between those lines. One of them was with me.

Mom was now silhouetted in the hallway light, and I thought about how beautiful she was and how I never told her and how I probably should because sometimes your life was *I was not Superman and the bus blew* and you weren't one of the

four who survived. I curled around my pillow and chewed the corner of the fabric.

She set two cookies and a glass of milk beside my bedside lamp, and said, "I thought I heard you crying."

"I wasn't crying."

When faced with my dry cheeks, she cocked her head to the side and dropped onto the edge of my bed. "Honey, what you did today—"

I assumed she meant my suspension. "I'm not sorry."

"I'm proud of you."

"You are?"

"Baby."

"Stop with the baby, Mom." She looked weary and beaten by my request, the glow of last night long gone. *Tell her you love her*, a voice said. "Okay, you can still call me baby," I said instead.

She tried smiling. "I wish you wouldn't sit in a dark room on your computer. And I wish you wouldn't dam your emotions. And I wish I knew how to help you."

I tapped the plate of cookies. "You help."

"Did you talk to Chan about the bomb threat?"

"I tried."

"Keep trying. Sometimes we don't know what we need."

I need you, I thought, but the words weren't there. Sometimes we can't say what we need either.

On her way from my room, Mom touched the edge of a framed photo. The New York skyline. Taken from the plane

with my phone. I got out of bed, walked across the room to shut the door, and traced the plastic frame with my finger. The night wasn't over. I was hours from sleep. Staring at those blue-gray clouds and skyscrapers, I wrote my own moment.

a micro-story by Golden Jennings

John William Jennings came through Ellis Island on June 16, 1907. He was my granddad's grandpapa. He bought the nine hundred acres I call home. John Jennings also bought the camera that I would shoot my first photo with—a No. 3 Kodak with a velvet red bellows and brown leather case. "Eight turns," my granddad would say. We'd crank the camera key together, counting each turn aloud. Have you ever heard film winding? It's a beautiful sound.

In the summers, when I was still young enough to nap and small enough for Gran to crowd my twin bed, she rubbed my back and chronicled family details until I fell asleep. Her grandparents were from Ireland. Granddad's were from England. She stocked me with marvelous stories, further feeding my obsession. In elementary school, I drew the Statue of Liberty; I sent my spit to Ancestry.com for my eighth birthday; I googled photos of Ellis Island. Whatever I could scrounge. None of the photos I googled were as awesome as the two from our family. The first of Great-Great-Grandpapa John and his family. The second of Gran and Granddad, shot with the same No. 3 Kodak, in the same pose at Ellis Island.

"Why didn't Mom and Dad do one?" I asked. I must have

been about ten. "Oh, honey, they're not as cool as us," Gran said with a wink. Even then, I understood my parents weren't into traveling beyond our farm or town. It could have been the cost too.

Gran will never go back to New York. Her arthritis and crumbling discs make long car trips painful, and her thoughts on planes are "If God gives me wings tomorrow, I'll be there. Until then, I'm grounded." But, in her heart of hearts, she wanted the two of us to go. For me to continue the family tradition and take a new photo. "You're my little wanderer," she told me when I was a little girl. "My greatest hope." I never forgot that. Despite her spunk, she's slowing down, and I feel the clock screaming, "You'd better do this soon if you want her to be alive to enjoy it."

For her seventy-fifth birthday, Chan and I planned the gift: I would get that third-generation photo on Ellis Island, shot with the same Kodak Grandpapa John had worn around his neck. Chan had sold two nativities, working day and night, to make the trip happen.

That's why I was in New York.

When I finished, I shared with Rudy.

Three minutes later, he pinged me back.

I assume you were going for the June 16 anniversary of when your great-great-grandpa came through? How did you end up heading to Ellis Island on the 15th instead?

I typed three responses:

Chandler got a one-day permit to cut logs on the Wey-meyers' land. We had to leave the city early to go back to Kentucky.

They were calling for rain the next day.

You and I met in the Down Yonder bathroom.

I erased them and wrote back a totally uncomplicated truth.

Golden: I decided the date didn't matter.

Rudy: Did you ever get your photo?

Golden: No.

Rudy: I hope you get it someday.

Golden: How about Sunday?

He didn't answer before I fell asleep.

I woke at 4:47. He'd written: If only I had a ride.

That's when I decided I was going back. With or without Chan.

CAROLINE

Because I wasn't stupid, I never googled how to make a bomb.

Instead, I searched where people frequently killed themselves in New York City, which ruled out the George Washington Bridge and all of Midtown as overpopulated options. I had a plan. I'd bum a ride to *my future college town*, Rochester, and then make the seven(ish)-hour train trip to Penn Station. From there, I'd pick my place. I couldn't die on Keuka Lake, not when I loved it so much.

The guys hadn't given up sourcing C-4. Whenever they got onto the topic of bombs, I kept my mouth shut. If they wanted to do something nasty, they didn't have to buy military-grade stuff. Not when ANFO (ammonia nitrate with fuel oil) or dynamite was easy to acquire.

"Why do you always look smug when we talk about this?" Simon asked.

"I'm not smug. I don't know anything about bombs."

Except I did. If they wanted a bomb, they needed a farmer with questionable morals and tree stumps he hadn't gotten around to removing.

Have you ever noticed when you think something no one else has thought of—no matter how simple—your face glows? Simon slapped the glow away.

To make him stop, I told him about the farmers.

When we met "Z" behind a no-tell motel in Ithaca—I was driving again, they were tanked *again*—he passed a heavy wooden box with misspelled Sharpie writing across the top. *Dangerus.* His face matched that spelling, wrong in more places than right. He'd welded an American flag to his rusty Ford; a ball sack hung from the hitch. His cab oozed McDonald's wrappers—two fluttered out his open window when he passed me the box. He was everything I expected him to be.

"You aren't buying a vest next, are you?" Z asked, hints of nervous laughter escaping his lips. "'Cause I can't be selling to *terrorists.*"

"No way. This is for shits and giggles," I said.

Z lifted a cell, snapped a photo of us. "Good, 'cause I'll nail your ass if you get me into anything." Which was stupid, because we could obviously nail his ass too, but whatever. He

tapped the side of his truck and said, "Don't forget. Shits and giggles are dangerous"—*dangerus*—and then drove off, ball sack swinging.

Back in the boathouse attic, I opened the box and made a grand gesture, "What did I tell you?", hoping the nonsense stopped here.

"Pure Science gets a gold star," they raved.

"Did anyone see you buy it?" Dozer asked, because he, like the rest of them, could barely remember his own name at the moment, much less Z's.

"Are you kidding? I'm a magician, same as the rest of you."

We say the things that people most want to hear.

13. You'd have made that same walk naked.

$49,333.00

Chan's breathing was perfectly even and his body was diagonal and twisted in the sheets. When I slid onto the bed beside him this morning and wrapped my body around his, he smelled like the absence of toothpaste and the presence of sweat. Familiar rather than unpleasant. I probably smelled like coffee beans and Crest. I blew my breath at his nose, smiling as he twitched awake.

"*Hey.*" He yawned.

"Hey."

He stretched—back arching; toes sticking out the sheets; his muscles and veins ropelike. God, I loved him like this. Groggy

and sweet. Squinting and squirming. It was like waking a lion cub. Chan's glasses weren't on the bedside table. I scooted closer, nearly nose to nose. I changed the part in his hair, smoothing it left and then right, searching absentmindedly for the amber sprinkled throughout the mahogany strands.

"Chan, you okay?"

"I am now. I'd kiss you except I haven't brushed my teeth."

"That was a serious question."

Our eyes locked. His were a green I never truly captured in a photograph. A green that you could tell were green in a black-and-white image.

"Why wouldn't I be okay?"

Deep breath. "Where did you put New York?"

"Put New York?" He made the city sound foreign. Like Kyrgyzstan or Djibouti.

Faced with the choice to disengage or double down, I doubled down. I moved my hand under the sheet, knowing my touch would be cold on his bare chest. He cringed as I drummed the skin over his heart. "June fifteenth. I want to talk about what happened. I want to talk about going back."

"We covered this."

Have we? Because on Sunday, there's a thing. "Can't you feel the weight? Everything we don't say lives between us. And it's changing us, or . . . I don't know, but I'm alone and you're right here. I need something from you."

I need something from you should have worked. If you say *I*

need something from you to someone you love and they don't say *What?* or *I'm listening*, it's problematic at best, relationship ending at worst. I'm not crazy to have this expectation.

Chan broke eye contact and moved my hand to my side of the bed. "I'm gonna brush my teeth." He stalked across the room in his boxer briefs.

During his absence, Mike, his dad, poked his head into the room and said, "You want any breakfast, Golden? I'm making biscuits."

"No, thanks. I made your coffee."

Chan reappeared on a mission, and Mike moved out of his way and disappeared down the hallway. Chan stood at his dresser, shimmying into jeans, jamming deodorant into his armpits.

"Brushing your teeth doesn't negate the question," I said.

He added a T-shirt, shoved his hat over his eyes, and planted himself in a gaming chair instead of returning to the bed. Bending over, he rested both elbows on his knees and cracked his knuckles. "We know each other, right?"

"Well enough you'd have made that same walk naked."

"Then why can't you understand I don't want to talk about New York City?"

"The same reason you can't understand that I need to."

"Golden, pick someone else to talk to before you drive me crazy."

"You don't mean that."

He gave a slow, deliberate nod. Recracked his knuckles. He walked across the room, kissed my cheek as violently as a cheek can be kissed. "No, I actually do. Now, I'm going to school. Have a good day."

He hadn't shaved. The kiss chafed. The whole thing chafed.

14. Beautiful but dark

$50,921.00

Three hours later, I was in Dolly Dodge with Becky Cable on my way to Florida, feeling guilty, feeling free. Emotions never played fair. I hadn't played fair either, and now I knew something about Chan he didn't want me to know.

After he stormed off this morning, I lay on the floor and reached under the headboard. Feeling around for the cigar box, my fingers also found a book. I slid Chandler's box toward me and snagged the book too. Chan had various sketchbooks; they were on his drafting table in the corner and crammed into the bookshelf by the bed. I'd never seen this particular one.

The first twenty or so pages had sketches of faces for his nativity carving. I kept flipping, wanting more, and hit a

second section. The drawings here were . . . frantic. Beautiful but dark. The first, a familiar-looking man. Big, bushy, salt-and-pepper beard. Middle Eastern, maybe? The charcoal captured every handsome feature. Next, a girl. Also someone I couldn't place. Five more who might have been students at my high school but weren't. They were *someone*, the details were specific—wrinkled Yankees T-shirt, butterfly headband, hooped earrings with dangling hearts—to be fabrications. Except for the first man, they all looked to be between sixteen and twenty. I hit the next drawing and dropped the journal.

Simon Westwood.

The picture on the following page: Caroline Ascott.

Chan had started the next drawing one page over but hadn't finished it. Rudy's eyes watched me. I stopped there.

"Oh, Chan."

I returned the journal and opened the cigar box, even more convinced I was right. He'd saved less cash than I anticipated. Or maybe he'd spent his reserves on my ring. Regardless, I placed into the box five hundred dollars with a little note that read, *Plane Money for New York*. It was everything I had that I wasn't using. And then I left.

15. More sides than a Rubik's Cube

$51,921.00

Dolly was a 1990 two-tone brown Dodge Ram with a camper shell that was sometimes off, sometimes on. Currently on. The animal was everything you ever wanted a station wagon to be with the height of a truck. The left windshield wiper didn't work, and the gas cap wouldn't screw tight. Those were her only deficiencies. Well, and Dolly peaked at sixty-five miles per hour. Not a significant problem in Braxton Springs. But things rattled on the interstate. Becky wrote Dolly's faults in the dashboard dust: no speed, no radio, no cruise control, one working seat belt, sliding cab window won't close, smells awful.

"Are you wishing we'd come in the Mustang?"

"No way." She swiped through the dust. "I like the *Titanic* even though it sank."

She'd been dicking around town this morning when I stopped at the ATM to take all the money out of my account. The computer screen had requested my PIN and it went about as well as usual.

1389.

Denied.

1893.

Denied.

3198.

Denied.

The car behind me honked.

9831.

Denied.

I'd screeched away from the machine into a spot so Honky McHonkerson behind me could use the ATM. The car was a Mustang. Electric blue. Becky Cable. She'd parked, straddling the lines, and ventured through the rain to my window. "Tough morning, Jennings?"

"Can't remember my PIN."

"Shocking. Were you needing something in particular? I can spot you the cash."

I don't know why I said it, but I did. "Not unless you want to spring for a trip to Florida."

Becky's dark hair was freshly showered and wet as an otter coming out of the creek. A strand stuck to her cheeks, and

her baby-doll shirt hiked toward her belly button. Even more so when she threw her hands in the air and whooped as only Becky could. "Hell, yeah, Jennings, I'll knick, knack, Kerouac with you any day. Let's blow this shitbox town."

"Hop in the cab," I'd said.

She'd slapped the door paneling triumphantly and hustled to the passenger side. "I've had three espressos," she admitted, one of them still in her hand. Her gray eyes were double their usual size. "Now tell me, who is in Florida? Your secret boyfriend? Secret girlfriend? Some lame second cousin on your mother's side who once asked you to do seven minutes in heaven? A sexual predator pretending to be your lame second cousin on your mother's side who you met on the internet the same way I met—"

"Becky."

Most people would apologize in a moment like that; Becky sipped more ten-dollar coffee, her eyes growing ever wider, ever probing. "Or is it a friend from summer camp? Or maybe, I know, a soldier you sent a Christmas box to who is home from Iraq? There are a ton of army bases in Florida."

"Becky Cable, you have more sides than a Rubik's Cube."

"That's the kindest thing anyone has ever said to me. What do they have, nine or six sides? Don't undershoot me, Jennings. Now, tell me the glorious details."

How about the glorious details of Rudy Guthrie? V-shaped face. Hollow cheekbones. Punchy jawline. High-arching eyebrows and prettiness you had to look for, but that was definitely

there. That description sounded more like a Gap model than a friend. I said, "Another survivor. That's who's in Florida."

"Ooooooo."

Becky realigned her internal Rubik's Cube and tamed her eyes. "Were you serious? Like, do you really want to go to Florida? 'Cause I was only screwing around, and now I feel like a royal dick. Like Charles-cheated-on-Diana-level dick. I love the royals; do you love the royals?"

Chandler screamed in my head. *Pick someone else to talk to.*

"Your nose is bleeding again, Jennings." Becky opened the glove box and found a napkin. I jammed the wad against the end of my nose. Stress bleeds were a fixture of my post-June life.

"Sorry," I said of the blood. She shrugged and waited on me to say something substantial. "Becky, I do want to go to Florida. And then, New York."

Because Becky is an extraordinary human, she had four words: "Your car or mine?"

We were already in Dolly, so that decision made itself. Becky pillaged the necessaries from her house and parked her Mustang at Gran's, and we hit the pavement at exactly sixty-five miles an hour.

Thank God her espresso high tapered somewhere around the Tennessee state line. I felt solid about including her on this crazy mission. She was now making a playlist she had aptly titled: Becky and Go Go. After a few vetoed songs, she announced, "I'm also making an anti-playlist. We'll fill it with

songs we hate and use it as punishment for all mistakes made. First song? I say 'Cotton-Eyed Joe.'"

"Do we really need more than that?"

"It's a *list*. A list must have more than one item."

I accidentally revved the engine above sixty-five; Dolly lurched. "I think in this case one will do."

Our musical tastes were similar. A selection of "oldies" we'd inherited from our parents, a fine collection of P!nk, Bruno, and Ed Sheeran, and then a whole set of songs that made us feel delighted to be driving. (But we couldn't name those artists without checking iTunes.) Sharing music was like sharing a diary. When you tell someone, "I love this song," you're giving a piece of your story to the person.

She said, "Stop at the Rocket, will you? I need to pee."

My blank expression told her I didn't know the Rocket.

"Houston, we have a problem. You know? The Alabama welcome center? NASA? The US Space and Rocket Center. There's a rocket along the interstate. They let you pee there."

I lifted my left shoulder in a half shrug.

"Jennings, if you spout some junk about how you've never liked space, just dump me on the side of the road and I'll hitch my way home."

"Becky?"

"Before you ask, the Rocket doesn't have astronaut ice cream in their vending machines. Major oversight, if you ask me."

"Becky?"

"Yeah."

"Why weren't we closer before now?"

Becky pressed Play on "Cotton-Eyed Joe" and laughed. As I didn't know what was suddenly hilarious, I didn't join her.

"Do you want this straight up or on the rocks?" she asked.

"Straight up, I guess."

When someone puts a question to you like that, whatever they say next has teeth. Becky's seat belt was the nonworking one, and she turned completely sideways and shoved her toes in my lap. She waited until I glanced sideways before she spoke. "You have two asses." She said this matter-of-factly.

"Excuse me."

"Two asses, Jennings. Your camera. Your boyfriend." She counted them off on her fingers. "You're always up one or the other. Makes it hard to know you. Add that to your notoriety, and, well, you're living in 'Cotton-Eyed Joe' Friendship Land. That is to say, everyone knows your song without having any idea what the words mean."

Ouch. Four hundred peers reduced me to camera, boyfriend, and Bus #21. I'd always thought seeing a person was like seeing a mountain. From a distance, it's a shape, mostly a triangle. Up close, it's crawling with moss and trees and animals. I'd never been sure who was responsible for the distance someone observed me from, but it couldn't all belong to me. I didn't attack Becky, but I asked my question as firmly as she'd

made her statement. "If you think I'm such a shallow well, why are you still here?"

"Oh." She swapped back to the Becky and Go Go playlist and made a selection; the melodic notes of Simon and Garfunkel emerged. "Because I'm clearly supposed to be. Synchronicity, my darling friend."

16. **Ship it.**

$52,291.00

Carter Stockton called after we stopped at the Rocket. I'd forgotten all about telling him I wanted to talk. We connected, and a siren blared in the background. And then beeping. "Golden, hold on a sec, will you?" Another man's voice said, "You off shift, Stock?" and Carter answered, "Just now."

"You there?" The background noise muted.

"I am."

"Thank you for emailing. Sorry for the delay in calling."

I was struck by how his phone voice matched his video voice, but didn't match my memory of June 15. I said, "You probably don't remember, but you were the medic who saved my life. I've been watching *Accelerant Orange*."

"I remember every kid I put on an ambulance that day, and I especially remember you. Who could forget a name like Golden? You're not a kid, so please don't be offended by the title. It's only, the longer I work on *Accelerant Orange*, the more personal it is."

"I'm not offended, Carter."

"Call me Stock. Everybody does."

"Tell me about Sunday."

"*Sunday?*" Becky mouthed excitedly. I waved her over, and she pressed her ear near mine. The beeping sounded again and Stock apologized before he continued. "You've seen some of the reassembly job in the videos, but what you can't tell is how much all the families have done to make the bus art. Everyone donated something. Photos and clothes and school bags. One lady brought me a signed baseball autographed by Babe Ruth because it was her son's favorite thing. Can you believe that? Thousands of dollars."

"That's unbelievable."

"I wish I had something from you. Not that I mean you any pressure by that. Only that you're a big part of that day. I reckon you're the reason I'm doing this."

I wiped my palms on my jeans and left a big sweaty smudge. *The reason he was doing this.* Becky's eyes went wide again.

"What if I brought you something?" I asked.

"Sure. Ship it, and if it doesn't arrive in time for the opening, I'll add it immediately. Rudy diagrammed the seats when I

was ordering replacements. I'll put whatever it is in your seat."

"I mean, what if I brought myself and Rudy Guthrie?"

Becky squealed with excitement, and I pinched her leg.

"To the opening?" Carter asked.

"Yes."

"Gosh, I'd be honored to have you attend."

"We don't need tickets?" Surely not, but I had to ask.

"On the house," Carter bellowed, and I knew he was excited about the possibility of our attending. "But . . . if you decide it's too much, I can put you in contact with the other families. They'd jump at the chance to hear final stories about their kids. Especially the Conner family. They've had it rough 'cause some person on the sidewalk claimed their kid was in a vest too. You know how social media junk gets going."

"Jim Conner wasn't a bomber."

"Ah, hell, I know. I only meant, it'd help to hear it from you too. They're the ones who gave me the idea about the college fund."

"Will the Conners be at *Accelerant Orange* on Sunday?"

"They will."

Deep breath. "Tell them I'll be there."

Becky squealed again.

17. SOME MORE THAN OTHERS.

$53,781.01

Need to get to know someone? Drive through Alabama. There is literally nothing else to do. The miles—326 of them—passed slowly, but we were fast approaching the delicate moment when I told Becky that (1) I didn't have an address for where we were going, and as "Florida" was a rather large place we would have to acquire that information sooner rather than later; (2) I hadn't specifically told Rudy we were making this jaunt; and (3) my connection with him was limited to Facebook.

The last part hung her up. "Facebook? Like *the* social network of grandmas and cousins in Tommy Bahama shirts who love their guns?"

"That's where I found him. And then he found me."

"Worrisome."

I explained my original search. How I had three pieces of information. Name. State. Approximate age. I gave verbal and written statements to the Bureau of Alcohol, Tobacco, Firearms, and Explosives, as did Chan, but they didn't reciprocate information. The bombing of Bus #21 was on front-page spreads from Washington to New York to London. Nineteen victims; faces and names listed in yearbook-looking spreads in print and online, and even on some billboards. One bomber: Simon Westwood. Profiles and speculative psychological reports. "What went wrong?" articles. Photos of him from high school yearbooks. His garage, where he'd first assembled the bombs. Emails indicated he sold three other vests. There was even a photo of Caroline and Simon on the deck of a boat with a two-word caption: *Keuka Lake*. I'd googled, but I'd come up empty.

Chan's names and mine were never released. We were minors, and we weren't on a passenger manifest. Our local paper agreed not to do a special interest piece. We'd been listed in community prayer requests, but someone would have to be investigating to find the print copy, as *Braxton Springs Weekly* wasn't online yet.

"That was a great initial decision, but it was oddly isolating," I said.

"So you followed the continued coverage looking for this other guy and girl?"

"Yeah. But there was nothing. As far as I could tell, they were as silent as Chan and me."

Becky admitted she hadn't previously paid attention to the minutiae—she rarely did—but she'd paid attention to me. I seemed *fake o-kay*. Chan was *a hurricane*. "But you had each other, so I didn't waltz into that shizz." There was something admirable in that. "Did the other victims—is that the right word?—know each other?"

"From what I read, some did."

"How did you and Chandler end up on that bus?"

"Rudy."

I fell under the scrutiny of her pensive eyes and heavy mascara. "Rudy from Facebook? Rudy who we're going to meet?"

"Yes."

"Do you hate him now?"

I'd never even thought to be angry. In fact, I worried that Rudy might feel guilty. He'd all but dared me to ride along. I'd seen his invitation as kind and mildly flirtatious. Chan and I weren't exactly rich, and New York had been way more expensive to negotiate than planned. Sneaking on the bus meant a free ride to Battery Park.

"No way," I said. "He was a way to get my photo."

"Come on! He radically changed your life."

"Everyone we meet changes our life."

"Dude." She turned "Cotton-Eyed Joe" to max volume. "SOME MORE THAN OTHERS."

We were quiet. The road was quiet. Dolly stayed loud as

ever, plugging away at the miles like a goat chewing cud. Becky asked me other questions about Rudy, the college fund—now at $53,781.01—and how mad Chan would be when he found out we were gone, and then wisely moved to safer topics. She chatted about the chapel where I lived and the new Bojangles coming to town and if my mom liked her newish aide job with special ed and whether I considered the Hive a cult; all while I relived the steps that preceded me boarding Bus #21.

Becky shoved her toes at the dash, smudging the window with her little piggies. "We're gonna get a ticket for going sooooo slow. Which I guess is fine, since there's no point in arriving somewhere unknown faster than we have to. We could be there right now." She pointed to a white house with black shutters alongside the interstate. "He could live there." Another brick mansion with a rolling wooden fence to the left. "Or there." She rolled down the window and called, "Rudy! Rudy! Where art thou?"

"You could drive."

She lit like a sun. I pulled off, and we swapped spots. I used the opportunity to send Rudy a message.

Golden: Where in Florida do you live?

Secretly, I was thinking, *Please don't say Key Largo or Miami.*

Rudy: Orlando.

"Set a course for Orlando," I told Becky.

And then I sent a text to Chan:

Call me when you get home. Something big to share.

"You know. I don't know what's scarier. That we're meeting

someone you don't know. Or he's on Facebook enough to answer you instantly."

"Don't make me play it!" I said, threatening the anti-playlist.

"I'm driving. I'm driving."

We drove toward Orlando.

CAROLINE

Five "vests" were draped over the shoulders of mannequins Johnny stole from the Salvation Army. They resembled a wicked episode of *Doctor Who*. I avoided their opaque faces as if eye contact might animate their pale, static limbs. I grew used to Mary, Peggy, Kathy, Althea, and Elizabeth; the mannequins, named after Larry Flynt's wives because when Johnny googled *celebs with five wives*, the founder of *Hustler* came up. None of us talked about the uniqueness of their clothing. None of us talked about how brazen it was to keep them on display in the boathouse attic even though we were the only ones who came up here. And none of us talked about those bombs living their lives fifty yards from where I slept. Damn close to tourists who flocked to our lake.

The boys had moved on to other projects to cure boredom;

I'd started talking to Angela again. Only when I was in the bathroom, shower running. Simon hadn't bugged my bedroom, I didn't think, but I didn't want him to find out and hurt her. He knew Angela was my ex. Knew she was beautiful and he couldn't compete when it came to attraction.

I didn't *love* love Angela anymore, but I missed estrogen. Missed friendship and conversations about politics and movies. Missed having someone tell me whether a pencil skirt was preferable to an A-line with my T. rex hips. I missed lying side by side on beach towels listening to seaplanes take off and land. Missed driving to Muranda Cheese tastings, and arguing over Aged British Cheddar and Gotcha Gouda. She always returned to Simon though.

"Your boyfriend moved in with you, yeah?" she asked.

"He doesn't technically *live* here."

She laughed, the kind that was at my expense. "Right. Right. He's just your boathouse buddy. I remember those days. I hope you're on birth control."

My turn to laugh. I couldn't remember how to have the conversations I longed to have.

Hey, Angela, I'm drowning.

Hey, Angela, Simon has five bombs.

Hey, Angela, he hits me with a plastic pipe.

"That's why we have Planned Parenthood, right?" I said.

"At least for now." And then we talked about the latest Pride march instead of me mentioning Mary, Kathy, Althea, and Elizabeth.

Dozer sold Peggy a month before the bombing of Bus #21, because Dozer was one of those eBay freaks who had his mom's Walmart dishes and his dad's screwdriver set from 1980 listed. If something was horizontal for three seconds, Dozer price-tagged it.

Simon freaked and hit Doze in the ribs. "Fifty bucks? What d'you think we are? A yard sale for munitions?"

Johnny paused the game system and set his droopy eyes on Simon. "You're going to get us arrested, man." He started it again, the fear already lost.

I said, "Who did you sell it to?" because I imagined a scenario that looped from person X to Dozer to us to Z and a photo of me from the motel holding dynamite. I could not, on that day, imagine Bus #21.

Dozer cradled his rib cage and explained, well, as much as he ever explained. "The guy said if this one worked, he'd buy the rest for five thousand. He's straight, dude. He won't tell." Dozer took a beer from the minifridge. He held it against his side. "Money's money. Larry's ladies can't live here forever, ya know?"

And if I remember correctly, we got dressed to slay and went to dinner at Union Block on Simon's credit card. Simon wasn't that amped about one rogue bomb. But then Dozer sold two more, and I decided Ellis Island might be the place to let go of the world.

18. A picture of a picture of himself

$55,822.00

Someone should make a phone that doesn't ring. Texting: great. Apps: great. Phone calls: unnecessary. At four thirty, my mother started calling. At seven, Dad. Who, in his history, had called only the bank and the no-solicitations-by-telemarketers number. Evidently, they found my "Gone Camping with Becky Cable" note unsatisfactory. Or maybe they were mad I took all the cookies. Gran would smooth things over tonight.

Chan didn't call.

Becky shifted sideways, squinted, and appeared unable to find a place where the setting sun didn't scorch her eyes. "You'll have to answer the parentals eventually."

"What did you tell *your* parents?"

"That I was running away to join the circus. This Rudy thing flops like a whale, I say we go to Harry Potter world."

"What did you actually tell them?"

She smiled a true Becky smile. Not the one she made when she cracked a joke. "That you needed me and I would be home eventually."

I examined the creature that was Becky Cable. My fast findings: she wore lipstick like ChapStick, had mastered the art of blending scarves and T-shirts, and never, ever seemed lonely. Underneath her sarcasm and hair products, Becky Cable was earnest. Add all that to a Mustang, and she was the Chick-fil-A of girls. I told her as much and she said, "They do have the best nuggets a kid can buy."

We stopped at the next Chick-fil-A we spotted and Becky sprang for two meals. Halfway through a large waffle fries, she said, "So, when you Facebook-stalked Rudy Patootie, what else did you learn? PS, this sun is brutal. *Set already!*" she yelled at the horizon.

I tossed her my sunglasses and savored another nugget.

"No posts prior to last June. No details on his About section. Three photos: a dog that is probably a Great Dane mix; a hard-boiled egg, which he made his profile photo at some point—kudos on that—and, a picture of a picture of himself."

"Let me see."

While traffic was light, I let her glance. Rudy leaned

against a waist-high concrete wall. He'd crossed his arms over his chest, probably to show off his shoulders and biceps, since he had enough to go around. The photo had been of a group, but he'd cropped the left and right sides, leaving two phantom arms draped behind his neck. The hot pink tank he wore worked on less than 1 percent of the population; he was in the 1 percent. The very tips of his black hair were frosted white-white.

"I think he was a soccer player," I said, meaning to sound serious.

"I think I'd check and see if Olympus reported one of their gods missing. Golden Jennings, you have done me a disservice. This boy is . . ." She whistled.

"I know."

"Has Chan seen him? I mean, you're not . . . This isn't . . . 'Cause you're wearing your ring . . . so I . . ."

"Oh, stop. This isn't a booty call."

"Well, not for you, but some of us are willing to swing that way for special occasions."

Becky's fan-your-face reaction matched a memory from Down Yonder Bar. I had never been an insta-crush girl. I didn't have movie boyfriends or guys on an "I'm allowed to cheat with him" list. Chan was enough. But something about Rudy waltzed into space that had always belonged to Chan. I couldn't figure out the specifics, but I'd been very careful to keep mental distance between us. "Is it cheating to have wondered if you

might want someone else?"

"Not if it's him," she said in a way that made me know she absolutely did think it was cheating. She popped a chicken nugget in her mouth and chewed slowly. "Friend, you need to tell me everything you didn't tell me in Alabama."

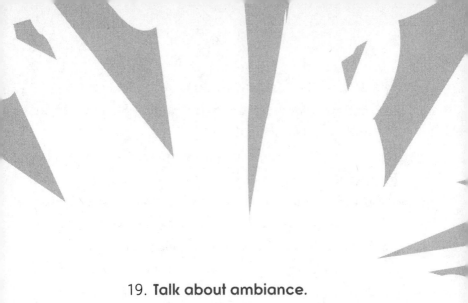

19. Talk about ambiance.

$55,912.00

I told Becky a story, each scene a photo.

The bar sat catty-cornered to our hostel and advertised half-priced appetizers. Our twenty-dollar-a-day food budget was pleased, and the atmosphere in Down Yonder was up, up, and away. Someone loaded the jukebox with peppy music, and after some quality "flirting" on Chandler's part, the waitress said, "Table's yours all night." She brought him a beer on the house. I wished she would bring him more than one. He was in a ratty mood and had been since we landed at JFK. The airline lost his bag, and although they'd promised to deliver it to the hostel pronto, he was in a spiral. His bag was probably halfway

around the world. His sketchbooks were lost forever.

"Southwest doesn't fly around the world," I reminded him.

Things devolved from there.

He was "It's the principle of the thing," and I was, "I'm checking out the bathroom until you're done sulking." The bag loss sucked for sure, but tomorrow we'd be in Times Square and then MoMA. The day after, Ellis Island. We were taking Gran's photo and no airline mishap could steal my joy.

Down Yonder's bathroom was on a sub-planet. Down the hall, down the steps, down another set of steps, down another hallway, through a curtain. Perhaps they'd named the bar after the bathroom's location. They should put water stations at the midpoint. Or urinals. Or both. Which turned out to be a bad thing, as the unisex stalls required a token and were occupied. The first door opened. A couple stumbled out. They shut the door behind them before I could ask them to hold it open.

"Count to thirty before you follow me," the redhead said.

They smelled like sex and french fry oil. Thirty seconds wouldn't change their flushed faces or gloriously messy sex manes. I don't remember their features very well, but she had on a black leather skirt I adored, and he had his hair partially hidden by a Waldo style cap. If Chan were in a better mood, we might have been them.

As I was in no rush, I waited for the other stall, planning to shove a foot in the door before the occupant (or occupants) let it close. I heard the dryer and leaped to action. I wedged my body into the door as a guy stepped out.

"I got in," he said.

"Actually, you're getting out, and I'm getting in. Thank you kindly."

He held a phone in his hand, his face brighter than the LED screen. "No, I got in. Well, not in-in; they won't let you sign until November of your senior year. But pretty much, per this email, I'm going to Emerson to play soccer."

I quickly grasped the gravity of the situation. "Oh. *Oh!* Congratulations. That's in . . . Boston?"

"Yeah. I can't . . . I, man . . . what an unbelievable night. Kiss me. Then I'll know if it's real."

"Does that work?"

"I'm sorry, what?"

"That pickup line."

He gave me an incredulous little nod. "I wasn't picking you up yet."

"You said kiss me."

"I said *pinch me*. Like, as in, am I dreaming?"

We stared, each reexamining the exchange, and the hilarious improbability registered. He smiled. I laughed. We were half-in, half-out of the bathroom. Inches from each other and also inches from a urinal and a trail of wadded toilet paper. Talk about ambiance. We shifted, subtly, as we simultaneously stopped assessing the situation and started assessing each other. Who exactly were we pinching?

I was not one of those girls who acted like I was completely unattractive. No, I wasn't top model skinny, pretty, or posh,

and that girl-next-door thing wasn't me either. I understood what I had going for me. Lips. Eyebrows. Hair that looked good dirty. Once, I asked Chandler, "On a scale of Hermione in *Harry Potter* one to Hermione in *Harry Potter* seven-point-two, what would you give me?" He stroked the bones on my face, kissed my nose, and said, "You're every scene where she dances."

Those were my favorite scenes, so an A++ answer from the boyfriend.

I'd never had to chart the difference between attractive and attractive to Chan, but I very quickly found myself wondering how this Emerson stranger saw me. I would put him (based only on looks) out of my league. Well, maybe not, if I had on Redhead's *Wait thirty seconds* leather skirt.

"I'm Rudy." He thrust his hand in my direction. "Washed it. I swear."

I pumped his hand twice. "Go." And then, realizing that didn't sound like a name, and added, "Golden."

"Go suits you."

"Bathroom joke?"

"Well, yes, but no." He leaned closer, nearly straddling me. The doorjamb dug through my shirt into my spine. I didn't mind. "Remember a moment ago when I said *pinch me* and you heard *kiss me*, what if we went with your version? Ever kissed a stranger, *Go*?"

"I've only ever kissed my boyfriend."

Mood killer. Thank God.

Rudy pressed his shoulder blades against the other side of the jamb. A respectful foot of air molecules between us. His tongue traced his bottom lip, presumably as he figured out whether he should be embarrassed by my rejection or respect that I was steadfast. I tried not to watch and ogled a crappy piece of art in the hallway. My eyes came back to his.

"Well," he said. "If you ditch Boyfriend tomorrow and wanna see the city with a Florida boy headed to Emerson, I'll be on Charter Bus Number Twenty-One. The curb outside the Green-Conwell. Nine a.m." Then he tugged the red beanie off my head and started down the long tunnel.

The half-lit hall. The curtain a portal. The boy going places. I was opening the camera, extending the billow, cranking the film, before I even registered the decision.

"Bandit," I called at his back, hoping he'd turn.

He spun on his Chucks, and I was ready.

Click.

Full of mischief and maybe even disappointment, he said, "Obviously, a better bandit would steal the girl instead of the cap." Then he laughed and launched the beanie at my chest.

As I leaned out to catch the cap, the bathroom door locked behind me.

20. Wildly vulnerable with a stranger

$58,912.00

Orlando traffic sucked big hairy bull balls.

We knew where we were going. A bar called Parkers on Highway 530. And we knew how to get there. Thank you, Waze. But we were stuck in that terrible time warp where the estimated time of arrival grew from a couple of minutes to twenty or thirty to *how does it take fifty minutes to travel two miles?*

"We might die here," Becky said.

I didn't disagree.

We were close to Disney World. Even without the signs, there was no missing the happiest place on earth. Families on

sidewalks. Families in minivans. Families riding our ass so closely they could get a drink out of our cooler.

In my last Facebook exchange with Rudy—the one with *I'm in Orlando, SURPRISE!*—we made the arrangements, and these were the arrangements. Parkers. Highway 530. 7:45. Becky and I were frayed from driving and buzzing with adrenaline. She'd been behind the wheel the last six hours, so I didn't bring up how close she cut her lane transitions and she didn't mention the number of times my phone rang. Still no word from Chan.

Parkers was on the right.

An old blue Mustang—maybe as old as Dolly—idled near the back in what my uncle Ash called the "Murder Section." None of the tires matched, and it had been wrecked in a way that had required the owner to scavenge a new, non-blue door. Rudy had said he'd be in an old 'Stang or a Pontiac GTO.

"You think that's him?"

"I mean, it's gotta be, right? Except . . ." I left my indecision hanging out there.

She looped the bar. The blue Mustang was the only 'Stang. Plenty of beater cars that spoke to the company Parkers kept. No Pontiacs. I'm not sure why, but I expected his car to be newer. Becky stalled Dolly in the drive-by-alcohol lane. She stretched the seat belt and heaved as if the belt had been choking her all day. "Remind me again how well you know Hannibal over there?"

"Would you prefer *We met in a bar bathroom* or *We're Face-book friends?*"

"I'd prefer you promise me we're not about to get sliced and diced. Can you see inside that rust bucket?"

There were no lights in the back of Parkers. There was only shadows and cat piss.

"Not from here."

This was where we decided if we drove eleven hours to pull into the space next to a fugly Mustang, roll down our windows, and get wildly vulnerable with a stranger, or if this is where we drove on to New York and wondered who was in that car.

"Are we doing this?" I asked.

"I have never felt like I was living in *The Matrix* more than right now."

Becky Cable was many things, but I was fairly sure her movie tastes were anything with a *Saturday Night Live* star and an occasional Avenger thrown in for sex appeal. "Have you even seen *The Matrix*?"

"No, but I know all the gifs, and this a green pill–pink pill moment."

"*Blue* pill–*red* pill."

She pinched my thigh for correcting her. I pinched her back for never watching *The Matrix*. Although I wouldn't have seen the film if Chan hadn't wanted to re-create an action shot that he claimed was epic and I decided was a good

way to die. Our knees were bruised for a solid week and the picture sucked.

"All right," I said. "Let's make this stranger-danger situation our bitch."

Becky swung Dolly one spot over from the Mustang and laid on the horn. Two heads snapped up from their reclined positions. Becky and I waved as the guys turned to check the disturbance. They waved back. Rudy Guthrie was in the passenger seat, and he was wearing my red beanie.

Becky asked, "Did you know he was bringing a friend?"

"No, but I didn't tell him you were with me either."

"That's definitely him."

"Definitely."

We rolled down the windows in unison. Florida air was dripping with humidity. Way too warm for the sweatshirt I'd been wearing all day. My heart slammed around like a rude houseguest and I leaned around Becky.

"Hi."

"Hi," Rudy said.

A lump that must have been visible from space formed in my throat, a camel hump bulging in my neck. Becky's mouth crept next to my cheek. She whispered in a very non-whispery voice, "And in the beginning, God created sex."

"You're going straight to hell, and they'll probably keep you," I replied.

Rudy hung his arms over the side of the car like he was

starring in a sixties movie about drag-strip racers. His hair poked out the front of the beanie. I'd seen Highland cattle with the same cut. I hugged my elbows, as if that would keep him farther from my heart.

"What are you doing in Orlando?" he asked.

"I heard you needed a ride to New York City."

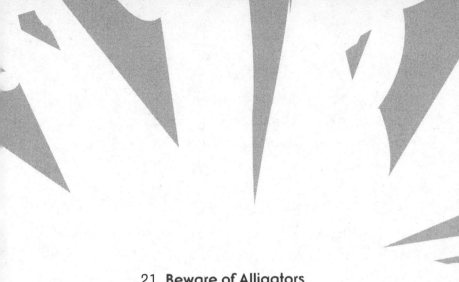

21. Beware of Alligators

$59,989.00

Necessary pleasantries occurred.

"This is Becky."

"This is Victor."

"Friend."

"Stepbrother."

Rudy was the same as before, and that was mostly a relief. I'd had hours to construct reunion narratives. The one where he didn't show at all. The one where he lived in Canada. The one where his family forbade him from seeing me. I should have written the narrative where he was here, one parking spot away. I thumbed toward Parkers. "One of your favorite establishments?"

Victor gave a mirthful laugh and flicked Rudy in the gut. "Told you we should have said Dollar Store."

Rudy stopped Victor from swatting him again, and said to us, "Parkers is easy to find if you're not from here."

"We've been to worse," I assured him.

Victor cast another gleeful, coy look at his stepbrother. "So have we," which I could have guessed, because their eyes were talking miles a minute. There were so many stories in the space between the boys, I'd never get to read them all, even if they handed me the book. I didn't have a great vantage point to assess Victor, but he was small, compact, and always smiling. My granddad would have called him "a pistol," my gran, "a card." His head was shaved, tan as the rest of him, and he had a cursive tattoo on his shoulder that read *Deuce*. I liked him immediately.

I released my elbows. Finally. "Thanks for meeting us."

The expression Rudy volleyed back was delightful. "Anytime."

Which made it easy to tease back at him. "I have a nasty habit of showing up when you invite me somewhere."

"No complaints on my end," he said.

I felt slightly queasy. Like I'd eaten some badly cured guilt this morning and my stomach was just beginning to spasm. Becky slipped her hand to my leg and lifted a wrinkle in my jeans. "Keep breathing, you."

What were we to do now?

Rudy sensed my question. "You bring your camera?"

I lifted the battered Canon into view. "Never without one."

This time Rudy hit Victor in the gut before Rudy turned to me and upnodded. There was something unspoken going on and no time to ask for clarity. "Let's hit the farm," he said, more to Victor than me. Then, a wicked grin curled Victor's lips. "You ladies wanna see something beautiful? Besides yourselves, I mean." He'd said this to other girls, and it had surely worked. Victor was sugar water, and we were meant to be the hummingbirds.

Becky revved Dolly's engine. "We do."

The boys squealed backward and spun toward the road. "Try to keep up," Victor yelled at Becky. Thank goodness the traffic was still mind-numbingly slow or we'd have lost them. The Mustang wove through neighborhoods and zipped across a major highway. We drove—God knows where—through canopies of Spanish moss and glades and reeds and past houses with big boats and houses with small boats and mansions with manicured lawns and shacks where the only income seemed to come from hot boiled peanuts. Two turns-offs later, we Y'd onto a furrowed dirt road and into a pull-out. A rusted chain stretched between two crooked wooden posts. The posted sign read:

PRIVATE PROPERTY
Beware of Alligators

Becky said, "Quaint," and I said, "The Farm."

"*A place for beautiful ladies*," Becky added, mocking Victor,

and clearly pleased with the compliment.

My insides were pacing. Not from fear. I never once felt like we were in danger. Well, not physical danger. Every minute we spent with Rudy and Victor felt like inching toward the ledge of the fire tower back home. Breathtaking and precarious. Becky expressed it best. "We're in it deep already, aren't we?"

Victor flung his door open, fiddled with a combination lock, and the chain collapsed to the ground. Two tire ruts led to the hilltop. Dolly and the 'Stang parked side by side under a Florida oak, its gnarled branches curling from the trunk like octopus legs. The clock rolled from 8:59 to 9:00. Rudy called, "Four. Three. Two. One. Look there," as fireworks lit the horizon. *Boom. Boom. Boom.* I recoiled, shrinking in the seat. Rudy passed something to Becky's outstretched hand. Noise-reduction headphones.

Victor winked at me. "My man, Ru, thinks of everything. Got his babies and bathwater in two separate containers."

Rudy smiled proudly. "I really love fireworks. And I thought you might want to shoot the famous nightly Magic Kingdom show."

I couldn't put my appreciation into coherent words. Instead, I made the necessary adjustments to camera settings, leaped from Dolly, and snapped photos in time with pyrotechnic beauty. The sky was in utter cooperation, night-black, the magical quality that makes you think of lampposts inside wardrobes and shifting staircases under castle spires. All that

firmament spent the day inhaling beauty, and this was its gloriously long exhale. I took a very deep breath, smelled the sulfur and copper, the hint of citrus permeating the air, and thought, *Am I awake?*

Headphones on, I walked to Rudy's side of the Mustang. "Thank you for this."

"What?"

I yelled over the explosions. "Thank *you!*"

He lifted the left earpiece from his face, grinned. "Say it again?"

I took his picture instead. Letting the camera catch around my neck, I gripped the door. Rudy covered my fingers with his; the weight of his body seemed to be in those hands. Victor turned toward the opposite window.

"Pinch me," Rudy whispered.

I eased the words out. "I still have Boyfriend."

His eyes cut downward toward the diamond hearts on my fourth finger. "That from him?"

"Yeah."

Rudy's hand limped away from mine. He scratched his scalp, the beanie shifting around to reveal more wayward dark hair. "Boyfriend not want to come along?"

I shrugged and looked skyward, not wanting to out Chan, and not feeling the urge to defend him either. My eyes stung, but I kept the tears inside my head.

"Hey! No worries. I swear. I'm very glad you're happy, Go. I've wanted that for you," Rudy said.

He'd considered me enough since June to want something for me, and I liked having occupied space in his life the same way he had occupied space in mine. "I've wanted happiness for you too."

"Guess there's some mutual wanting going on." Before I responded, Rudy leaned around so Becky heard him. "We really moving this party to New York?"

"If you're willing," she said for us.

"Willing and . . . able."

Victor cut in. "Where are you lovely ladies staying tonight?"

I made a grand gesture at the cab. "Top reservation at Hotel Dolly Dodge."

That's the moment Rudy realized I hadn't planned this out. He checked with Victor, who flipped his hat around and gripped the wheel. Rudy looked off toward the Magic Kingdom and said, "Follow us. We'll see about parking that reservation somewhere safer than an alligator farm."

22. All-wheel drives

$61,469.00

We played follow the leader for the second time, and Becky did a bang-up job of not asking, "Jennings, what the hell are we doing?"

Wise on her. I had a very short list of things I *knew*. Four in total.

I knew Chan hadn't called and that if I were home right now, and everything were normal, we'd be nice and cozy watching a nineties movie with soft action and glaringly bad CGI. My head would be pillowed on his thighs; one of his hands resting heavy on my head, the other sketching.

I knew Carter's fund had collected more than sixty thousand dollars.

I knew a boy I'd met twice handed me noise-reduction headphones during a fireworks show.

And I knew I was still terrified of buses.

We passed Parkers, and Becky ran out of grace. "Those fireworks. That was *some* show," she said in a way that was 90 percent *Charlotte's Web* and 10 percent asshole.

"It's nothing."

"You keep telling yourself that, Jennings."

There was no time to tell myself anything else. The Mustang stopped along a curb in a neighborhood where the roofs needed repairs and the paint peeled off in large dandruffy flakes. The house directly in front of us had two front windows, one broken, and one apparently added for the sole purpose of holding a window unit. Two baseball bats braced the AC.

"This is us," Rudy yelled. "Pull into the yard."

At home, we had bent grass for acres, a luscious green that fused to the knees of your jeans and wouldn't wash out. If not for the ants, you could roll around and mistake the lawn for your bed. The yard here was scrubby sand with a few pimples of grass. It was packed with parked cars and plastic toys. The aforementioned Pontiac and a rusted-out yellow Jeep lacking a back left tire lurked beside the remnant of a wooden fence. Victor honked the horn and a neighbor across the street yelled, "Victor!"

"Marco!" Victor called jovially and whipped out of the Mustang like a gunshot. A curly-haired baby toddled onto the

porch and pinched the air to wave at us while licking a push-up ice cream pop. In a well-practiced move, Victor pinned the kid to his hip and blew a zerbert on his reddened belly. "Auntie Jane put you to bed at eight o'clock, Little Man."

The kid cackled.

"Victor's son, Deuce," Rudy said to us from his passenger seat.

Victor called over his shoulder to Rudy, "I'm coming, man," and deposited Deuce inside the house, hustling back to the Mustang. Rudy didn't move until his stepbrother lifted a low-profile wheelchair from the trunk and positioned it close to the passenger door, wheels locked. Rudy transitioned from the car to the chair, the motion graceful and easy.

"Nice ride," I said admiringly.

He picked at the edge of a fitness sticker wrapping the lime-green frame. "I should have told you about my highly specialized wheels."

"No," Becky answered for us. "It's fine. We love all-wheel drives."

Becky made a scene while trying not to make a scene. I slid down the cab and fell into step beside Rudy. "I should have told you I was coming to Orlando today."

He popped a wheelie and spun a full circle. "I'm glad you're here."

"I can't believe I am."

"I can't believe you want to go to New York."

"How can we not try?" I said, thinking of everything Carter and the viewers had done. "All those strangers. They're being so amazing."

"All we did was live. I don't deserve college money for that, but I'm really stoked."

A *very* large gray dog—the one from Facebook—broke loose from inside. With wild abandon, the animal flung himself onto Rudy's lap as if they'd been separated for years. "This is Buddy Holly." Rudy wrapped the Great Dane in a hug and patted his muscular haunches. Buddy Holly wiggled into a better position. The dog must have weighed eighty or ninety pounds.

"Buddy Holly?" I repeated. In 1959 Buddy Holly, the rock star, not the dog, died in an explosion. On a plane, not a bus.

Buddy Holly's ears thrust straight into the air like triangular satellites searching for a signal at the sound of his name.

Rudy said, "Not what you're probably thinking. He's named after a Weezer song. Fairly one-hit wonderish, but Mom played their CD when she made lasagna. And you know how that goes? You like something weird and it's connected to something happy and then all of a sudden you're naming your dog Buddy Holly and smelling pesto in his dander." He buried his face in the dog's great neck and nuzzled him. "Isn't that right, Buddy?" The dog nibbled his ear. "So, y'all want to come meet some of my family? You can even crash inside if you want."

"Give us a minute. We'll be right behind you." I was watching the dog.

Rudy rolled from the road to the sidewalk to a rather steep wooden ramp. He turned back and looked at me, full grin. "You should see me at the skate park," he said, and moved up the ramp in a few swift pulls. Victor and another dude appeared on the porch. The other guy gave a crooked, gap-toothed smile and waved. "We got beers if you're thirsty," he called before disappearing through the screen door.

Becky traced her lips with her favorite brick shade. "I handled that pretty well, yeah?" Her sarcasm dripped all over us.

"He has a dog named Buddy Holly," I said.

"Jennings"—she gave me a conspiratorial look—"do you *also* have a Great Dane named Buddy Holly?"

"No, I had a Lab mutt named Weezer. Named after the same obscure nineties group, whom I liked . . . because—get this—my mother listened to their CD."

She scratched lipstick from her tooth. "A. Play your mom some real music. And B. You're stretching synchronicity pretty thin, my friend."

"Come on. It *is* ironic."

"Careful, honey. You can't marry him over a nineties band connection. Hardly anything worthwhile came out of the nineties."

Considering the sheer number of Red Hot Chili Peppers T-shirts Becky owned, this didn't seem to be a serious statement. "Are you sure?" I teased, poking her in the ribs. "Don't tell anyone, but we drove to Florida . . . so I could marry my Facebook boyfriend . . . because he has a dog named"—I

lowered my voice to a seductive quality—"Buddy Holly."

"Golden Jennings, I love you."

"Why?" I asked, which is never the proper response when someone says I love you.

"For starters, you find out your *Facebook boyfriend*—your word choice, not mine—is in a wheelchair and you're going on about a dog and a nineties band? That's grade A refreshing."

"Why does it matter if he's in a wheelchair?"

"Doesn't. Just seemed like late-breaking news."

Rudy lived through Bus #21 when nineteen others hadn't. I wasn't about to place restraints on miracles. "Becky, everything about this trip is late-breaking news."

"True. So, hey, maybe you should call your *fiancé* before we shack up here for the night."

"I want him to call me first."

"Said every girl ever." Becky lifted her Vera Bradley duffel, gave her eyes and lips one last check in the side mirror, and then followed my *Facebook boyfriend* and his sugar-and-spicy stepbrother into their Orlando house.

CAROLINE

I hurled moments before the air particles compressed. Rudy and I tumbled down the well, soaked in my breakfast. Two eggs. Three strips of bacon. A glass of orange juice. The shock waves carried energy like jet engines. The shrapnel—screws Dozer and John had crammed into the vests—rocketed outward and vacuumed inward.

When a bomb goes off, if you're the one who bought the dynamite, you're thinking about Taco Bell quesadillas, farmers named "Z," plump sweet lips wearing Hot Tamale Sparkle pressed against yours, a second mouth inside your mouth probing and whispering, "Boom. Boom. Boom," the thunking sound a PVC pipe makes when it strikes your temple because your boyfriend thinks you're leaving him for a girl. You are. You were. You wanted to. You didn't. You curled on the shower

tile, beneath a teak seat covered in Moroccan argan oil and Neutrogena face wash, wondering about the effects of ingesting shampoo.

You're thinking, *Let death be swift*, and *God forgive me*, and *If I'd already killed myself, would any of this have happened?*

Because you know everyone else is dead.

And that's your fault.

And it will always be your fault.

23. The next logical choice

$61,769.00

Over the years, Chandler and I have held court on a number of things. Cars. His aspirations included power-train warranties with backup cameras. I want vehicles to move forward, backward, and occasionally diagonally. Church. I like to attend. He likes Sunday mornings relegated for sleep. Children. I want them. He doesn't. (Too many unpredictable factors to suit his taste.) Our latest bout: cities. He'd strike their existence from earth. I was currently traveling to the one that never slept.

Apparently, we disagreed over things that started with the letter C.

I already knew we disagreed about Carter Stockton and non-C-word Rudy Guthrie.

Because I disliked war on all levels, especially with Chan, I developed a peacemaking trick for conversations that had nuclear potential. Before impending confrontations, I listed reasons the person was in my life. I jotted a list about Chan on several rogue glove-box napkins—the list was too short to encompass Chan but long enough to encapsulate his humanity—and made the call.

He answered.

I opened with "I sent you a text," instead of *Why haven't you called?* A victory. For a phone connection traveling miles to space and back, Chan crossed the distance quickly.

"Where are you?"

"Orlando."

"What's in *Orlando?*"

"Another survivor."

Silence on a cell phone isn't actual silence. Plenty of noise boomeranged between us. The breathing. The rising of his hackles. "Golden." My name sounded like a weapon.

I stared at my list and then crumpled it in my fist. "You said find someone else to talk to."

"I meant your mom."

"Yeah right."

"I meant Gran."

"Gran wasn't with us last June."

"So the next logical choice was to drive to Florida?"

Try New York.

"I guess."

"You guess. Anything else I need to know about you two?"

"No. God no. It's nothing like that."

"Seems to me like this is the second time you've followed him somewhere that got us in trouble."

"That's not fair." But wasn't it?

"We've far exceeded fair."

"There's nothing romantic between Rudy and me."

"I wish I could believe that, but . . . fool me once . . ." He stopped.

I had no idea what *fool me once* meant. I said, more a breath than a sentence, "I wish you were here." What I meant: *I wish you'd been the one willing to listen.*

"Funny enough, I was thinking the same thing." There was another long, dreadful sigh. "I love you, Golden, but you have to see this from my side. This morning you were in my bed. Tonight, are you in Rudy's?"

"I am not in Rudy's bed."

I imagined Chan seated on the gray-and-black-checked rug beside his bed, pressing the top of his spine into the mattress, his face tipped toward the fan. His chain saw Christmas ornament spun from the string and clanked quietly against the light fixture. He was seeing the faces from the bus, the ones he drew. He was seeing me with Rudy.

"I believe you. But . . ."

I wanted to separate his pain from mine. To see it as its

own entity, but I didn't have the bandwidth for that much generosity and I suspected he didn't either.

"But what?" I asked.

"We'll talk when you get back."

The call ended there.

24. Westwood is a fairly common surname.

$61,969.00

If you dissect anger, do you find fear?

I texted Chan: I don't want to lose you.

Chan: We survived one breakup.

So he counted our three-day tiff last week as a breakup. Was that supposed to be encouraging? *We survived one. We'll survive another?* Or *We're already broken so you better be extra careful?*

I kicked Dolly's tires. How could Bus #21 keep taking things from us?

Me: This trip is about facing what happened and finishing what I started with Gran's photo.

Chan: Are you taking the photo with him instead of me?

I typed *Should I?* but didn't press Send. Partly because that was cruel and partly because Becky leaned out the door and called, "Jennings! Get your ass in here."

The neighbor gave her a two-finger salute.

Becky raised a hand like she lived here, forever comfortable. "Marco," she yelled before she disappeared inside. If you dropped that girl in a pit of vipers, they'd weave her wardrobes from their molting skin.

I told Chan no, I was not taking the photo with Rudy, and lifted my luggage. A raised El Camino inched down Chamberlain Street, music thumping so hard the shocks couldn't keep the car level. The Elky's high beams caught the reflective tape on two mailboxes across the street, names: Richards and Westwood. The *W* on Westwood was damaged, like someone had tried scraping it away. Seeing those gold-and-black weathered letters worked me over instantly.

Westwood is a fairly common surname in the United States. Open a phone book—any phone book—and you'll find at least two or three. Type Westwood into White Pages: entries galore. There were even three Westwood siblings who attended Braxton Springs High School. I went the other way when I saw one. Logically, they had nothing to do with Bus #21, and percentage wise, bus bombings were quite low. According to a statistic from 2016, one in every 160,487 people was killed in bus, train, or streetcar incidents. That's super low. Especially when you consider that one in every 10,785 died from heat and one in every 3,409 died from choking. Logic wasn't always logical. I

knew nineteen people who died on Bus #21.

My nose was bleeding again.

Buddy Holly wagged his way over to where I crouched beside Dolly's tire, hiding from a mailbox. His tongue tickled my cheek, and his love was the kindness I needed to holster my anger. I'd traveled eleven hours today; I would travel many more if Rudy and Becky remained willing. Facing *Accelerant Orange* would be harder than sighting a mailbox. I looked again at the Westwood name. Made myself stay on those letters.

I nearly passed out.

Was Chan in his room at home, *SportsCenter* on, drawing *my* photo from that day on the bus? Did he draw our hands? I'd held him so tightly I'd fractured his pinkie. I considered the other drawings in his journal. The details clear as photographs. Could I handle New York if an onslaught of faces zombied around in my brain?

Could I handle New York without Chan?

I sent him a message.

Golden: I want to take that photo with YOU. Watch Accelerant Orange. Buy a Saturday ticket to NYC with the money I left in your cigar box.

I wanted him to meet me halfway to healing.

He didn't answer.

I jammed the underside of my sweatshirt against my nose and went inside.

25. Plenty of humor available

$62,255.00

Raucous laughter billowed from the kitchen and there was no doubting why when I got inside. The foursome gathered in the one air-conditioned room in the house and Becky galloped around the table impersonating either the Flintstones' vehicle or a rodeo. In the most hick voice I'd ever heard, she explained how we'd slid down a dinosaur back and run here barefoot from Kentucky. They gobbled it up. By "they" I meant Rudy, Victor, and *Jane?*, if I'd heard her name correctly.

Jane saw the blood first. "Good God. Did my brothers leave you dying in the yard?"

"Fountain started after they left," I said.

Jane popped Victor and then Rudy with a kitchen towel

and tossed it my way. "Probably because of them."

"Not at all," I assured her.

I pressed the rag against my nostrils and declined a beer. There must be adult-adults around here somewhere—folks who might care about an invasion from Kentucky—but they weren't in the kitchen, and none of the other teenaged occupants seemed particularly concerned about underage drinking. Victor had three bottles lining the rim of his placemat. Becky had two. Rudy was drinking a Gatorade and eating carrot chips. The air was kicking, and kicking hard. I put my sweatshirt back on and sat next to Rudy.

Facts slotted into place as I stole carrots from Rudy's plate. This wasn't the Guthrie house. This was Rudy's dad's girlfriend's place. I didn't catch her name, which made me feel guilty, as I was staying the night. Jane was Rudy's half sister. Victor was their dad's girlfriend's son. Not even a true stepbrother, but they didn't care. Except for being tan in the same perfect Orlando way, Rudy didn't look like Jane, but Victor somehow looked like Rudy. Nurture over nature. They'd been together since Jane was fourteen and Rudy was twelve and living here for nearly as long. Jane's boyfriend, Josef, lay sacked out on the couch because he had to be at work early. They called him Jane's *husband*, but he wasn't. Evidently, he was the only one among them who could coax Deuce to fall asleep in his own bed or eat a food group that didn't involve sugar. Jane had been warned. If she broke with the *husband*, Victor and Rudy were keeping the *husband* in the divorce.

"You met the girls *where*?" Jane asked.

When Victor and Rudy said Parkers, they buried their heads in the crooks of their right elbows to avoid Jane's wrath. "Parkers is *not* suitable." Her disdain worsened when they copped to hitting the farm for fireworks. "These two wombats warn you there were alligators, like big frickin' alligators, at the fireworks spot?"

"There was a sign," I said, and Becky asked, "That was for real?"

Victor held his left hand up for us to see; his ring and pinkie fingers were partially missing. "One of them got me."

"And it was a baby."

"Four or five foot long."

Rudy finished off his drink and tossed the bottle across the room into the trash bin.

"Two points," cooed Becky, when the bottle rimmed the trash can and fell in. She must have a decent buzz going.

Rudy was still on the alligators. "Tell them what you were doing, Vic."

"I may or may not have been taking a selfie. I didn't think the little ones could run that fast."

"Was the photo good?" I asked.

Victor offered me his knuckles. "Thata girl, you know it was."

"That photo was a blurry mess," Rudy said.

"But I looked very handsome. Am I right? Give me three

and half." Rudy smacked Victor's hand hard. They laughed even harder.

They'd clearly recounted this story many times to others and still enjoyed it. They'd enjoy it twenty years from now. There was plenty of humor available, because two fingers were something Victor could live without. Two fingers—well, one and a half—was worth the glory. "You really don't care?" Becky asked.

Rudy cocked his head toward Victor. "Better to lose two fingers than the rest of him."

Jane explained. "Vic was supposed to be with Rudy in New York. Their fairy godteacher, Ms. Jay, paid for them to attend after Aunt Linda started her *culture campaign*."

"But then I stopped being able to count to five on my right hand and had to bail."

"We gave that alligator a big-ass medal," Jane said, looping an arm around Victor's neck and squeezing his face against hers. She turned to me. "Ru says we should give you one too. That he wouldn't have gotten off the bus without your encouragement."

All three of them eyed me, but it was Victor who said, "Do you need a medal, Golden Jennings?"

The only thing I gave Rudy was my beanie. "Lord, no, but I'll take a beer."

We had another round of drinks and conversations, and then Victor and Jane said they were too tired to exist and must

depart to bed. There was some discussion of how zapped Becky and I must be after our day of driving. And it was true, my eyes were on fire and there was a low-grade hum happening behind my temples. The clock on the stove read 2:03 a.m. when Jane dragged a groggy Josef off the couch. She paused, supporting his weight on her shoulder, and said, "The sofa doesn't pull out, but it's better than your truck," and that seemed true enough to accept the offer.

Becky tromped to the kitchen sink with her toothbrush and Rudy rolled behind me into the living room. It was the first time we'd been alone since the bathroom at Down Yonder.

"Your mom should have named you Penny. You keep turning up."

I probably shouldn't have asked, but I did. "Is your mom around?"

"Nah, but Charlotte will get home about the time we leave. She works nights at Waffle House down the strip. She won't mind that you're here if you were worrying about it."

"Where do you sleep?"

"Upstairs." He grinned; he seemed to be made of grins, like there was an insatiable spring of grins inside him. But then I caught on and smacked his arm for teasing me. "I'm down that hall. You can wake me if you need anything," he said.

I'd been down the hall on an earlier trip to the bathroom. There were only four doors. If one of those doors was a closet, then I guessed all those rooms were filled to the brink with beds and kids. A dormitory family. A teeny commune. And I

figured, we were not so different.

This guy, the one who rolled back and forth in his two-hundred-square-foot living room, and the one who had stood at Down Yonder's bathroom door, were the same, despite the changed circumstances. He had to have known his world was enlarging with that unofficial acceptance to Emerson. That his days of evening drinking with Victor and Jane might be paused or over; that to charge ahead was to leave them behind. But he'd gone on to New York without Victor, so maybe that was something he knew how to do. I wanted to ask him about Emerson, if he was moving to Boston in the fall, but I didn't.

"You doing okay, Golden?"

I was. My head was an aquarium stocked with swimming thoughts. I gave him a resolute nod. "You?"

When he raised his head, doggedness and determination twinned through his eyes. "Tomorrow morning, let's visit Caroline before we hit the road. We should try convincing her to come along. It would mean a lot to Carter to have the three of us there. And maybe even to the crowds. I do think there'll be crowds. And if the donation thing is an indicator, they're going to be overwhelming. What about the boyfriend? Could you change his mind?"

"I don't think so," I said.

Becky was flashing her freshly polished teeth at me from the kitchen sink. I was thinking of people at their computer desks sliding credit cards from their wallets and typing sixteen digits of their hard-earned cash into a GoFundMe with

my name on it. I was thinking of those same people boarding subways, Ubers, taxis, planes toward the Green-Conwell. How they'd file through *Accelerant Orange* on Sunday. And then Caroline's name registered. "Caroline?" I asked.

Rudy gave me a look that said: *The only Caroline we know.* "She's my cousin. Moved down to live with our aunt over Christmas. Lives about ten miles from here now."

Oh.

CAROLINE

Palace Theatre has the best popcorn. It's the butter, even though Johnny always claimed it was the oil. Let me tell you, it's not that orange salty shit they leave on the counter by the straws. Sometimes, to punish myself, I eat the stale puffs and kernels off the sticky, concrete theater floor. Then, I sink into a stadium seat, eyes closed while the movie reels, and think about how a trip to Ithaca became a bloody dripping battle of screws. I think about melted metal and the broken stained glass Jesus of New Wesley Church. The explosion punched holes in the panes, directly into Jesus's side, and a pastor there was quoted as saying, "Jesus knows our very sorrows," which might be true, but I was more interested in a Jesus who stopped our sorrows, and He didn't seem to do that for me.

"Caroline, did you know Simon had a bomb?" the

investigators had asked. "Do you know where he got a bomb? Do you know what made him snap? Was he supposed to sell the bombs to someone in New York? Is that why the two of you drove into the city?" The interrogations are never-ending. Local police. ATF. FBI. Everyone had nearly the same questions. How and why?

"Caroline."

"Caroline!"

"CAROLINE."

The inside of my head grinds and grinds. I answer in short, nearly inaudible bursts. *Simon had the dynamite for months. I made him snap. He told me his dad was trading the Porsche to a dealer in NYC.* The investigation confirms my story. His computer is seized, his emails read, his text messages examined; he was supposed to sell the vests. He kept pictures of the bruises he made on my face.

Their questions change after that. I am a victim again.

"Z" will put details together eventually. Or maybe he won't. Maybe he was one of those men who only watched fishing channels and *Wheel of Fortune*, and I was stuck with the knowledge that we'd created a monster together.

I think about the Caroline I used to be and how she launched popcorn in the air at Angela. How that Caroline laughed when her girlfriend bumped into strangers to catch wayward kernels. I think about us buying Gobstoppers and crunching the candy so loudly other moviegoers asked us to stop. That used to be me watching the next *Fast and Furious*.

And now, I'm licking the floor.

I do not call Angela.

I do not call anyone.

I try college and fail.

When I return home, the sun is too bright, Keuka Lake is too blue, the tourists too drunk and chipper. I sleep in the cabin of our neighbor's boat for a week before Dad sends me to live with my mom's sister in Florida. "You need a change of scenery," he says. But really, I am the only failure in his life. Small towns have keen memories for scandals. They have something entirely worse for me.

If I had the energy—thank Jesus *who knows our sorrows* I don't—I'd drive to New York and end this the way I meant to the first time I got on Bus #21.

26. Semi-typical night

$67,255.00

Nightmares have the legs of Olympic sprinters. They chased me all night long; they caught me around three.

My blood spreads into the sidewalk cracks and runs down to the street. It was a proper nightmare, so the blood became a river. A man in a buttoned-up trench coat paddled a kayak across the street when the sign read *Walk Now*. The paddles were dismembered arms.

Chan lay on the sidewalk beside me.

"I'm tired of always being second to your agenda. We're done," I said. Tears welled in his eyes. I was merciless. "I mean it," dream-me said.

Bus #21 was now a marooned train on Third Avenue. Near the middle of the vehicle was a digital clock that looked as if it belonged to Times Square on New Year's Eve. The numbers counted up. One. Two. Three. Four. They became a voice. "One. Two. Three. Four." They became a scream. "ONE. TWO. THREE. FOUR." The numbers grew louder than a scream. "SEVEN. EIGHT. NINE."

The world was ash. A cool wind blew down the street and the ash lifted off the ground. The man in the kayak traded one dismembered arm for another. I watched him row away.

Becky woke me.

"Did I scream?" I asked when I was finally aware that she was holding me and singing softly. My hair was a damp, tangled mess, and she finger-combed the strands. "You were moaning," she told me.

"I'm sorry."

"Shhhh." She kept singing.

I fell back into the haze.

Three hours later the house awoke. Coffee perked. A two-year-old clapped. A Great Dane licked his paws and then our faces. "We're awake," I told Buddy Holly, but Becky and I didn't budge. We slept like lovers, spooning on the couch, because we'd decided we were too tired to care about the conditions and I suspected Becky felt majorly protective after my nightmare.

She flopped toward me, our faces inches apart. "Rough night?"

"Semi-typical night."

Becky was about to say something, when Rudy's voice sifted through the wall. "I know, Ms. Jay. I know."

"That's his teacher, right?" Becky whispered.

"Yeah."

We listened again.

"Two survivors, maybe even three, return to the scene. . . . Yep. . . . I can't turn anything in until I get back, but I'll send you updates. . . . The heart of the story. . . . Thanks for covering me. . . . Yes, I have all my equipment. They'll understand. . . . Will you let Dad know when he calls? . . . You're the best, Ms. Jay."

Becky dug her elbow into my side. "Is he writing about this?"

"Maybe."

I wasn't sure how I felt about that.

Rudy rolled into the living room. He wore black fingerless gloves that he hadn't the night before. "My dad's working the oil rig for another six days, but Ms. Jay's handling him. Victor's mom won't care as long as I'm with good people. We run our own little boat around here. I've got all the things that make me work these days, and, you know, a toothbrush. So, I guess travel is settled on my end," he said agreeably. "Oh, the bathroom is free for the next six minutes if you want to hop in."

Becky and I utilized our six minutes while Victor and Rudy learned the easiest way for Rudy to enter and exit the truck. Dolly was significantly higher than the Mustang. I wasn't there

to watch, but he mastered the maneuver by the time my teeth were brushed and my hair was in a sloppy bun, the back of my T-shirt soaked from not bothering to towel it dry. Becky and I took a quick lesson on the proper way to store his wheelchair in Dolly, because it was *flippin' expensive* and a donation. And that was that. I was plus a Rudy and minus a Chan.

On a final trip into the house, Victor trapped me in the kitchen. "He's a pro at workarounds. Assume he's unbreakable."

I assured Victor I understood. And although he smiled and deemed me capable, he offered a warning. "If he needs help, he'll hate it."

"Don't we all."

Victor wrapped my shoulder with his three-and-a-half-fingered hand and squeezed. We stood there in a solemn agreement that this trip was a good thing without using a single word. Becky honked, and I ran out the door. Deuce sat on Victor's hip; father and son waved Dolly away from the curb. Rudy pointed at the mailbox across the street. "In case you were wondering, they're not the same Westwoods."

I pinched my nose in case it started to trickle, and we were off.

27. The token bathroom at the bottom of the world

$67,955.00

Between Rudy's and Caroline's houses, I remembered the girl I'd shared a few seconds of life with last June. I'd envied her— that swanky leather skirt hitting five or six inches above the knee, the swagger of a woman who knew what she wanted. We were in sensory overload—the Down Yonder jukebox too loud, the din of laughter in the bar striking like CPR compressions. Bodies knocked into our table. Into me. You couldn't leave New York on the sidewalk. She accompanied you inside no matter which store you popped into.

I'd pointed Caroline out to Chan across the crowded Down Yonder bar. "You see that girl?" he'd said. "The one with the flames?"—meaning her hair, not her body. In nearly any group

Chan could accurately guess who or what I meant with only so much as a nod. And vice versa. Which was very satiating. "That's the one," I had said.

I went on to tell him about the sexcapade in the token bathroom at the bottom of the world. "Which guy?" he'd asked, and I'd let him guess. Chan picked Jim Conner on his first try. When I asked how he knew, he explained, "It was either the guy staring at her ass or the one catching her eye, and I figured the ass dude hadn't gotten any recently. Look at his hips. He's angling to use them later."

We'd peddled a theory about hip location indicating sexual frustration. He'd even drawn a lewd cartoon on the cocktail napkin. I didn't think about Caroline until the next day. When Simon—the guy Chan claimed had been staring at her ass—tugged his sweatshirt to his nipples and showed us a bomb.

I considered now that Caroline had faked the swagger in the hallway. That the skirt and the sex were a costume for a life she wanted, rather than a life she had.

Simon Westwood had been her boyfriend. That's a helluva thing, when you think about it. She'd probably loved him. She'd certainly screwed him. *"No one screws my girlfriend but me,"* he'd screamed at Bus #21. He'd loathed her by that point. Had he ever loved her?

"How did she survive?" I asked.

Rudy tapped his chest.

There was a story, but we arrived in her driveway. Caroline Ascott lived in an estate large enough to hold four Methodist

chapels. There was even a gatehouse at the bottom of the drive that could swallow Dolly Dodge whole. The smell of sweet oranges filtered through the cab when I lowered the window.

A voice crackled through the intercom box. Rudy leaned around me to speak. "Hey, it's Rudy. Can you buzz me through?"

The barrier bar lifted.

On our way down the driveway, Rudy gave us the family rundown. His mom had two sisters who married up. Caroline's mom to a wine tycoon in the Finger Lakes area in upstate New York, and his aunt Linda, who owned the sprawling Spanish colonial before us. He didn't mention his mom, but there was an understanding that she had not followed in the family betterment plan. "The New York tour was Aunt Linda's idea. Linda convinced Caroline's mom. Caroline's mom called Ms. Jay and said she thought Victor, Jane, and I ought to tag along. Jane had to work, and you know why Victor bailed."

"Anything we should know about your cousin?" Becky asked, eyes sweeping the property.

"Oh, you'll peg her in about three seconds."

We left Dolly unlocked and Rudy led us around the house, toward the edge of the grove. He rolled through the manicured lawn, over sprinkler heads and soggy soil, over oranges that had fallen early and rotted. The one time I moved toward his chair, he said, "Uh, uh. I've done this before." He had, but the going wasn't easy.

June-fifteenth Caroline Ascott was not the Caroline Ascott

of today. Where her red hair had been long and glorious, shiny in that shampoo-commercial way, it was shaved. Off and gone. Beneath a bright purple headband, her scalp had a nasty sunburn. The ass she'd expertly swiveled at Jim was parked in an aluminum lawn chair under a Valencia orange tree. From behind, she appeared to be reading a book or listening to music or knitting, something stationary. Up close, I could see she was gazing at bark.

I probably shouldn't have, but I raised my camera. Loneliness usually lived in the eyes. Hers was visible from behind. I was glad I didn't look that way from the outside, even more glad there wasn't an X-ray machine for my soul.

"Caroline," Rudy said to his cousin's back.

"Go away."

"Turn around, please."

Caroline turned around. She sipped from the tumbler and glanced at Rudy's entourage, seemingly without recognition, and turned back to the tree. "Go away, Rudy."

"This is Golden Jennings."

"I'm not an idiot."

Wow. Caroline Ascott hated me.

Rudy rolled closer and maneuvered between Caroline and the tree. "We're going to New York today."

"For pleasure or masochism?"

"We're going to tell the devil to eff off in person," he said.

"Tell him I said hi."

"Care!"

"Ru!"

"We want you to come with us."

"*We want you to come with us*," she mocked Rudy. Then she shoved him in the chest. His chair rocked sideways on the uneven ground, teetered. He tumbled onto the grass, an inelegant pile of limbs. Rudy waved me off as he righted the chair. Every muscle flexed with the effort of returning to his seat.

That was when I decided Caroline wasn't just lonely, she was stuck in a rut, and I was willing to help with the unsticking. "Look," I said. "I'm not going to judge your pain. I wasn't on the bus in those last few seconds. But I do know *that*"—I pointed at Rudy dusting dirt off his clothes and arms—"and this"—I indicated her general dishevelment—"means you need help."

"Don't pretend you know me."

"I'm not. But I've spent ten months in a bubble where most of my family and friends refused to talk about what happened and—I thought you might understand."

Caroline laughed.

"You think this is funny?"

"I think you're entertaining," she said.

I have a good ear for veneer and hers cracked. I gambled that I was reaching her.

"Look, I have static in my head too. Questions. Answers. I have gaps, big *Titanic*-size gaps. Like I couldn't remember what Simon was wearing over the vest until Rudy told me, even

though I know his left eye was blue, his right eye was brown. That's some bullshit, right? But I swear, part of my brain from June fifteenth is an Andy Warhol painting and part is spray-painted black. I don't know how any of us got here, but here is where we are."

"Here?" she said flippantly.

"Yeah, *here*. Him in a wheelchair, you staring at a tree, and me and my boyfriend with so much to say we can't say anything at all. It's like the bus blew our tongues and your decency and his legs. And maybe that's fine with you. Maybe you like your cushy aluminum sippy-cup life in your McMansion with your ridiculously interesting fruit tree, but I'd like some new scenery. You can come with us, see the installation of Bus #21, or you can sit in the truck until we get to Ellis Island. I don't care which, but that's the last invite you're getting. Take it or leave it."

She mocked me with her tone and her *Screw you to kingdom come* face. "Don't you just look like one of Carter's precious scholarship babies! No wonder Rudy brought you here."

"And don't you just look like you feel sorry for yourself."

"I lost everything."

"Yeah, well, join the club."

She repeated the phrase the way she'd repeated Rudy's earlier. Her vitriol draining with every word.

"Hey," I said. "I don't know if anyone has told you lately, but you lived through the bombing. Don't you want to live the rest of your life?"

That question broke her.

Caroline curled into the crook of the tree, letting the bark punish her skin. When she started to cringe from the pain, she tugged the bottom of her sundress over her bald head. Her abs clenched with grief. I looked away from the red bra and underwear, but not before seeing that she was tattooed in a few places and thin. Bone thin.

I squatted, tugging on the fringes in the knees of my jeans, saying nothing. I did not think she wanted comfort—a hand on the back or to be pulled into a hug. She was more creature than girl, made of scales and a soft underbelly. I hovered, considering what might reach her. Or what would reach me if I had a dress over my head in an orange grove.

Sometimes when you watched a person, you had an uncanny sensation that they were an alternate version of you. I did not want pity, so I didn't offer such to Caroline. I offered community. She was going through these emotional wind sprints of guilt and anger, but she did not have to go through them alone. I thought of taking her hand but touched her arm instead. She tried to rip away; I tightened my grip.

A few steps away, the sun starbursted through the grove and fell on Rudy and Becky. They shielded their eyes from its punishment, each a saluting silhouette. Caroline and I were in the shade, and the shade was made of gray light and weak shadows. She could stay here, but I couldn't. I wanted to get back to the light. I patted her twice on the side. The universal sign for tapping out.

She asked, almost where I couldn't hear, "You're going to Ellis Island?"

"Like I planned to last June."

From beneath the ModCloth dress, Caroline whispered, "Let me pack a bag."

28. Capture it just right.

$68,279.00

There was nothing legal or wise about our travel arrangements. We arrived at Dolly, realized four people didn't fit in the cab—a fact that had previously escaped us—and decided we didn't care. Becky dropped the tailgate and nested our sleeping bags. Dolly had only one seat belt to begin with. Riding under the camper top wasn't much more dangerous than riding in the cab. Plus, as Becky noted, "If God wanted you guys dead, He missed His big opportunity."

With no further discussion, Rudy and I seized the front. We planned to swap drivers in three hours. I leaned across the bench and said, "Your cousin's a barrel of monkeys," but I forgot the sliding glass between the cab and the back didn't close.

Caroline knocked her knuckles at us and said, "I heard that." Then she thrust her head through the gap. "I've got two rules. One, I hate road trips. So, this isn't a road trip, and anyone who calls it a road trip is getting their head shaved the first time they fall asleep. The second: no one talks about Simon."

"Fine by me."

Rudy and Becky agreed. No one wanted to discuss Caroline's bomb-making, life-destroying ex-boyfriend anyway.

Rudy wedged himself closer to the door and gripped the battered handle in his fist.

"Are you comfortable enough?" I asked.

"Can you not ask me that?" he said, although not unkindly. "As a general rule, if you wouldn't ask Becky, don't ask me."

I nodded, embarrassed. "Is it okay if I say I'm here if you do need anything?"

"Only on Wednesdays," he said with a scowl that immediately broke into a wide smile, and then a laugh. "I'm just kidding, Go. Thanks for the offer. I'll let you know."

"You laugh a lot," I said, because he did. More than anyone I knew. And he was laughing now, and it was beautiful.

"By-product of living," he said. "And it keeps my abs nice and tight."

Now I was laughing. We had this great lightheartedness between us, but I still worried I would say or do the wrong thing and we'd lose this energy. If Chan were here, I'd turn the vents toward him, set the air conditioner to high, and find an NPR entertainment interview. He'd ask me to locate a gas

station before the highway, where he'd stroll from the store moments later with a Coke and some shelled peanuts. I was intimately acquainted with the rut of Chan and me in this truck. I had no idea about Rudy.

We rolled northeast with Disney at our back and New York City somewhere on tomorrow's horizon. I'd call Stock when we had more miles under our belts and let him know I had three of four in tow, which felt like an unbelievable victory. Rudy caught me gawking at the ocean and said, "It's even better without the clouds." But I liked the clouds. I would like the ocean best if I could get her alone for a few hours. All my favorite ocean photos were taken at sunset or sunrise, in remote locations. Some with slow exposures, so you saw the stars stretching toward earth. Today, families and retirees cluttered the sand and horizon with colors.

"You stopping for photos?" he asked.

"This is not a road trip."

"Golden, have you ever had your toes in the surf?"

"No."

"Don't make a regret," he warned.

When the next public beach access came, I zipped Dolly toward the dunes. Caroline was napping in the back. "She won't even know," Rudy promised.

"Are you com—" I planned to say *coming with me* and caught myself too late. I worried that I'd soured the moment, but he flashed a gracious smile and said, "I'll come along if you capture it just right."

I crossed the seagrass and sand with the Canon around my neck. Each time I looked through the lens, I didn't press the shutter. This particular slice of world, so very different from my towering oaks and billowing Kentucky bluegrass, was a deployment of water and wind, moving in perfect unison. Row on row of colorful umbrellas flapped like round butterflies in the wind. Hints of jumping silver fish. Twinges of salt. Driftwood and seaweed. Bits of sharp shells biting and massaging my feet. The mist waved in off the water and coated my sunglasses in a fine foggy film. Sand lapped over my toes, soft and cool.

I was in love.

Chan should be here for this.

Chan could have been here for this.

I took a picture for Rudy.

29. **For your trouble**

$69,450.00

Caroline and Becky stayed asleep in their camper nest, curled together like kittens in a cardboard box. We planned to wake them for lunch and didn't. "Don't go 'round poking bears," Gran always says.

Rudy asked, "Is what you said to Caroline true? You and the fiancé aren't on the best terms?"

"He's not my *fiancé.*"

Rudy's eyes fell on my ring. "Okay. I assume your *boyfriend* knows what you're doing and isn't wild about the idea?"

"That's about right."

"*About?* Not that you have to talk to me about him, but you can."

"He's not speaking to me."

Rudy scratched a place on his cheek and stared at a billboard for Savannah. We were close, twenty miles maybe, from the edge of the city. Ten miles out he asked, "Did the trouble start before or after Bus Twenty-One?"

"Does it matter?"

"A little."

"Why?"

"You came to the Green-Conwell on my invitation. You got on Bus Twenty-one because I asked. . . . Let's just say every day, I think about you in that bathroom doorway and my taunting you to come along, and I've questioned what would have happened if I just kept my mouth shut. If I'd thought, *Rudy, that's a pretty girl* instead of showing you my cell phone or stealing your beanie. Would you be here if I'd kept my mouth shut? Would I?"

"Playing that game will kill you," I said, with the expert tone of someone who'd played.

"Do you believe in the butterfly effect?"

"That a yes in a dirty bathroom in New York knocks a pebble off the Great Wall of China?"

"That a yes in a dirty bathroom saved my life?"

I tried not to roll my eyes. "Come on, Rudy, I didn't save your life."

"Did I ruin yours?"

"No."

But there was rubble.

"On Facebook you said you came to the bus for Ellis Island.

But for a couple of bucks, you could have caught a subway. There were a million ways to snag that picture for your gran that didn't involve me."

He was right. "So?"

"So that makes me think you had an ulterior motive and it's hard not having answers to a question like that."

I sympathized.

Did I want to tell Rudy about the morning of June 15?

Chan's bag hadn't been delivered. Or it had, but to a different room at the hostel. We didn't find out until a week later, when the owner mailed the bag to the Hive with an apology and twenty dollars "for your trouble," the note claimed.

Chan droned on and on about the luggage—how the drawings were irreplaceable—and while I understood his great loss, that his plan had gone utterly awry, his ongoing rants drove me bonkers.

"I'm sorry, Chan, but no one can magic your bag to us."

My comments didn't suit. He threw a pillow against the headboard and put his hands on his hips. "Is that what you want me to tell you when your computer crashes and you lose all of your photos?"

"First of all, I back up my photos."

He shot me a *Yeah, right* look.

"Forget the photos," I snapped. "What I'm really pissed about—"

"I lose something irreplaceable and you're pissed at me."

"I'm not pissed you lost something. I'm pissed about your attitude."

Our adjoining neighbor pounded the wall.

And then Chan, pacing back and forth across our tiny room, said, "I'm doing all this for you."

For me rather than *with* me. Sure, the timing was bad. And yes, the trip was expensive. Did I realize he might need to be at home carving or felling logs so he could finish his latest nativity project by deadline? Sure. But what was three days?

"Do I need to remind you that it was *your* idea to get this photo for Gran?" I let the words bite. "This was not some pity trip that I forced you to attend. So you can put that passive-aggressive shit back up your ass."

"Go, that's not what I meant."

"What *did* you mean then?"

"I needed this to go differently. My bags were . . ." He shook with a frustration I hadn't seen on him since we were in middle school. Squeezing the rolled brim of his hat as he spoke, he bit out words. "They were supposed to be with me. So I could . . . sketch. I need to sketch."

It was childish, but I threw the free memo pad at him and said, "I'm going to shower. Sketch all you want."

This was one of the few times we'd let our words get away from us.

When I returned from the shower, wrapped in my towel, I expected things to improve. He'd admit he'd been an obsessive ass, and I would apologize for not being sensitive about his

sketchbooks. We'd get rid of my towel in a creative way and then head to MoMA.

But Chan was on his phone and he was joyfully effervescing to someone, taking notes, as if our previous argument hadn't occurred. He said, "You're saying if I catch a flight home on the sixteenth instead of the seventeenth I'll be able to harvest from the Weymeyers' land. . . . Yeah, it's terrible timing. . . . I've been sending the man emails for months. . . . Right. Right. I get that he wants to be there. . . . You're sure there are no other dates? None at all. . . . All right. Yeah. I'll meet you there. This is fantastic."

And then he saw me and remembered it was only fantastic for him.

Without a consultation, the decision had been made, a new plan forged: we were heading home a day early so Chan could cut down trees.

He knew it was awful, so he didn't try to bake his crap into a brownie and pass it off as something edible.

"I'm sorry about this," he said. The words sounded true, but his face was glowing. "Look, if I cut those logs, I'll be able to afford to bring us back next year. Then everything will be perfect. Every detail exact. I'll make this up in a way you'll never forget." He tried to touch me, and I shook him off.

"We were seeing MoMA *today*. And Central Park. And Times Square. And *Wicked* tonight. What about our plans for this year?" How could Chan, who never handled a change in the schedule without weeks of warning, shift this fast?

"The tickets were in the missing bag, so it's not like—"

"Shut up."

"I said I'm sorry."

"Great. Excellent. I'll take a picture of that apology and label it Times Square."

"You're being a jerk."

That's when I remembered Rudy's invitation to ditch my boyfriend and see the city. I seized it. "Well, this ass is catching a bus to Battery Park and taking the ferry to Ellis Island today. Alone."

"Which bus?"

"Who cares? You have planes to catch and trees to cut. I, on the other hand, have one day to do this photo for Gran— remember, Gran? The whole reason we came on this trip."

"But the day will be off. It's the fifteenth. We should come back next year. On the sixteenth. When it's perfect."

"Whose fault is that?"

"The airline's. I'm coming with you."

We dressed for the day. Well, I dressed for the day. Chan wore the same thing because he had nothing else. There was a moment when I nearly forgot how much I despised him. He was sitting in a straight-back chair in the corner, legs crossed, tugging his T-shirt taut to eliminate the wrinkles, and I actually thought, *Chan, we should blow dollars at a street vendor and get you an NYC T-shirt*. Then I remembered Chan was going home. And even if we weren't, he'd want that shirt washed before he wore it.

"Your hair looks pretty," he said, trying to mend some fences.

I pulled my knitted red beanie over my hair as a response.

I said to Rudy, "Our fight started before the bus."

"Before we met?"

"The airline lost his bag and he was out of sorts from the very beginning."

And then I told Rudy an abbreviated version of our argument. When I finished, he said, "That blows!" and pulled my red beanie over his eyes.

From the back, Becky said, "I'm hungry," and Caroline said, "There are worse things a boyfriend can do."

30. Starting was harder.

$69,540.00

When it was time to swap drivers, Rudy assured us riding in the nest was safe. No one agreed, and Caroline told him he had "shit for brains," and he said, "Shit for legs, Care, get it right," and hauled himself through the sliding window and tumbled into a heap. Becky gave me a glare that meant, *Put the cousins in the back*, but I followed Rudy through the window. He wiggled deeper into the nest, and I put my spine against the truck bed so I could feel the road vibrating.

"I'm driving over sixty-five," Becky threatened.

"We'll see how that works for you," I said through the glass, but then I put an arm through and choked her neck. "I love you, Becky Cable."

She did the perfect thing again. She said, "Why?" because I had said "Why" the night before and that's what we said. I played Paul Simon as loud as my phone allowed.

"I hate this song," Caroline said.

"You hate everything," Rudy told her.

I let that comment hang in the ether before I asked, "Do you really? Hate everything."

"Wouldn't you?"

That reply made everyone dive into pools of unspoken thoughts. In the wake, Rudy opened an ancient laptop and clacked the keys—presumably on some article for Ms. Jay. Caroline went back to humming, Becky turned on our playlist, and I closed my eyes to think about hate.

Hate made things ugly.

Simon had defended his hate because he thought the circumstances warranted it—hate was his passion; hate was his movement; hate would change his world. And it had. Hate had spiraled like an airborne toxin and crawled inside us all. I felt the infection.

I wanted to talk about what happened, but when I played that conversation with Caroline in my head, it went like this:

Me: What good will hate do us?

Caroline: It's all that gets me up in the morning.

Me: But if we hate, how are we different from Simon?

Caroline: Maybe we're not.

Me: What if hate like his starts with hate like ours?

Caroline: Screw you, Mary Sunshine.

That *Screw you* was why I didn't start the conversation. When you knew something might end poorly, starting was harder. But maybe that's how everyone felt, and that was why no one pulled Simon Westwood aside years before, when he was setting puppies on fire or jabbing the skin on his thigh with a butcher knife or whatever the hell he'd done that indicated he was catapulting toward violence. Maybe no one asked Simon, "Hey, what are you doing with your hate?" If Carter Stockton were in this truck, he'd do something. He wasn't here, so that left me.

"Caroline," I said. "Tell me why you shaved your head."

31. It's time to talk about your vocabulary.

$70,005.00

Caroline's purple headband had a seam where the narrow fabric gathered. When she was nervous or self-conscious, she adjusted the seam to the center of her forehead and palmed her skull like a basketball. I watched her slide that seam around for nearly sixty seconds. "Ask me about shaving in South Carolina," she said.

"Why?"

"Because I like Georgia, and I don't want that to change." She stopped fidgeting with the headband and curled against the passenger window. That was all. She was done.

"What do you love, Go?" Rudy asked to keep some semblance of conversation.

"Lots of things."

"Tell me."

"Well, my camera." I whisked the Canon into my hands, removed the lens cap, and made a few adjustments before pointing at Caroline. She didn't smile, but she let me see her through the lens without turning away. "The way a photo captures history before it's even history. And . . . I love our house. It's an old Methodist chapel we're slowly restoring. Watching movies with Chan is pretty awesome. Let's see. I love my kooky little town and our kooky little community. And I love the idea of leaving my kooky little town and our kooky little community, even though my gran is one of the best people on the planet."

"Where do you want to go?"

I looked over at Rudy, wishing we were alone somewhere instead of trapped in this cab. My response would matter to him. "I was thinking of Boston. Well, maybe."

Rudy beamed. "Boston, eh?"

I was incredibly pleased that I had spoken the desire out loud. So much so I said it again, just to hear it roll off my lips. "Yeah, Boston."

"I like Boston too," he said.

And then there was Caroline, inserting her opinion. "Aren't you two more precious than words," because it wasn't like they couldn't tell we were talking about far more than a city.

It crossed my mind to confess how I felt when I realized Emerson had a degree in media studies. That the school was

just as good a fit for me as it was for Rudy. The degree excited me. The city excited me, or at least googling it did. Boston was home to museums, baseball, history. I could shoot North Church, ducks on the water, cobblestone streets, the Gardner. I'd missed the application deadline for this year, but if I was able to face Bus #21 and if Carter's scholarship money was a real thing—possibly, I could apply by November 1 and transfer in next fall. Golden Jennings, girl about New England.

Those were big ifs.

"Guys, I have bad news." Becky didn't wait for us to say, *what*? She said, "Dolly is getting dodgy. Like seriously dodgy."

The truck lurched.

"I do not love car trouble," I said.

"Anyone here mechanical?" Becky asked.

Caroline said, "I made a birdhouse in shop class."

A loud pop drowned out *class*. The day had cleared, so when clouds of smoke rose from seams in the hood, they were like cotton balls on a bright blue canvas. Something hissed like an exorcised demon and Becky eased Dolly to the shoulder. I scrambled from the back with a water bottle. Becky popped the hood, emitting a much larger cloud and flames large enough to roast marshmallows. The two of us doused the fire and coughed away smoke.

"I told you not to drive over sixty-five."

"And I told you I was going to anyway." Becky snapped out the response, but I knew she was angry at herself instead of me.

"It's okay," I said, even though it sucked. Dolly Dodge had been Granddad's truck—a prized possession—and I'd killed it on a highway in South Carolina, miles from our final destination.

Caroline was already on the phone to AAA giving them our location. After a few minutes of sitting without the engine running, the temperature spiked to 94, felt like 108. The average temperature under the camper cab was seventy-eight when Dolly was running. Exiting seemed preferable to heat stroke. We stripped down to tank tops. Truckers and cars whipped by, batting us with wind tunnels of baked air.

"This isn't better," Caroline said.

"We could play a game while we wait," Becky suggested.

"No. Games are for road trips. This is not a road trip."

"Maybe it's time to talk about your vocabulary, Care. Because this is a road"—Rudy gesticulated to the highway—"and we seem to be traveling it."

"Well, not right now," she insisted.

Immediately following their exchange, Becky's face lit. "I feel like we've been here before," she said, at the precise moment Caroline said, "Does anyone feel like we've all been here before?" The girls turned toward each other in a spasm. "Hey, whoa, déjà vu!" And then there was a four-person chorus of "Jinx," and then another, "Double jinx."

That was the first time we all cracked a smile. The first time we'd all been on the same page. The second came later,

when the AAA dude pulled alongside Dolly. We went through the particulars, arranged to tow the truck to the closest town, which was only a mile away, but when the time came to climb into the cab, the AAA man thrust out his hand and said, "Oh, by the way, my name is Simon," and all of us said, "No, thanks, we'll walk" at the same time. Except Rudy, who said he'd roll.

32. An unmarked grave in Bath

72,754.00

Four kids, one in a wheelchair, walking the shoulder of the interstate drew the attention of passing motorists. Semis slowed. Young, bright-eyed muscle cars rubbernecked and then revved off. Half a mile from our exit, a lady in a black Lexus two-seater pulled off and suggested one of us ride with her to a nearby service station. She was insistent, even after Caroline said, "We've already called AAA." With her high ponytail and hot pink yoga outfit, she didn't appear dangerous. Still, we looked at each other like none of us were sure if stranger danger was still a thing, but perhaps it was. "If only serial killers wore uniforms," Becky whispered laughingly in my ear. I shushed her, highly doubting Lexus Two-Seater was

a serial killer, but Simon hadn't looked evil either. Accepting the ride meant we'd have to split into two groups, and I wasn't comfortable with that. Her Lexus zipped onto the highway and two bumper stickers stated her loud and proud second-amendment rights.

Rudy wheeled out in front and spun in wild circles, making a passing motorist honk with delight. "Boy, that was close!" he said, completely animated.

Becky, who had never hitched in her life, said, "Man, I remember when hitchin' used to be safe."

I threw in, "Watch out for those yoga moms," and cocked a fake handgun.

"You guys go on and laugh, but that's how all the horror movies start." Caroline almost pulled off her seriousness, but a smile crept in at the last moment. And then we were all doubled over laughing again.

Considering Dolly went kaput and we were huffing I-95 in eighty-nine-degree weather, we were in remarkably good moods. The conversation turned not to Dolly's malfunction or the cost to fix her or even the long, muggy walk, but to the déjà vu we experienced in the aftermath.

"Why does déjà vu happen?" Becky asked.

Rudy's hands paused on the wheels. With all the traffic, holding a conversation was difficult, and his voice often matched pitch with the rumblings of large trucks. We came in closer. He said, "I don't know about why, but if déjà vu is

feeling like you've lived through something in the past, what do you call that sensation when you're sure you've already lived through something in the future?"

"Premonition," I said.

Becky said, "I'm not sure that happens to me."

Caroline *tsk*ed. "Oh, sure it does. Say you're driving and you think *I shouldn't take Miller Lane home*. You take Lakewood instead and wind up at your house in time to watch *Law and Order*, believing you dodged some cosmic bullet."

"But there's no way to know if that's true or not," Becky argued.

"There is if you take Miller Lane and life goes sideways," Caroline said.

"But who does that?"

I shrugged at Becky. "Lots of people."

Caroline seemed intent to prove her point. She darted directly in front of Rudy and dropped onto his lap. "Rudy, list three things you knew were going to happen before they happened."

Rudy popped a wheelie and then used the forward movement to dump Caroline out of his chair onto the grass. The cousins poked at each other, and he acquiesced. "I knew Victor was going to tell me his girlfriend was pregnant with Deuce. And . . . the day I won the Bob Reid Journalism Award, I felt like something good was going to happen even though I didn't know what. I can't think of a third." He smoothed the leather

across his palms. "Oh, wait, yeah. Remember when Jane and I lived over on Calderon?" he was asking Caroline, who nodded. "I took a bag of my favorite stuff to school the day the house burned and it wasn't even show-and-tell day. Something told me to take them."

"Something? Or *someone*?" I asked.

He responded, "Are we getting religious?"

"I don't know. Are we?"

Becky shooed us forward with a loose wave of her hand. "How did a question about déjà vu turn into whether there's an official puppet master of the universe?"

Caroline answered, "Because for us to have premonitions of a future event, there has to be someone bigger who exists outside of time who already knows what will occur."

Becky's *Why?* was all over her face, but she didn't ask.

"Knows that it will, *preknowledge*? Or forces his will to be done, *predestined*?" Rudy said.

I liked these questions. They were mildly threatening and simultaneously harmless. My insides inched around like worms, but exploring philosophical mysteries added context. And it certainly improved our moods. I said, "We're really wondering: Is everything orchestrated? Was Stacy always going to get pregnant? Were we always going to take this non–road trip road trip? Was Dolly destined to break down?"

Which left Becky to ask the unasked question. "Was Simon Westwood always going to blow your bus? And if so, did any of you sense it was coming?"

"We're not talking about him!" Caroline snapped, her tone back to *I'll shave you in your sleep* status. She moved the headband round and round her head.

"But we are, Cuz. He's here whether we name him or not."

"No. He's in a million pieces in an unmarked grave in Bath because his dad doesn't want vandals pissing on him. And I, for one, am happy to blame the puppet master. God, if that's what you want to call Him."

Rudy cut her off with his chair. "Because it's easier than blaming Simon?"

"No, douchebag. Because it's easier than blaming myself."

I curbed us far off the interstate. Sheer walls of white granite and limestone rose thirty feet like we were at the base of a mountain. A metal net covered the facing to prevent rockslides. "Caroline," I said. "Did you know Simon was going to blow Bus Twenty-One?"

"Did I have a premonition?" she asked.

"Did you know?"

She backed farther into the rocks, her fingers twisting through the chicken wire barrier. "Would I have gotten on if I did?"

I followed her. Weeds stabbed at my legs. "Maybe so," I said. "I think you're into destructive things, and Simon might have been one of them."

She pitched into me like a limp doll and laid her forehead against my breastbone. From this view, I saw the thin scars left from the razor covering her skull. She took one deep breath,

and I considered what I should do with my hands. Hold her head? Wrap her up? In the end, I lifted her face, held her jaws with my thumbs, and looked inside her. "Caroline, why did you stay with him?"

We must have been a sight. Traffic slowed. Life slowed too.

"Why do you stay with Chan?" she asked. "Because you love him, or because you can't get away?"

"Because I love him."

"Well." She sighed, her gaze refusing to meet my eyes. "Congrats on your perfect life."

Caroline's knees bent and I worried she might collapse and knock us to the ground. But her toes grew into the cement and though she wavered, she did not fall. I wrapped my arms around her slight frame. "This was never your fault," I whispered.

"This was always my fault," she whispered back.

33. Who got up this hullaballoo anyway?

$75,110.00

No one said much after Caroline's meltdown. Only Rudy, who offered her a ride, which she accepted. Her added weight, although slight, must have been an extra workout for his arms. They fell behind a little—her being cautious the fabric of her dress didn't catch in the wheel, him making sure she didn't slide off his lap—but I knew he was glad he could do this for her. Chan always wore the same prideful non-smiles when he took care of something for me. Another guy in a long list of guys who liked his hero status. I questioned if I'd pushed Caroline too hard. She was angry, but sometimes anger kept people alive. Becky was on my hip, asking me to lag back long enough to say, "I'm worried about her." I was too.

Simon, the AAA driver, had promised the body shop was directly off the ramp, beside the Shoney's. I saw Shoney's. Mercurys and Lincolns dotted the lot. The Open sign flashed above the front door.

Behind me, Becky asked, "Do people still eat at Shoney's?"

I lifted my shoulders. "My gran likes their strawberry pie."

"I thought they'd all closed."

Becky dug a rock from her flats and used the back of her cell phone like a mirror. While applying lipstick that was somehow miraculously not melted, she said, "I say we find out about Dolly and then split one of those pies. I gotta feed the monster." She rubbed her stomach, and it growled on cue.

Caroline, raised with more money than any of us, was opposed to the idea on principle. Her face twisted around the word *Shoney's* like Becky was asking her to lunch on sour prunes. Let them duke it out over food; low-grade fighting brought color to Caroline's cheeks, and God knows, she needed to be a shade above puke green. Rudy flashed me a thumbs-up behind her back as she slid from his lap to volley disparaging remarks with Becky.

It was full-throttle Shoney's assault until we reached Auto Fix Nation. When the decision of where to wait became Shoney's or hell, Shoney's won hand and foot. Among Auto Fix Nation's many amenities were ripped pleather couches, a Skittles machine, and the very finest selection of *Bikers and Babes* magazine (with the Christmas pullout poster). The desk clerk's pale-blue button-up service shirt was embroidered with the

name Digger on the pocket. Digger wrote my phone number on his arm with a Sharpie and promised to call "after Roddy got her all tinkered out."

"How long might the tinkering take?" I asked, knowing the question was folly before the answer came.

"We close at six." Digger told me after checking his watch. "So you'll hear from us by, well, six."

"Fantastic."

"Don't you go washin' that arm, Digger," Becky said, probably because she couldn't help herself.

"Ah, don't worry, darlin', I keep all the pretty numbers."

"Jesus Christ," Rudy whispered.

"To Shoney's," Caroline said.

Our sudden appearance in the Shoney's waiting area disturbed the fabric of the restaurant. A young hostess with bangles from wrists to elbows leaned over the counter and whispered, "There's an Applebee's at the next exit."

"We came for strawberry pie," Becky announced.

"Okeydokey, artichokey."

That was a real quote from a real human even though it didn't seem possible. She tucked us in a rounded corner booth away from the tables of senior citizens, who were mostly seated near the restrooms or salad bar. Rudy rolled to the open spot and checked the menu. "I say we order breakfast first."

We had just placed our order when we heard air brakes. Caroline parted the miniblinds wide, and then wider. "Tour bus."

The second coming of the senior siege descended upon

us, and the volume in the room quadrupled. Shoney's quickly proved why it existed. For every polyester knit suit and nylon sweater, there were smiling waitresses with coffee cups ready to flirt with men four times their age. I imagined a manager in the back saying, "This is our moment, troops. Go out there and get two-dollar tips like your life depends on their Depends."

Our table filled with plates and drinks, and our hostess swung by our table and said, "Y'all ordered just in time." Since we hadn't done much more than snack for lunch, the food was exceptional.

With her mouth full of pancakes, Caroline asked, "Which of you got this thing up?" She volleyed a glare at me and then Rudy.

"This what?" I asked.

"Global warming! The destruction of the Great Barrier Reef." Massive eye roll. "This trip."

Our eyes scraped each other's plates. There was a busy silence between us. My head stayed bent. I started with an easy, palatable answer. "I always wanted to see Ellis Island. So does Rudy. So we thought—"

"We'd try," Rudy finished.

"And then there's the art installation. We just—"

Rudy again. "Feel like we—"

"Should be there," I said.

"For Carter," we said together.

"Did y'all practice that?" Caroline asked.

"Oh, shush," Rudy said.

Becky moved the topic from *Accelerant Orange*. "Well, I got suspended because of Go and came along for the ride."

"What did y'all get suspended for?"

My cheeks were flames and the flames were spreading into my chest. "Cutting school during a bomb threat. They wanted to put us on a bus for *safety* and I said hell no."

Caroline turned her fork upside down and sucked syrup from the tines. I expected her to poke fun at me, but instead she said, "Tell me: What's your obsession with Ellis Island? Because I also have an obsession, but I'm betting ours are different."

"I want to replicate a family picture. My gran—man, I wish you could meet her—does this thing with replicating photos. I was trying to do the same so we'd have three generations of the same photo, taken with the same camera. Probably sounds stupid if you haven't seen her wall of photos, but that's what I was doing in June. Unfortunately, I lost our family camera, a very old Kodak, in the explosion."

Caroline folded her napkin into a square. A tiny square. The tiniest square possible. "Tell me about the bomb threat at your school."

I sipped my coffee. "I think anyone that has anything to do with bombs—fake or real—should be strung between a couple of trees."

Caroline parted the miniblinds again. A layer of dust poofed into the air. "You're right about that. So, Jennings, if you ran from the general vicinity of a *school bus*, what makes you think you can handle *Accelerant Orange*?"

"I don't know. Maybe, I really want that photo at Ellis Island."

"No."

"Okay. Fine. I want to take any photo I please."

"No."

"All right. New York broke me and Chan. And what do you do when you get lost? You go back to the last place you were found."

There it was. Well, most of it.

Caroline kept pressing. "You sure New York was the last place you were found?"

"Yes."

Caroline jabbed her fork at my chest. "If that's true, board that bus out there. Test her out. Show us you have the stones to take back what you lost."

"I don't have to prove anything to you."

"Yeah, you do. Come on, Jennings. What's the worst that could happen?"

In 1993 a car bomb detonated below the World Trade Center North Tower. Six people died. Many more were injured. I'd bet my red beanie there were spouses who begged their partners to stay home the next morning. I imagined their conversation. The husband said, "Honey, we always said we'd raise our kids out of the city." The wife, after attempting to shower PTSD down the drain, argued, "This is my job. I have to go." Maybe he made the coffee and tried again—this time,

pleading desperately. "Do this for me, please!" But that ill-fated woman grabbed a North Tower badge, and said, "What are the odds that this will happen again?"

Eight years later, the answer came. One hundred percent.

One tragedy didn't buy you cosmic leeway.

"That bus out there could blow too," I said.

"You really know how to play worst-case scenario. Here's the thing: I'm not going another mile unless you find that driver and ask him for a tour."

"Care—"

I held a hand up to Rudy, knowing what to say to Caroline. "Keep that up, and we'll leave you at Shoney's."

Caroline laughed in my face. "You don't think anyone is expendable. Your bleeding heart probably weeps for Simon and curses the mommy who made him the man he became." *How did she know that when I'd just said bombers should be strung up?* "Don't give, Jennings, if you can't get."

I had pushed her to the brink twice today. Bullied her, even.

"Watch it, Care."

"Ru, you weren't telling her to ease up on me earlier, now, were you?" To me she said, "There is no point in driving to New York if you can't board the senior trolley tour of South Carolina. Or, at least, attempt it. Think of all those generous people out there watching *Accelerant Orange* episode forty-five." She gave the *five* her best Southern twang. "They're probably typing their credit card numbers in right now, believing their

hard-earned money will go to someone with a spine. Do you really want to let all those suckers down?"

"You're being a bitch," Rudy said. "This is hard enough without heaping extra guilt on her."

Caroline looked satisfied by the accusation. "Please. Every single one of us dresses in rags of guilt. Way before there was a dollar amount attached to our potential healing. Way before there was an *art installation*. Plus, look at all that brimming determination." She pointed at the vein pulsing in my forehead. "Our golden girl's going to try it."

"You *are* a bitch," I said. "And you're right. I'll try."

God, I missed Chan. But I had to get used to the idea of doing hard things without him.

I stepped toward the driver. And nearly fell over from the rush.

34. Ride, Sally, ride.

$78,880.00

A middle-aged bus driver hunched over the end of the counter. He ate sausage links like he'd never eat again, and when I climbed atop the stool beside him, he didn't notice. I watched as he tapped his paper check with his yellowed fingernails. "Bus driver eats for free," he reminded the waitress. He had not one but two cigarettes above his left ear.

"Um, sir," I said.

"Oh yeah," he said, the words stretched with a Midwestern accent.

"My gran's considering a bus tour to Philadelphia, and I wondered if I might hop on your bus and check the seats

for her. She had a hip replacement." I feigned deep concern. "We all want her to go, but we're worried. You could ease our minds."

"Sure, kid. Lemme hoover this down, and I'll unlock her."

I nodded and swiveled in the opposite direction so he wouldn't feel pressed. Rudy was there. He gave me a cheesy smile I couldn't return. My stomach was roiling from the sausages and the idea that I was about to be up close and personal with a bus. I put my chin on the counter and took a deep breath.

"Ya ready, kid?"

"She is," Rudy answered, thrusting out his hand.

The man popped the cigarette he was holding into the corner of his mouth and shook Rudy's hand. "You the brother?"

"I'm the friend," Rudy answered.

He slapped Rudy on the back and said, "Good on you. Let's head outside to Sally. Ya know, like 'ride, Sally, ride.'" He laughed heartily at his own joke and slapped Rudy between the shoulder blades again.

Rudy tugged me off the stool and we followed the driver out the front door. The smell of tobacco wafted toward our nostrils and Sally beamed in the late-afternoon sun. Her diesel engine ran like a purring jungle cat. When I closed my eyes, the image distorted. The bus flipped sideways. Melted metal. Crumpled steel. Burning skin. Rudy screamed.

When I opened them again: the aqua-blue bus, the black steering wheel, the gray, swaying steps. Cigarettes and diesel.

Closed. A bus in pieces. I touched my side, blood escaped from a hole near my hip.

Opened. An empty, innocuous charter bus. Ride, Sally, ride.

The driver, who had by now told us that his name was Dennis and that he was married with five kids and he'd once been a rodeo clown in Fort Worth, stepped clear for me to enter. "I'll have to pat you down when you leave," he said, but he took an embroidered hankie from his back pocket and pressed it into my hand. "Nose is bleeding, tiger. Don't drip on the seats."

"You don't have to do this. Caroline's daring you because you dared her."

"She's not wrong."

"What if something happens to you in there?"

"I have to make it up there before we worry about that."

Rudy accepted this answer with grace. His lip even curled into a smile. "Ride, Sally, ride," he said, but I couldn't bring myself to enjoy the joke. The bottom step lay six inches away. The standard-issue grooved rubber flooring from Bus #21 covered the three-step well. The driver's seat loomed. Next to that, a shiny aluminum pole ran floor to ceiling. The fire extinguisher was bolted to the floor. Its red metal loomed into focus and out again.

I lifted my foot, pawing at the step.

Everything blurred.

Everything swayed.

A rush of emotions thrashed by like straight-line winds.

Chan and me kissing. Chan and me fighting. Chan and me alive.

The ringing in my ears shook my balance. Endless, endless ringing. I gripped the rail inside the well. A tsunami crested and fell. Heat.

Nothing.

I awoke stretched across Rudy's lap, feet dangling over the side, head lolling on his shoulder. He pressed the driver's bloodstained hankie against my nose.

"How long?" I asked.

"A few seconds," he said, but Becky and Caroline were there. Unless they'd slipped outside to watch me board the bus, they couldn't have made the dash so quickly.

"You were right," I said to Caroline. "I'm not ready for this."

"'The attempt and not the deed confounds us,'" Rudy said.

"Churchill?" Becky asked.

"Shakespeare," said Rudy at the same time that I said, "Stock's people, the crowds, the crowds that believe in you and me and all of us, will measure the deed, not the attempt."

"I'm about to 'Cotton-Eyed Joe' your ass, Jennings."

"Do it," I told Becky.

She clutched my chin the way Granddad used to. "You tried something huge."

And failed. In front of my crew. I liked my role as shining example and pillar of fortitude, and *this*, whatever I was right now, was like being gnawed to death by a rat. I did not want to

faint at the steps of *Accelerant Orange*, and at this rate, I thought I might.

"I've got to figure this out," I said.

"Two days ago, you refused to even look at a bus. Today, you nearly put your foot on the bottom step. That's progress. And we're celebrating. Now let's get back inside so we can eat strawberry pie like senior citizens," Becky said.

35. Society's prodigious metaphor for love

$81,200.00

Digger phoned on our way inside: 5:58. "See, now, here's the problem, we need a part we can't get till morning. Hole up somewhere nearby, and we'll have you back on the tarmac bright and early."

I muted the call and translated Digger's news to the group. "We'll see you at eight a.m.," I promised, and clicked the red End button. Becky yelled toward the phone, "Don't you wash that arm tonight, Digger." He probably heard her across the Shoney's parking lot.

Caroline was already online renting us a room at the Comfort Inn. I told her I'd pay our part and was relieved when she said it was no biggie. Gas expenses had put a serious dent in

my wallet. Plus, I expected to take another hit from Auto Fix Nation the next morning. I'd have to use Gran's credit card, and I knew my parents had put new truck tires on it last month.

Because my family rarely ventured off-Hive, the last time I'd stayed away from home was in New York, and that was in a hostel. Here, there were two queen beds, a minifridge, and a closet safe. I explored the corners while Caroline flung herself on the bed. "You don't get out much, Jennings?"

"And you do?"

"I used to get out *a lot.*"

She situated pillows against the headboard and settled in. TNT had a *Princess Bride* marathon and that fast became the soundtrack of the room. Becky perched on the corner of Caroline's bed, and then slowly scooted back to watch the movie. Within minutes, Caroline had her head in Becky's lap and Becky was removing her purple headband and claiming everyone should feel how soft her head was. Rudy announced he was finding the gym, and I opted for a long shower. We were stuck, and there was nothing we could do about it until morning.

After showering, I slipped from the room, rode the elevator to the eighth floor, and cruised to the end of a long hallway. Two windows looked over a great wide nothing. A glorious spring exploded right to left in the fading daylight. Back home, the tallest thing we had other than the old fire tower was my grain bin. I'd climbed the bin many times, Chan on my heels. Sitting high in the sky, away from everyone, watching the land

wave in the wind. Touching heaven with our fingertips.

"Can't do this in a city!" Chan would say, resting his hat on his knee.

"Can't do what?" I'd asked, though I already knew.

He'd closed his eyes and taken a deep life-giving breath. He'd watch the world below us the way adults watched their children speak for the first time. Finally, he'd said, "You ever think we're sitting in the orchestra pit and those fields over there are the violins and the creek is the cello—"

"And the deer hooves are drums—"

"And the cicadas are—"

"Castanets?" I'd finished.

We'd stared at each other, and there'd be plenty of longing—the sort that bubbles up when you feel known.

"I'm glad for this place," I'd said.

"I'm glad for you," he'd said. And then he'd pulled our fingers to his lips and kissed the back of my hand . . . my wrist . . . my elbow . . . my collarbone . . . jawline . . . lips, all while I lay there tingling, the metal roof hot on my back and Chan's breath heating everywhere he touched. I'd never felt so warm.

If he were on this trip, he'd have found his way here too. Chan loved people and camaraderie, especially on the Hive, but he was equally connected to the land. He was always the guy saying, "Let's get outside this weekend." We'd be standing in an overcrowded room of bees milling around some queen, and he'd find my eyes. Out he'd go. Into the trees. Along a cornrow, his hands grazing silky stalks as he ran. Up the grain

bin with a telescope. Countless times, I excused myself from conversations and followed him. Or he followed me. That was how we first kissed. Not because we were running to each other, but because we were escaping at the same time.

Frequently, my inner voice told me there was no one better than Chan. But sometimes there was another thought—how would I even know? I'd never looked farther away than a house I could see from my kitchen window. Would it be luck that I was born a thousand feet from where I was meant to be? Did God not trust me to explore? Or was Chan a gift and should I shut up and be thankful?

Mom used to say, "Honey, you'll know forever material when you do what you want to do and then look to your right and left and see who else is doing it."

I stared at my ring—society's metaphor for *love*—and wondered if loving someone was a reason to stay with him. And . . . if love wasn't enough, what was? How did anyone ever stay together?

I felt shallow for being angry with Chan when I was also angry with myself. I'd passed out this afternoon a foot away from a bus. When I stared at his refusal to leave the Hive, it probably wasn't an unwillingness to come with *me*. He was scared of the city the way I was scared of buses. That made me an arrogant ass, which made me bone-sad. And tired. I've always been my greatest critic, and when I looked at my recent behavior, there was hardly anything here to be proud of.

I remembered Rudy's wisdom from the beach that

morning—*I can come along if you capture it just right*—and I texted Chan a photo of the snaking river outside the window, hoping he'd know I was somewhere he would like and I was thinking of him.

Maybe he'd buy a plane ticket with thoughts like that.

Or maybe he wouldn't.

36. What happened in Simon Westwood's brain?

$81,210.00

According to a map on the elevator door, the fitness center lived on the lobby level. I rode to the main floor, stole two oranges from the breakfast nook basket, and followed the chlorine smell of the pool, hoping to find the fitness center nearby. Rudy was there, hair slicked back and handsome in that post-practice way football players always are.

I tossed him an orange.

"Hey, thanks." His fingernails dug into the pulp. "You needing a workout?"

"I'm needing not to be in a small room with Caroline."

"Yeah. She's hard."

"I'm glad she came with us, but she worries me."

"Simon messed her up way before he messed us up."

"I'm sure. I keep trying to imagine who I'd be if Chan treated me the way Simon must have treated her. It's not pretty. Chan's not perfect, but he's good, you know? He'd never hurt someone on purpose. Much less me."

Rudy half laughed, half sighed. "I was actually just thinking about the way I treat people." He held paper and a pen. "I stole this from the business center printer after my workout and was writing a little before I hit the shower."

"Can I read what you wrote?"

Rudy chewed an orange wedge. He looked torn, and I understood that whatever was on the paper was personal.

"I don't have to," I said. But he rolled closer and trusted me with his words.

"It's not finished. See you back in the room."

I stretched out on a treadmill to read.

When I was twelve, I broke up with Kelly O'Leary because she got on my nerves. She didn't shed a tear at my departure. I didn't shed a tear at hers.

When I was thirteen, I broke up with Abby Bell, Rachel Feinmach, and Kayla Somebody. (I can't remember her last name, but we met at the skate park.) Abby cried and called me a faggot. Rachel and Kayla were hanging off other guys within the hour.

Fourteen was a backward year. Four girls broke up with me, and none of them gave reasons.

When I was fifteen, I fell "in love" for the first time. Her name

was Honey Granger. We went out the whole year, said I love you, fooled around, and nearly had sex (but she was thirteen and thought she should wait until fourteen). I bought her a cool watch for Christmas, and she got me new jeans. Expensive gifts for poor kids. In April, she told me she didn't love me anymore. When I asked why, she said, "I don't know. I just don't." That was that.

I got over Honey by dating Taylor, who I promptly dumped, because she had a thing for my brother, Victor, and we don't jack around.

That was when I fell in love for the second time: Crystal Abernathy. If she said "Jump," I didn't ask, "How high?" I hard-lined the moon and hurled my body at the sky. For seven months, I thought: I'm going to marry this girl someday. I fantasized about it too. The house where we'd live. Our kids with her eyes. Making Hamburger Helper in our kitchen.

Christmas Day she accidentally swapped my gift with her other boyfriend's. Victor hauled me over to Parkers and got me smashed. I stopped taking her calls and felt like an Olympian for my discipline.

By the time I was seventeen, I'd sworn off serious relationships. High school girls were players, I told myself. High school girls liked breaking hearts. High school girls wanted to stay in Orlando, and I was moving to Boston. Love and dating were brutal and tragic, and I accepted that they were brutal and tragic, because that was high school. And perhaps my heart was an organ that would function better with age. College, that would be my season. Maybe it will, maybe it won't.

Here is what I don't understand: Why do some people, who are in

the same circumstances, respond so differently?

What happened in Simon Westwood's brain when he found out Caroline had cheated on him—same as Crystal Abernathy cheated on me; same as lots of people cheat—and he thought the solution was to kill a bunch of people? To bomb a busload who weren't involved?

Hurting Crystal never occurred to me. Ever.

Hurting Tommie the sleazebag burnt-orange Civic driver did. But not seriously. I might have bloodied his nose if I'd seen them together right after we broke up, but I wouldn't have hurt him or anyone else. I was altogether happy to let them hurt each other (which I was convinced they would do. And I was correct).

What makes people snap? Do they know it's happening while it's happening? Did Simon, for instance, believe his brain was firing along, business as usual, and that blowing the bus was a logical punishment for Caroline?

I want to understand how the world that produced Carter Stockton also produced Simon Westwood.

CAROLINE

We lie in a queen bed in the Comfort Inn.

My head is in Becky's lap. Her fingers massage my scalp. She is singing a song for me, so my heart will not race. But it races.

Becky is unafraid; Go is a wonder; Rudy is a marvel.

My brain is a chorus.

I like them all. I like them

all. I like them all. Dammit, dammit, I like them all.

37. Butter on a skillet

$83,250.75

I stayed in the gym for a long time, rereading Rudy's words. All the lights were off except for the bathroom's. *The Princess Bride* started again. Caroline and Becky occupied one bed and a single lump filled the other. I stumbled toward the television, nearly tripped on a shoe, and groped for the remote. The picture shrank, and I followed a sliver of light to the sink, where I brushed my teeth, washed my face, and tried not to think about getting into bed with Rudy Guthrie.

Maybe he's asleep. Chan often fell asleep before his eyes closed.

When I crawled into bed, Rudy whispered, "We can swap them."

They were snoring. "It's only sleep," I said.

"I don't want you uncomfortable."

"I'm not," I said, but we both fidgeted. "I liked what you wrote. What's it for?"

"My sanity."

I'd expected him to say Ms. Jay. When I turned slightly, the outline of his nose and the curve of his forehead were in dark silhouette. That incredible mop of hair fell onto the pillow and I resisted the urge to part it the way I would if he were Chan.

"Give me a micro-moment?" he asked.

"From when?"

"From whenever."

I chose a time I'd rarely spoken about.

"Carter Stockton was my medic. He loaded me into the ambulance, started an IV, wiped the trickle of blood from my ears. He wrote *Bellevue* on a clipboard pad because I couldn't read his lips. I asked him to call my mother."

"I don't remember my ambulance ride at all."

"Most of the sounds from that day are dulled, practically wiped, but some of the images are seared. When I close my eyes, Carter's smiling at me."

"I . . . that's amazing. I'm still remembering things from that day," Rudy says.

"You can't blame your brain for protecting you until you're ready."

His head bobbed against the pillow. He curled more to his left, more toward me. He was shirtless, which wasn't

surprising, but it was distracting. I made sure to stay flat on my back and stare at the ceiling. But no matter how much distance I kept between our bodies, my voice betrayed me. "I didn't know you'd lived," I said.

Mom tried to hide the special edition *People* magazine under a newspaper in her hospital chair. When she left for a coffee refill, I forced myself to search for Rudy's face. The issue reminded me of the coverage of Sandy Hook. Nineteen square photos on a black glossy cover. A yearbook of Bus #21. There was a boy that could have been Rudy. For twelve long minutes I imagined him in a sleek black casket. I lay there praying and squeezing the rails of the bed, unable to read the article. When Mom came back with a Danish and decaf, I begged her to check the names.

"I was so relieved you weren't on that list. I didn't even know you and . . ."

"Ms. Jay did the same for me. I listened for you, Golden, and I thought about you when I was in rehab."

"You did?"

"Yeah." He coughed quietly, self-consciously. "Tell me more about Carter the medic."

"We managed a decent conversation between lip reading and his clipboard. I probably screamed at him." It had taken days for the ringing to stop. "He'd been a medic for twenty years and he swore he'd never seen anything like our bus. I told him I'd been in New York less than twenty-four hours and I wasn't impressed. I tried to laugh, but I coughed myself into

a fit. Carter squeezed my hand and walked me through my injuries. Burned feet, fractured jaw. I lost a lot of blood from a laceration near my hip." I remembered thinking about how much money all that blood would cost my family. That Mom and Dad might not be able to work if I lived and were seriously injured. And they'd have to afford a funeral if I died. I thought caskets were fairly expensive, but the Hive would pitch in and help.

"Did you think you were going to die?" he asked.

"Yeah."

"What did you do?"

"I prayed."

"Me too."

"Who told your dad?" I asked.

"I don't know. Maybe a cop? Maybe Caroline? I never asked. I only have a twenty- or thirty-second memory following the bombing. Seeing . . . bodies. Caroline on the ground. Screaming that I couldn't move my legs."

We were stilled by this memory.

He asked, "How come you didn't tell me you knew Stock?"

"I don't know him know him. He was just there."

"What made you reach out on Tuesday?"

"Chan's *engagement* request. Stock announcing opening day. What made you?"

"No one else to talk to."

"How do you feel about *Accelerant Orange*?"

"You've seen the videos; you know what Stock's doing is a

tribute to us and the others. I trust that. His heart is first-class. I guess . . . apart from that . . . I'm nervous. It's not just the bus itself; it's all those people. I've played soccer in front of several thousand, half the stadium hoping you fail, half wanting you to succeed. Guess which side is more pressure?"

I already knew. "Your fans."

"You bet. A hundred percent of the time. Because you go home with them. Because they'll see you again. They'll follow your story. *Accelerant Orange* doesn't feel very different from running out on the field, hearing the crowd scream, and knowing you're playing a team full of Goliaths."

"Does the money make it worse?" The number was still climbing: $83,250.75.

"Not really. That money is the only way college is an option now. Does it for you?"

"I don't know yet. Maybe. Pretty unnerving to think about. I watched my gran put a hundred dollars in the till, so I have an image of people seeing our story and deciding they'll give to our futures. It makes me think that's a shit ton of money . . . I'd better build a future they'd like. If I have another day like today, they'll ask for a refund."

"Go, the future is tough to control. Those people know that." I knew what he meant. I'd lived it. But then he added, "Ideally, the future was me kicking a black-and-white ball. It's not. I have a cathing bag, a digital stim machine, and I actually need the handicapped bathroom because infections are a real thing. I have to live with the future the past gave me."

"Rudy, what's wrong with your legs?" He heard the question below the question. *Would he ever walk again?*

He shifted his torso and repositioned his thighs. "The explosion threw me into a street sign and injured my spinal cord. Doctors call it an incomplete injury, so there's some hope of healing, of the paralysis lifting, but there's been no improvement over the last year in PT. It's not likely." I watched the definition of his chest as he exhaled. "What was wrong with your feet?"

"Third-degree burns. A random piece of metal. Melted right through my soles like butter on a skillet. 'Butter on a skillet.' That's what the doctor at Bellevue told my parents later. He was from the South, doing a residency in the city, and was delighted to hear my parents' accents."

"And the cut?"

"Shrapnel. Technically, part of the handrail. Went right through"—I found his hand and placed it near my hip—"this area."

"Through the bone?"

"No." It spiked my right ovary.

"Can you have children?" he asked, removing his hand from my hip bone.

"Probably. Can you?"

"Probably."

"That's good."

His breath caught and he turned his face toward me.

I lay there feeling sacred things—things I'd only ever felt

for Chan. Attraction. Anticipation. Maybe even desire. Did I want Rudy to inch closer, to touch my face, to kiss me, to see what his bare stomach felt like against mine?

Sometimes, after Chan and I were together, I'd lie almost covering him, two bodies stacked like bricks on a wall, and I'd press my ear to his heart and listen for the downbeat. What did Rudy's downbeat sound like? Did each heart have a signature sound? I didn't know, but I clutched the sheets so I wouldn't move or give myself away. The sensation didn't pass.

"Rudy?"

"Yeah."

"I'm gonna sleep on the floor, okay?"

"Me too."

I rolled off my side of the bed and listened as he moved to the floor on the other side. Was sleeping on the floor bad for his body? *If you wouldn't ask Becky, don't ask me.* I left his decision alone. He knew how to take care of himself better than I did.

"Good night," I said, the queen bed now between us.

He didn't answer.

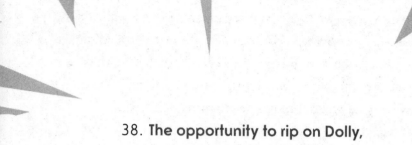

38. The opportunity to rip on Dolly, Roddy, and communes

$89,100.00

A sliver of cream-colored moon hung in the morning sky when I parted the hotel curtains. I had a theory about days where you saw the sun and the moon in the morning. God sent you extra light.

He was also sending extra heat. Outside, the air was muggy, reminding me of the night before. Rudy's fingers against my hip bone. The pressure in my chest. There was nothing erotic about my medical history, but what happened in my brain turned chemical and potent and very unmedical. I'd put Rudy's hand near the most vulnerable region on my body. My parents, doctors, Chandler Clayton: that was the exhaustive

list of people who had touched my hip bones. I repeated the gesture now to remind myself a hip was only a hip. We'd done nothing wrong. Rudy had bags under his eyes from not sleeping. The floor must have sucked for him too.

We'd brushed our teeth at the same time. Afterward, he'd sat quietly in his chair, watching me dab concealer under my eyes. He'd said, "Sometimes I wish guys wore makeup."

"You always can."

Even that sounded sexual.

He'd left with his bag in his lap and I waited to follow so we didn't go down the hallway together. Five minutes and a trip across the street later, Auto Fix Nation hit me with the old one-two punch. The bill for Dolly was a whopping six hundred dollars, and Digger said, "I hope y'all aren't taking her far."

"New York."

"That truck makes North Carolina, Roddy's a fuggin' wizard."

When we were in the parking lot, Becky tossed an indignant hand at Auto Fix Nation. "Does anyone want to trust *Roddy the fuggin' wizard* on a single seat belt and a truck older than our combined ages?"

"Dolly's from 1990."

Becky said, "I told you a long time ago I was bad at math. But I am very good at vehicles, and this one isn't up to the task."

She was right, and I was on fire with frustration, pacing along the yellow parking space line. Back and forth. Back and

forth. This wasn't right. We couldn't end the trip here. We hadn't gone anywhere. No offense to the people of Wherever the Hell We Were, South Carolina. Becky placed her body in front of mine so I was forced to stop. She clamped my shoulders tight as a vise. "I'm sorry. This sucks like Orlando traffic."

"Are y'all saying we're done?" Caroline suddenly sounded desperate to be on the trip she'd disdained at every turn.

"Roddy and Digger say we are."

Caroline said, "I have a personal rule about letting people named Roddy and Digger dictate my life."

Becky provided logic. "None of us are old enough to rent a car. If Dolly can't make it, our option is drive to one of our houses and swap vehicles. If we pick Orlando, we'd have to figure a way back to Kentucky. If we pick Kentucky, I'll donate the Mustang to the cause. But there's still the trouble of getting them home." She pointed to Rudy and Caroline.

Either choice made New York by Sunday more difficult, a fact Becky already knew, no matter how bad her math skills were. After everything had been so hard, why couldn't this part just be easy? I was feeling pretty sorry for us when Rudy backed into the shade; he'd been turning anxious wheelies as I paced. "If we hit Orlando, you'd probably have to tow Dolly home. Roddy and Digger might be dumb as dirt, but every mile we put on this Dodge is a stretch. Let's gamble on Kentucky. It's not that far out of the way, and I don't want to be done yet."

His bolstered resolve helped me. Caroline was looking

waify and slight, like she might fall over if Becky wasn't serving as a human buttress. But she was almost smiling.

"My place is probably ten hours from here," I said.

Becky struck a Supergirl pose. "PS, my girl here lives on a commune."

"Yes, and you're going to love it," I said matter-of-factly. "Speaking of, I need to call Gran."

That concluded the big discussion. We were going to New York by way of Kentucky. The three of them disappeared to Shoney's for to-go breakfast. Which gave me a minute to call Gran and gave them the opportunity to rip on Dolly, Roddy, and communes. I assumed Becky would fill them in on the latter. Not a cult. Not religious. Not dangerous.

Gran answered right away. "Hey, chickadee!" She loved talking on the phone, even when we could easily speak in person. I didn't have to be present to see her sitting at the breakfast table, the long spiral telephone cord stretched from the wall. Her Bible was open, her prayer list beside it. My name was written there. The commune wasn't religious, but Gran was steadfast.

I ripped the Band-Aid fast. "I've got bad news about Dolly. Transmission problems. I'm not done with my trip yet, but I wanted to let you know on account of how much we love the truck and . . . I might need to use the credit card you gave me."

She gave me permission straightaway. I was lucky; when I called home to ask for help, someone was there to give it. Not just one someone, thirty someones, if I were counting. That

was the benefit of living where I lived.

"By the way," Gran said. "Chan told your mom and dad that you and Becky went to *Disney World*."

"He said *what*?"

"That camping was a bust and you were at Disney World having a ball. I didn't call him on it, but I thought you should know."

I shook my head and stared at my group, who were emerging from Shoney's laden with bags. Chan had invented a narrative and spread it like mayo on a bun. Maybe he was protecting me, but I found the decision strange.

"So *is* Disney World wonderful?" Gran asked facetiously.

I thought of fireworks and alligators and the empty hotel bed between Rudy and me. "Let's say it's eventful."

"Sounds true. And is this snafu with Dolly big or small? Do you need me to put you on a plane or something?" Gran asked. I heard her bustling about the kitchen making something. Probably coffee at this time of day. I imagined her red cup and saucer with the dainty blue flowers.

"We're driving home to trade vehicles. Will you tell Mom and Dad I'll be there for supper and I'm bringing friends?"

She giggled. "I'll set the table, chickadee. Do you want me to tell Chan you had a great time at Disney World?"

Under my breath, I dropped a few indelicate curses. "No, leave that for me."

39. Dickheads are like geysers.

$89,500.00

Tall, nearly naked pines lined the interstate, and somewhere nearby workers set controlled burns in the Carolina forests. Digital road signs warned of smoke and slowdowns. I tasted ash in the air. I drove because no one wanted to be responsible if Dolly broke again. Caroline rode in the camper nest with Rudy. We'd been cruising the highway for fifteen minutes when Becky said, "Caroline has something to say." Caroline glared at Becky, who smiled cunningly in return. "Don't you, Caroline?"

Perhaps Becky and Caroline had had an emotionally active night in their hotel bed too.

A reluctant Caroline said, "I'm telling a story now." When

she spoke, the words were aimed at my eyes in the rearview mirror. "I'm going to ruin South Carolina," she said, not cruelly, but like this was a helluva story.

Rudy knew pieces, the cousins shared some things, but he twisted until his face was near Caroline's, and the four of us made a strange circle in the truck.

"I'm not going to cry," she announced. "So if you're thinking I'm about to be all waterworks and weepy and you'll have to pull over, it will not happen."

I kept my eyes on the road. "Okay." Fine by me. I didn't plan to cry either.

Becky echoed me.

Rudy said nothing, and Caroline began.

"Mom and Dad went along with Aunt Linda's suggestion of a summer tour of New York. They were heading to Italy with the Westwoods to investigate some new grape hybrid and thought the trip would keep me occupied. Generous, right?" She didn't pause for a response. "Simon's parents signed him up about two seconds later. *The Westwoods and Ascotts are vital to each other.*" She was mimicking someone; I suspected her father. "They're *Pour me another shot of Pappy Van Winkle's* sailing buddies. If you don't know the bourbon, it's, well, God-only-buys-one-bottle-a-year expensive."

My body tensed. I tried to remain a blank slate while she was willing to talk, but Simon, rich? One of the newspaper articles said he made the vests to sell, and I always assumed that

was for enterprise rather than boredom. I also never thought of him as someone who might have the means to lounge on a sailboat in the Finger Lakes or drink expensive bourbon. In my brain, he was a poor, angry racist who zipped that second vest onto Jim Conner's chest.

"We went on the trip. Bada bing, bada boom. You were all there. Yada yada. Explosion."

Rudy watched his cousin closely, like a cobra that might strike her own tail. The urge to interrupt and say something like *Seriously? Bada bing, bada boom? He's paralyzed* edged my tongue. I bit down and studied Caroline in the mirror.

She'd shaved her eyebrows to stubs, which enhanced the freckles across the bridge of her nose. We'd all awakened to an electric razor buzzing and shared a collective sigh. I hadn't realized she'd shaved more than her head until that pretty purple headband was framed in Dolly's mirror. There was even a small cut above her eye.

She continued, "After Bus Twenty-One, Mom thought it best to keep everything quote, unquote"—Caroline laughed bitterly—"*normal*. As if that were possible for them or me. Still, she made me enroll at the University of Rochester as previously planned. 'They would be close but not too close,' she said, as if they'd always been present and supportive. I would live in the dorm instead of this massive house they'd already bought. 'You'll be around *good people*,' she said. I'd be around people who didn't know everything, is what she meant. Turns

out, I was around people who knew plenty."

Those early days had been hell. When I finally went back to school, acquaintances checked on me in the hallway and I stumbled away, assuring them I was fine. Classmates dropped questions about violence into world history discussions, baiting Chan and me to answer. Everyone wanted the real story.

"College was always going to be rough." Caroline paused again. "Especially since my roommate was tangentially connected to a victim. The distant cousin of a girl who lost her boyfriend on Bus Twenty-One. You all know him." Caroline disappeared from view.

"I didn't know anyone on the bus," I said.

"You knew *him*."

Jim Conner.

"Did you tell your mom you didn't want to go to school?" Becky asked.

"I hardly spoke for a month after the bus, so, no. I bought a duvet from Pottery Barn and went off into the wild blue yonder of higher education. As the Ascotts all do."

Mom and Dad hadn't made me do anything. I even had a little sit-down after my wounds healed to explain that I wanted, in fact needed, to leave the Hive. But that was months later. My first sixty days of senior year were homebound.

"It went like you'd expect. As word spread, people harassed me about Simon. They harassed me about me. They were grieving and pissed, and I didn't blame them. I left the theater

one night—I like to watch late shows alone—and one of them warned me, 'You can't sweep this under the rug, Ascott.' To which I said, 'No kidding.' But they didn't think I took them seriously enough."

Caroline said all this with zero emotion. As if she were talking about someone else's life.

"Dickheads are like geysers. They go off every few days. I got used to their slurs and icy glares. Until one night I came back to my dorm and there were three people in ski masks. One of them had to be my roommate—I recognized her perfume—and someone had to let them in."

"Jesus, Care, you should have told me," Rudy said.

My fingers ached from holding the wheel. Beside me, Becky Cable cried quietly into the collar of her shirt.

"They duct-taped me to a chair and played barber. First, with scissors. Everyone took a turn. Then, an electric razor. There wasn't anything left, but they dumped a pail of water over my head, lathered, and shaved my skull with a blade."

"My God!" Becky's voice squeaked.

In a clinical, measured tempo, Caroline finished the story. "One of them, I don't know which, wrote 'I date bombers' in superglue along here"—she drew a half-moon between her ears—"and then glittered the letters. They left me taped to a chair in the shower."

Becky faced Caroline, her hand stretching through the glass toward Caroline's shoulder for contact. "Did you turn

them in to campus security?"

Caroline shoved Becky away, and curled into the nest. From the fetal position she answered, "No. I decided they were right. People should probably know straightaway I'm toxic as hell."

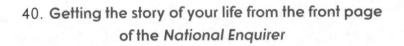

40. Getting the story of your life from the front page of the *National Enquirer*

$90,140.00

Caroline's story ruined South Carolina *and* Tennessee, and had the steam to destroy future states as well. Stories could be thieves. I wanted to do something besides drive, but we needed to get home and switch cars. I rolled down the window and leaned into the air. Across from me, Becky did the same. A tunnel of wind wreaked havoc on her bangs and my curls. Neither of us said a word. We didn't have to.

She hated those kids who hurt Caroline, and I hated them too.

I wanted to hurt them.

For one long minute I imagined MMA versions of Becky and me beating those college kids with tennis rackets until

they were unrecognizable. And then I pulled over and hurled Shoney's bacon and eggs into the weeds.

When I was driving again, I said Caroline's name.

"Don't say you're sorry," she said, her voice mildly threatening.

I was sorry, but that wasn't what I planned to say. I didn't know what I planned to say. Not only had an atrocious thing happened in the wake of the bombing, she'd adopted that atrocity as truth. The ghosts of those roommates had placed a razor in her hand this morning. The ghost of an enemy had whispered, "Be ashamed. Be ashamed. Be ashamed." The ghost of Simon had wrapped her brain like jellyfish tendrils—long and poisonous—saying, *This was your fault.*

Was there really anything I could say to that?

I wanted to tell her to stop. To explain that life didn't have to be toxic because she dated a bomber in high school. I wanted to shove Rudy's free writing into her hands and demand that she see the whirlwind of dates and heartbreak, and how no one thought of him as Crystal Abernathy's ex anymore. Surely, if Caroline waited, no one would think of her and Simon together. Listening to her attackers was like getting the story of your life from the front page of the *National Enquirer.*

Caroline didn't need two-cent wisdom for a million-dollar problem. She needed something better than words, better than an argument.

All I could hope was this trip would heal her insides.

That was what Stock said in episode 41. He had a do-rag

on his head and a toothpick in the corner of his mouth. He'd looked into the camera and said, "Empathy is the antidote of hate, people. I can't bring anybody back to life, but if I can bring life back to people through honoring everyone injured by this tragedy, well, I'll have done my job."

I prayed then, because my gran says God is a doctor at heart. Dear God, save her insides. Bring life back.

And then I was quiet some more, and so was everyone else.

Maybe they were praying too.

41. Gird your loins.

$94,267.00

On the west side of Nashville, Tennessee, I received a text from Chan. I got you something & dinner will be ready by 7:00. The problem with text messages was the lack of tone.

We hadn't spoken since he'd hung up on me. I'd texted him. I'd left messages. Hell, I'd left money for a flight, and he hadn't acknowledged me. And then, out of the blue, when I was nearly home, I received *this* text. He was either trying to make peace. Or . . . I didn't know what else, but I had a hard time trusting my homecoming would be simple.

The sky was a shade of purple-pink that existed only between seven and eight p.m. Each mile brought us within reach of home. Fallow winter fields made a corridor along the

highway as we left the interstate behind. I was so close to the steeple of home that I could feel the rumble of gravel beneath our tires before we turned onto Tobacco Road. I couldn't stop chewing my lips. I couldn't stop pushing Dolly to sixty-five.

"This is it," I said.

Caroline and Rudy pressed their faces to the center glass and strained their eyes against the hazy gray dusk. The Hive's entrance had a beautiful country formality. Long curving road. Cattle grates that rattled under tires. Land as far as the eye could see. There was a ramshackle produce stand to the right where I occasionally sold fruits and veggies, an enclosed information kiosk with brochures about the community to the left, and a ranch-style gate you had to get out and move. A carved sign hung from crossbeams:

THE HIVE COMMUNITY
established 1962.

It looked like something out of a *Halloween* movie if you weren't used to it.

I explained the dynamic of families living here. In exchange for housing, they contributed to the community financially and creatively. On the grounds were a craft shop with the world's largest checkerboard and one of Chan's nativities, Gran's paint studio, my grain bin, cattle, land . . . all the usual things.

Caroline was quick to remind me, "Those are not usual."

"They are if you live here," I said.

The place was handsome as hell, even in the semidarkness. They were wowed immediately, which was deeply satisfying. I don't know what it was that made me want people to love where I came from, but I always did.

Becky smacked the dash with delight. "Also, there's a baby-blue Mustang with my name on it."

"You're staying for dinner." I wasn't asking.

She glanced at Caroline, a peculiar expression on her face. "Yeah. Sure. Why not?"

We rolled past the chapel, past Gran's, and parked Dolly in the lean-to barn. My parents would have heard us drive by; the screen door opened at the first crunch of gravel. They probably planned to greet us as if I were a soldier returning from war.

"Gird your loins," I told the crew, and climbed from the truck.

"Will it be that bad?" Becky asked.

"Probably worse."

We were a back-door family. Something about the front porch was undeniably off-putting and yet . . . there was my family plus Chan on the steps of the chapel, about to escort us through the double oak doors.

Wearily, we stretched and then lugged duffels from the camper. Chan stepped off the porch, crossed the lawn, and took my bag. "Welcome home, my prodigal love, I have killed the fatted calf for you and your friends." He was not happy, but a stranger wouldn't know. He also wasn't unhappy. If I had to

guess, he was scared. We embraced, and I held on longer than he did. After everything Caroline said this afternoon, hugging him felt like a luxury.

"This is Chan, everyone." I gave quick indications, aware he didn't need them.

Caroline stared hard at Chan's boots and hat, like she'd never seen a Kentucky boy in real life, and said, "We've heard a lot about *you*."

"I'm sure you have," Chan said grimly.

There was a round of formal handshakes, fierce pumps, like they were drawing water from a well, and then my family descended, and we had to repeat the process. Dad, ever quiet, wandered to Dolly and popped the hood. Mom called him back. "Peter, dinner's ready," and he left the antique to its whines and coughs.

"She did fine today," I told him, and as was his habit, he tucked me under his arm and pressed a kiss against my temple. That was his *I missed you, I love you, and I'm glad you're back safely.*

"You need a hand?" Chan asked Rudy when he reached the porch steps.

"I'll take him through the kitchen," I said. The grass was relatively flat from here to there, and I sensed Rudy would not want strangers lifting his chair. I hoped the back door was wide enough.

Chan tipped the brim of his hat like he'd been dismissed from a saloon. He stayed with the group, and as Rudy and I

parted toward the back, I overheard Mom ask, "Now, how did all y'all meet?"

I whirled on the spot, curious at this first hurdle.

Caroline pepped her voice to an annoying level. "I believe the answer we're going with today is Disney World."

"Well, that's lovely," Gran cooed. She had her blue eyes on me and then Chan. "Happiest place on earth, right, Chan?"

42. That's what was in my bag.

$81,766.00

In our brief moment alone, Rudy took my hand and squeezed once. "They're nice."

"They are."

Hospitality is important to them. Without being asked, they'll set another place at the table, bring seconds, make sure visitors have enough quilts on the beds, explain there's a night-light in the bathroom, and let them know they can run the shower at the same time as someone else in the house because they have great pressure and a continuous hot-water heater. (My dad's really proud of his new hot-water heater.)

But I do not have parents who will support a return trip to New York City. Not for their baby.

"Your house is legit," Rudy said.

"You should hear the organ."

Rudy wore my red beanie, which was a gift from Gran the Christmas before last. She thought it would set off my hair and smooth my coloring. I tugged on the fabric. "My gran'll probably recognize this." Chan might recognize it too. His near-photographic memory would likely register that this wasn't *a* red beanie, but *my* red beanie, which I told him I'd lost in the bombing. Not a lie. An elastic truth.

"I can take it off."

I hesitated. It was already too late.

"No."

"Can I ask you something?" We were in the mudroom— the door was plenty wide for his chair; everyone else was in formal dining room. His question would be private. I nodded that he could. "When you tossed me this cap before you left the bus, what did you say?"

"I don't remember. I know that's terrible. What did you think I said?"

He didn't look wounded from lack of memory and that was a relief.

"Bandit," he said, which was what I called him in Down Yonder. "What do you wish you'd said?" he asked.

"I like you a lot. Don't die."

"That's basically the same as bandit, right?"

He removed the beanie. If I weren't with Chan, I'd have kissed him right then. Instead, I leaned against the washer and

watched him twist the red fabric. Rudy looked like a manne-
quin. He was perfectly dressed. The lime-green stickers on his
chair matched a stripe in his shirt. His jeans—frayed and dark
denim—hung to the edge of his sneakers, his sneakers rested
against a single plate across the bottom frame of the chair. I
remembered precisely how tall he had been in the Down Yonder bathroom. The top of my head met his clavicle. Now, we
were precisely reversed. His height preserved by a long torso.
He was staring at my chest, working that beanie like a baker
kneading dough.

The past doesn't exactly repeat itself. People said that it did.
But to me, the past was wise. It knew how to repackage itself
again and again, so each time felt original and familiar. I'd been
tempted by Rudy before and it hadn't led me to a good place.

"They're probably waiting," he said, looking away.

"I'll be right behind you."

He left, and I turned on the mudroom sink. I soaped my
hands, scrubbing hard, abusing them, buying time. My ring
slipped off. I trapped the golden hearts against the drain. A
millisecond slower and my engagement ring would be in the
pipe. That ring. I didn't know whether to solder it to the bone
or give it back.

"Golden! Honey! We're starving."

"Coming, Mom."

I slid the ring over my knuckle, dried my hands, and
entered the kitchen.

Chan wasn't kidding about the calf. Food to feed armies

covered the table's center. Mom had everyone holding hands in the dining room, because Gran insisted we pray as a group. Dad moved an end chair away from the table so Rudy would have a place.

Chan held the circle open for me. I left Rudy with Caroline, who was latched to Becky, and took my rightful place. His hand was warm as a fever and as familiar as my own. His thumb traced the bones in my fingers the way they always did. The prayer was short and everyone bumbled to his or her seat. We passed potatoes. Scooped hearty portions of mac and cheese. Raved about the homemade biscuits and beef shoulder. Another expensive meal. Chan and my family talked to us and around us.

I was the stranger at our table. Lonely among my dearest.

I wished I were back in the dingy linoleum kitchen in Orlando. Talking and laughing with Victor and Jane over beer. Or even, God forbid, at Shoney's eating strawberry pie. Caroline tilted and mouthed, "Dude, this is your electric razor." And then pantomimed buzzing my hair.

That did it.

I busted up a nothing conversation about Chan's biology homework with an announcement. "We weren't at Disney World."

"Epcot?" Dad asked.

"No."

"Camping?"

"We never camped," I said.

Chandler squeezed my leg under the table. "Don't do this," he pleaded. *Or what?* Rudy and Caroline clearly wished to escape, but I gave them a *You're staying* nod. Becky pumped her fist and mouthed the first words of "Eye of the Tiger," which was tops on our Becky and Go Go playlist.

I blurted out the truth. "Rudy and Caroline are the other two survivors of Bus Twenty-One."

"Oh," said my father.

"Oh," said my mother.

Gran ate another spoonful of potatoes; the show was just getting good. Chandler gripped his steak knife tighter.

"But Chan said—"

"Mom, Chan lied because we're fighting."

Chan butted in. "I *lied* to keep you from getting in trouble."

"You lied because you're unhappy with our relationship and don't want anyone to know."

"Golden, you're the one always going on about talking, but I don't see you talking. I see you demanding that I talk, that I be 'vulnerable,' and I gotta tell you, I'm not looking forward to you sliding off the back end of that high horse you're riding."

I snapped. "Don't make this about me. You stopped answering your phone. You lied to my parents. You told me to find someone else to talk to. You pushed me away. Since"—and then out popped the truth—"New York."

"That's what you think?"

"Maybe this is a conversation you and Chan should have," Mom whispered delicately, "*in private.*"

"No, Mother! Chan's the one who invited you into our relationship with a public display of commitment. At this very table." I flat-palmed my place setting and water shook in all the glasses. "So we can have a civil, truthful conversation that I've been trying to have for months."

Chan gestured with his hand. "Go for it."

My eyes were like a minute hand touching each number on the clock as I leveled my gaze around the table. "The bombing isn't a secret. You are sitting at a table with the only four survivors of Bus Twenty-One. Let's stop talking around what happened."

"Honey. I don't think we need to revisit painful topics."

Revisit? Who was she kidding? "You never ever asked me *how* we survived."

Silence.

I smacked my palms against the table again. "Ask me *how*, Mom."

"That's enough," my father said from the head of the table.

"Dad, you realize we lived through something that made the president of the United States fly a flag at half-staff? That there are memorial funds and hashtags and senators who ran for office on the political gasoline of my grief? *Our* grief. This is a real thing. You can't unhappen it by ignoring the details. So unless you go deaf or I go mute in the next ten seconds, I'm talking."

"Okay. Okay." Mom steadied her wineglass. "Tell us how, baby."

I began. "The bomber was very upset with his girlfriend. He wanted to punish her for cheating on him. Publicly humiliate and terrify her. He strapped a vest to himself and then a vest to the guy she'd cheated with and forced her to confess her indiscretions. Except, she was in shock and couldn't speak. To help with her failing tongue, this guy, this selfish asshole, Simon Westwood, made Chan and me stand."

I was in the memory now. I didn't care if they heard me; I cared if I heard me.

"The bomber said, 'LOOK AT THIS COUPLE. THEY DON'T CHEAT ON EACH OTHER. DO YOU?'"

I screamed at them the way Simon screamed at us. Chan slipped down the chair, his shoulders folding together in an uncomfortable *u*. He'd said *Go for it* without realizing how going for it would feel. Caroline laid her face on the table and swaddled her head with her arms.

"'DO YOU?'" I screamed. Every word of Simon's etched in my brain. "'HONEY, THEY'RE GOING TO SHOW YOU HOW IT'S DONE. WHAT'S YOUR NAME?' I told him my name. Chan told him his. Simon yelled again, his hand crashing into my back each time he finished a sentence. 'GOLDEN, CHANDLER! LOOK LOVINGLY INTO EACH OTHER'S EYES AND SAY, 'I'LL NEVER EVER SCREW ANYONE ELSE. I'LL LOVE ONLY YOU FOREVER.'"

My mother covered her hand with her mouth.

My father's eyes never blinked.

Chan trembled in the chair beside me.

"We said the magic words. And the bomber said, 'GET OFF THE BUS. YOUR MONOGOMY HAS SAVED YOU.' We didn't move. I was frozen. 'GET OFF MY BUS,' he yelled. He blew Bus Twenty-one when I had one foot on the side-walk." Gran gave me a nod from across the table. "Go on," she mouthed. "He made us believe we were leaving everyone there. And for what? We didn't deserve to live any more than anyone else deserved to die."

My father had tears in his eyes. He did not typically cry.

"You hate me for making us leave," Chan said quietly.

"I've never hated you. Not for an instant. I hate living with this . . . whatever it is . . . every day. And I think you do too. I don't understand why you won't. . . . Part of you never got off that bus, Chan. You're stuck. We're stuck. That's why I'm going back to New York. I have to move on from that moment in June, and I think the only way to do it is to get back on Bus Twenty-One."

"Honey."

"The only way to do it is to be honest with yourself," Chan said.

"I am being honest. You should try it." I locked eyes with Rudy. "Mom. Dad. We're getting on Carter Stockton's recon-struction of Bus Twenty-One and it's going to be abysmal, but it is necessary."

Dad reared back, hands clutched in prayer, and looked helplessly at my mother. Mom was sputtering, unable to man-age a full sentence.

"Mr. Jennings," Rudy said, "a medic on the scene that day, the same one who called you about Golden, got permission from the city to build an exhibit from the rubble. The exhibit opens on Sunday. That's what she's talking about."

Mom applied her *You're being ridiculous* stance. Hands on hips, head cocked to the side, patronizing tone. *"Now, Go—"*

I cut her off. "We're going. Tomorrow morning! All the families are coming. Everyone who lost someone. They're attending to honor their kids. And so are some of the people who've followed the video series. They've raised eighty-one thousand dollars so far"—I watched Chan for a response, but he was blank—"to help with college. That's how much strangers believe we can move on. Look it up. *Accelerant Orange.* It's . . . astounding. I can't believe people are pulling for us like that, but they are. Is it too much to ask my family to do the same?"

"I donated," Gran said. "I'm pulling."

I smiled triumphantly at Gran. At my new friends. Mom was slack-jawed.

"And when we're done, Gran, I'm taking the best picture of Ellis Island you've ever seen."

A question came from Chan. "And if I don't go?" He stretched his hand to mine and touched the diamonds on my ring finger.

I shrugged. "You didn't want to go the first time. I'll try to get over it."

"That's still what you think? That I didn't want to go?"

"It sure seemed that way."

"Things aren't always as they seem."

"Chan, I don't want to fight anymore. Just tell me. Why did you give me this ring? Because you love me? Because you don't want to lose me? Because Simon screwed with your head about us?"

"Golden Jennings, ask me why I was irate about my bags in New York."

This was a futile question. I'd known the reason since we were eleven years old. Chandler Clayton was shit at handling changes.

"Ask me."

I gave in. *"Fine.* Fine. Why were you irate about your bags in New York?"

"Because . . ." Chan tapped the ring and then worked it over my knuckle and off my finger. Holding it out for everyone to see, he swallowed hard. "This ring is a replica of the one in the photo of Grandpapa John. Gran helped me with a drawing and I had a jeweler make it. I had all the clothes replicated too. That's what was in my bag. I was trying to give you the best Ellis Island shot with your Kodak."

43. You have this much baggage, you should stay put.

$83,888.00

I hated being wrong. I especially hated being wrong when it mattered.

Now Chan's acute disappointment and frustration toward the airline made sense. His ratty attitude in the restaurant: the trip he'd planned for months ruined. His telling me, "It's irreplaceable." My believing he meant his sketchbook. My believing he was selfish. *This ring is a replica of the one in the photo of Grandpapa John.*

I stumbled over words. "I'm sorry I ruined dinner," I said, and escaped through the front door with Chan on my heels.

This farm had a million uneven places. Water pumps and

drain covers. Five forking gravel roads jutting off the central lane. Hundreds of tree roots. I ran fearlessly into the night until my lungs burned. Chan caught me at the maples.

The summer after middle school, we planted two dozen red maples alongside the farmhouse driveway. Gran sold a memoir about the Hive and from the proceeds Granddad sprang for larger trees. Ten-footers with burlap-wrapped root balls. They were terrible to plant, especially compared to the tiny seedlings we sowed in previous years. And we couldn't afford to rent the backhoe that would have made planting easy.

As I put my hands on the bark of the maples, bending to catch my breath, I remembered Chan saying, "Buying them with roots feels like cheating. You have this much baggage, you should stay put."

And I had said, "So when you leave here someday you'll go as a seedling?" Chandler's answer had been a peal of laughter, and then, "I'm keeping my gigantic roots balls right here."

He was fourteen. I had been stupidly charmed by his crudeness. But now I wondered if his feet were roots stretching into the ground. If he was another Hive kid who became a Hive adult. And I just couldn't bear it. I lay on the damp ground and stared at the midnight-blue gauze of clouds covering the stars.

"Will you talk to me?" Chan asked.

"You're the one who stopped talking."

"Why did you bring them here?"

"Are you serious?"

"They aren't part of *this*."

"They *are* this, Chan. No one else is more *this* than them. We were all on a bus together. That's never going to change. Five years from now, that bus blew up. Ten years. Know what happened on June fifteenth? Twenty years—"

"Stop, Go. I'm not an idiot."

I reached out to touch him, apologize, but he moved slightly, and I pulled back.

"I understand hiding from your fears. I've been hiding from mine. But why are you hiding from me?" I'd tried to say this before, but only with anger and frustration and selfishness. I'd wanted Chan to talk so *I* would feel better. But seeing Chan, the anguish, knowing him the way no one else did, I said everything now with the vision of someone who loved him without wanting anything in return.

"Please, trust me."

Chan squeezed his temples with the tips of his fingers. And without looking at me, said, "We need some space. I need to think."

Heat rushed to my face. My heart rate spiked. Everything moved faster except words. "You don't mean that."

I watched his reaction and he watched mine. And then he said, "I do."

"You're quitting me?"

"I'm quitting us. Like I should have right after the bombing."

He didn't mean that. I changed tactics. "Screw New York,

Chan. We'll go some other time, but don't do this. Don't throw everything away because you're scared."

Chan touched my knee and glanced sideways, catching my eye. "If you could stop yourself from doing this, you would have already. I might not be able to come with you, but I won't keep you here anymore." His arm curled around my shoulders, and I leaned into him the way I always had. My heart was adrift. It was like I'd had it removed from my body and I could see it beating in the air. He kissed my cheek, and his voice caught. "We always said we'd want the best for each other. And . . . this . . . this feels like an impasse. Go on to New York. Meet those families. Tell them I'm sorry." He sounded so logical. So done. When had he decided this? Everyone had impasses. But then he said, "Go on and choose him too." His muscles slacked; his posture fell. "If that's what you need."

God, it hurt to have him say that and mean it.

"I'm not choosing him."

"You already did."

"Come on, Chan. Rudy isn't the reason we're here. You can't give up because it's hard."

"And you can't hold on because we're easy."

"You gave me a ring in front of the Hive." I put my left hand on his knee. "Why bother if you thought we were finished?"

"I gave you a ring for the same reason you put *five hundred dollars* in my cigar box. We tilt toward each other. And that's probably not our faults—look at where we were raised.

We've been the only two people on our planet our whole lives. But it would be our fault if we stayed together for the wrong reason. I shouldn't have asked you in front of the Hive. I shouldn't have asked at all. I just . . . God, Go, I didn't want to lose you."

"You haven't."

"Go."

"You haven't," I repeated.

Chan stared longingly in the direction of the chapel. He pulled his hat as low as it would go, where I couldn't see his eyes. "We lost each other in June."

"Then let's fix it in April. This Sunday."

"You drove to Florida for someone else."

"Chan, I drove to Florida because you wouldn't talk to me."

"I'm sorry I failed you. That I keep failing you." His fingers clenched mine. He brought our hands to his lips and brushed kisses on my knuckles. "I'll tell the Hive so you don't have to."

"I don't care about the Hive."

I was boneless and empty, a mold of skin in the shape of me.

"It might be asking too much, but will you come with me for a minute?" he asked.

Chan led me zombielike over the hill, past the greenhouse, through the valley where we used to make dandelion crowns, and toward the barn Granddad raised the year he died. I rarely visited here anymore. When the barn was under construction,

I'd sat on the roof across from him and Chan, hauling sheet metal, handing over screws, and running extension cords for the drill.

Chan paused and said, "I told you I had a gift for you." He slid the big barn doors sideways in their tracks and fumbled for the fluorescent lights. The light popped from dim blue to ultra-white. An old, gray Mount Zion Methodist Church bus sat in the barn's biggest bay. A big dent in the grill, but otherwise intact.

"They were going to send her to a salvage yard. I talked them into towing it here instead. You said you needed to be able to get on a bus. Here, you could practice with no one watching."

I was gobsmacked.

Always, when I thought he wasn't hearing me, he was listening the hardest.

He wiped his eyes with his sleeves. "You need photos of the world. And I'm just Chan."

Just Chan?

I hated Simon Westwood.

Hated him.

He'd done this to us with his stupid hate-filled vests.

When I was finally able to speak, I said, "This is the most outstanding gift of my life. I have to believe that something in you understands how important this is. I know I asked you before, but I'm asking again. Come with me. Come with

us. Please. I need you. I don't think I can get on that bus without you."

He held my face in his hands the way he'd done since we were kids. "When you get back, we'll talk. And Go"—sadness turned the corners of his mouth down—"no matter what, I'll always know the way home."

44. The wooden congregants

$85,025.00

Four years ago, I got lost in the woods behind the Hive.

The Claude Ridge Fire Tower was built in the eighties after a tornado tossed the old structure into the forest. In winter, when the trees were stripped naked, you could see the tower from our living room. I was as enamored as a tourist in London or Paris catching sight of the London Eye or the Eiffel Tower.

All the older Hive kids bragged about climbing to the top. They also bragged about their sexual conquests. The mile-high club, they called it. At that age, I didn't care about the mile-high club, but I was insanely curious about the view. A photograph of the chapel from that vantage point would be spectacular.

Getting there was complicated. In some sections of Gran's

nine hundred acres I could map individual trees, but once I crossed the creek into the national forest, the territory was unfamiliar and expansive. Forty thousand acres. Chan was in a phase where incessant rule following made him feel safe. Which meant he would never (1) skip chores on a Saturday, or (2) head to the tower without permission. We'd been given strict instructions by Gran to "never go anywhere near that thing." Probably her idea of birth control.

Armed for the below-freezing temps in my coveralls, coat, and double socks, I strapped my camera around my neck and walked into the woods and over the creek. Hours passed in camera clicks and almond snacks. There was no way to track progress from inside the foliage.

The tower rose out of a clearing like a very large accessory to a G.I. Joe play set. One story up, I felt the wind. Five stories, the tower swayed. Seven stories, I reached the trapdoor to the wooden six-by-six fort. It was decorated with the trash of teenagers: a ripped condom wrapper was caught in a corner crevice, five of a six-pack of Pabst Blue Ribbon were on the floor—that decision was either charity or the inability to continue—and a lone toothpick was wedged into a notch along the rail. Below me, miles and miles of forest made mountain shapes as if they were the wooden congregants gathered together for the tower's Sunday worship service.

I propped myself against the railing, eyes roaming the inky, magnificent darkness. It was too dark for a photo, and considering all that land between home and me catapulted

my fears. I'd been cold. For hours. I'd warmed myself by the quest of the tower, the delight of an adventure. After, the wind struck my bones and singed my throat. The sun was down. There was no sign of the snaking creek, and I'd thought that would be my ticket home. There was nothing to do but pick a direction and walk.

I walked twenty miles that day.

Chan walked another twenty searching for me.

He found me at three a.m., curled under a sycamore, waiting for morning light. "You wandered a little off path, Jennings," he said, knocking the snow from my hair and dropping his hat on my head. "Lucky for you, I memorized the way home."

CAROLINE

This evening made me reconsider everything. Go and Rudy were wandering the way they do even when they're sitting still. The Hive smelled of clean growing things. Honeysuckle? Jasmine, maybe? There was no light pollution; the night was a vast black dome, punctured by light. As if God were a boy intent on playing with his star collection, cataloging each name alphabetically: Altair, Arcturus, Europa, Hyades, Pleiades . . .

Becky and I walked to her Mustang. We drove without ever discussing if we wanted to or not.

She is the only person I've met who always seems free to come and go.

She was smacking her gum, putting on lipstick, and going a million miles an hour on a road that warned *Speed Limit 35* and *Dangerous Curve Ahead*. That's apparently how everyone

drives in Kentucky. We took the "five-dollar tour," in which she showed me *town* and their school. We drove by her house, and she pointed out a pink playhouse her dad built when she was little. I thought about dads who built playhouses versus dads who built bank accounts and how much I prefer the former.

We ended up at the community tennis courts. Her at the net. Me standing against the fence. She lobbed a flat tennis ball she found in the grass in my direction. It died before reaching me, and I lay flat on the court and launched the ball at myself a few times. My scalp was cold against the red clay.

Becky lay beside me.

We held hands in silence until a cloud covered the moon and she said, "We should get back," and I said, "Okay," but really I was thinking, *What if we just sleep here?*

On the way back, Becky said, "So, yeah, I sort of love the hell out of you, and if you die on me anytime soon, I'll kill you." Her eyes were on me instead of the road.

We were heading toward another curve. The car going faster than my heart.

"What did you say?"

"I'm not saying it again, but just so you know, me handing out love is like a dentist giving away lollipops."

There was no room in my life for life, much less love.

"You don't have to say it back yet." The *yet* was so Becky.

Yet implied a future.

Part of me wanted that future, but . . . if she knew me, she wouldn't have said it.

I slipped off my headband and put it around her gearshift. "I sort of love you too," I said, because I didn't know if there would be another opportunity for her to have something to remember me by.

45. A poor kid's treasure hunt

$86,350.00

When you live in the country, the sounds of night are a welcome refrain. Bullfrog songs bubbled from nearby ponds while the coyotes and bobcats howled their existence to the forest. A vehicle rumbled down Tobacco Road. Chan? Out driving off this awful love hangover? But then I heard the low growl of his chain saw and noticed the light in his workshop. He was in there, carving Mary the Mother of Jesus.

I did not have to search each Hive cranny and crook to know every square foot of this land was tied to Chan. Chan was the swings under the pavilion, diving off the rocks in a summer heat wave, fishing for crawdads in the ditches, homework at Gran's table. He was stepping on a hornet, tobacco salve in

the wound; there is no Santa Claus; I got an F in algebra. He was sneaking through a window, memorizing Beyoncé lyrics incorrectly, catching the grill on fire, fessing up.

Chan was my childhood.

I had anger next to my sadness, and that snapped me back to reality. I called Stock and gave him the facts.

"Hey, there," he said in his low country drawl.

"Hey, Stock. Will you leave four tickets for me at the hotel?"

"Your family making the trip?"

"Caroline Ascott and Rudy Guthrie. Our friend Becky is coming too. I tried to . . ." My voice nearly broke. "I tried to get Chandler Clayton, but he's not ready."

"That's understandable."

Maybe for you, Stock.

Stock must have sensed my frustration. "Golden, can't nobody tell anybody what's good for them. You be proud of you now. He can be proud later."

"Thanks."

"No, thank you. People are gonna be grateful you're coming."

I was thinking about people, all the watching people. How they'd line up on the sidewalk with their cell phones held out, taking videos and photos of me standing beside Bus #21. I tried to see myself putting a foot on the bottom step and I couldn't do it.

I made my way to the barn and took the shovel off a hook. On the right side, where Granddad's boat used to be parked,

I put my back against the Cooper Feed sign and counted ten paces toward the silo. I sidestepped right the length of a yardstick and dug until I hit metal.

The summer Chan moved here we buried "geocaches" all over the Hive—a poor kid's treasure hunt. He hid four boxes; I hid four boxes. We turned each other loose with clues. I found all of his, but he never found this last one of mine. Every now and then, he'd remember the lost geocache and snuggle beside me. "When will you tell me where you hid the last box?" he'd say. And I'd kiss the end of his nose and say, "When we break up or when you marry me."

That's the sort of thing you said when you thought your names would end up side by side on a tombstone one day.

The box was rusted and the hinges fussy. I pried the lid open with the shovel. Remnants of Lisa Frank stickers lined the interior. The Ziploc bag was still sealed. Our photos were safe from the weather. A whole roll of Kodak 110 exposures. Mostly silly up-the-nose and wooly thumb shots. Chan was chunky. Hell, I was chunky. We wore more mismatched sweatpants than a colorblind baseball team. We were such kids. It was hard to know those kids would grow up to be us.

I should take the box to Chan's house and leave it on the porch. He'd know immediately we'd reached the real end.

But I buried the box and returned the shovel to the barn.

I could always tell him tomorrow.

46. Summer in an upside-down spoonful

$88,880.00

Rudy's voice traveled from the shadow of the red maples. "Your mom's in there showing Caroline and Becky how to knit." He thumbed over his shoulder. "I asked to learn, but they wouldn't let me."

He wanted to make me smile, and while it didn't work, I appreciated the effort.

He stretched in his chair and twisted his neck from side to side until it crackled. "Things go badly with Chandler?" A pause. "You don't have to answer that."

I sleeved off my dripping nose. "The worst."

"Want a distraction?"

"Sure," I said, because I could not bear facing my mother's invasive questions yet.

"Give me the Golden tour of the Hive?"

I adopted what I assumed was a Realtor's voice. "Well, sir, you are standing on one of the most beautiful properties in Kentucky." I cringed at my use of the word *standing*, but he didn't react. "What would you like to see?"

"Somewhere you love. Somewhere that makes you happy."

There were many places I loved. Too many to count even. These trees. The blue hole. A little table in the greenhouse where the light filtered through the plastic sheeting and made rainbows. The lightning bug valley. I chose the grain bin. "Can you stomach a walk?"

He flexed his bicep. "I can walk for days on these babies."

I appreciated this about him. He was proud, but he didn't trip over his arrogance very often. Certainly not now.

"This is different from where I grew up. 'Course you know that. You've seen it."

"*This* is different than where people around here grew up."

Luckily, it hadn't rained since Wednesday and the terrain between the maples and the bin would be paved or packed earth. I didn't ever want to be guilty of underestimating Rudy's abilities, but I also didn't want to lead him somewhere he couldn't go. Victor had said, "He'll hate needing help," but he'd been the one helping me.

"You're pensive," he said. "That from Chandler or me?"

"You're strong," I answered.

"Well"—he beamed—"I work out."

"That's not what I meant."

"I knew what you meant."

"How did you get that way?"

"Cheated the system. I came this way. You cut off my hands tomorrow morning and I'll figure out how to roll this thing with my chin. Or at least, that's what I tell myself. Part of being strong is faking yourself out when its necessary."

"I love that about you," I said.

"And here I thought you kept me around for a red knitted beanie."

We changed the subject. I told him about Sunday mornings. How the Hive hummed and buzzed, a symphony of tasks and noisy projects. How at odd intervals, saws turned on and off and woodworking crews set about their crafts and tasks. I told him about building decks and pergolas. How people shared the mowers. And, even though I was supposed to be working alongside people, I often climbed the hill behind the Grable Cabin and took their pictures.

"Sometimes on a Saturday afternoon, you can look clear across the Hive and count twenty people out and about. John Paul and Uncle Ash might be adding gravel to a washed out place in the road. On the big field by the quad, Bill Lovelace and Chan sometimes scrounge a touch football game for anyone interested. And there's a group of young kids . . . Sophie Grable is their headmistress. Eleven going on forty. She's gonna be a ballbuster. And right now, much to everyone's dismay, she's

addicted to remarkably bad music. Not that you care about all that, but these folks made me who I am."

"Sounds really nice."

"It's not an easy place to leave."

"Because it's safe?" he asked.

I didn't answer.

Ivy circled the grain bin like strings of old Christmas lights, and rust covered the corrugated metal roof. No structure was creepier. No structure more gorgeous than this dying tower. When we neared the outer ladder, Rudy said, "I don't think—"

"I want you to see inside."

When my photography became more sophisticated, Mom told me it was time to make a gallery. If there was one thing the Hive had, it was room. In a matter of weeks, I transformed the abandoned grain bin into my art museum. Chan did most of the high scaffolding jobs. Affixing cheap eight-and-a-half-by-elevens to the circular walls, rising thirty feet.

I flipped the layers of shop lights Chan and I hung from the roof. Rudy paused by the front door.

"My chair won't fit."

The door wasn't a real door, just a cutout in the metal. I'd sawed the opening myself.

"Oh, God, Rudy, I'm sorry."

He bent and peered through to see one wall, smiled determinedly.

"If you'll turn off the light and wait outside, I'll fix this."

I did what he asked.

"Okay, come back."

The chair was parked outside and a scattered trail of hay and grain stretched from the door to the center of the room. He lay stretched out, arms laced behind his head, eyes on the ceiling. "Lights, please," he said, in the same intonation Linus used when he read the Christmas story to Charlie Brown.

As the lights popped to life, I joined him. My gallery rose in circular rows around us—a library of work. Near the top, some of them were faded or ripped from moisture, but that only added to the effect. We didn't speak. We spun, observing every angle.

"I didn't know you were a magician," he said.

"Only with a Number Three Kodak," I said.

"You haven't replaced it?"

"Some things get lost and stay lost."

"This is your *Accelerant Orange*?"

His jeans touched the exposed skin of my legs.

"It's me making sense of life."

He said, "It's beautiful," but his eyes were on me instead of the walls. The air thrummed. Each breath charged and roared with curiosity.

We stared at each other, noses inches apart.

"Thank you," I whispered.

He used his hands to scoot his leg closer to mine.

"You have words," I said. "These are my words."

"How many prints are there?"

"I don't know."

He pointed to a photo of Dolly Dodge. "One." He lost count in the thirties about four rows up. "Why is all of this in a grain bin that no one sees?"

"Because privacy is the only control I have."

His hands were no longer pillowing his head.

Mine weren't in my pockets.

Two fingers crept toward the fabric of my T-shirt.

The choice existed. His hand was there for holding.

I touched my pinkie to his. They overlapped.

I exhaled and pulled my hand back.

He turned his head sideways again. Neither of us smiled. "Am I still a bandit?"

Go on and choose him too.

"Yes," I told him. "You're a suitable bandit."

Rudy's lips, his breath, were so close. I smelled the banana pudding he'd had for dessert. Sweet. Vanilla. Summer in an upside-down spoonful. One decadent, sugary moment after all the bitter bites. It could be mine. His face was an invitation, a green light to cross the street.

"You're hurting," he said.

"Yes."

"You're scared."

"Yes."

"Me too."

"I know."

He cupped my face with his hands. His forehead touched mine. His hair fell across my skin and I put my hands around

his jaws. Jaws that were so different than Chan's. We breathed deep into each other, the moment hanging heavy as overripe oranges in Caroline's grove.

"You don't need this right now," he said.

"No," I agreed, because he was right. "Pinch me."

That was all the permission he needed. He kissed below my ear, and around my chin, working his way slowly to my lips. He was confident and soft. When his mouth met mine he said, "No buses. No monsters. No guilt. Okay?"

"No buses. No monsters. No guilt," I repeated, knowing good and well there would be guilt. There was always guilt.

47. It's not like a Sherlockian leap.

$88,950.00

Mom fussed over Rudy when we returned. Did he want water? Was the house warm enough, cool enough? Had Pete shown him how to work the shower? "There's a hidden button behind the nozzle," she explained. I was mildly annoyed and hoped he understood the excess attention had nothing to do with his wheelchair and everything to do with hospitality. He reveled in her affection. I watched them, their ease with each other, and felt a little envious. She led him to a converted Sunday school room where we sorted our laundry and where the seniors of old used to read their Bibles and say their prayers.

I called, "Eight a.m.?"

He spun in his chair and tipped an imaginary hat. "Wheels up at eight."

Mom had made Becky and Caroline a blanket pallet on the floor of my room. It was empty because they were in my bed. They wore beanies from my bedpost and huddled together like baby meerkats on the Discovery Channel. They looked like *friends*. When had that happened, not just to them, but to all of us? Is that what driving did? Or Shoney's? Or the back of a 1990 two-tone Dodge with transmission problems?

I culled all the strange and improbable events that precipitated Caroline Ascott and Becky Cable cuddling beneath a quilt stitched by my gran, under a roof constructed by the Methodist men of the 1920s, and nearly laughed. I read enough fantasy books when I was younger to understand how time folded over on itself like a packaged sheet from JCPenney, and how the really wise characters poked holes in the fabric and rode shortcuts through the middle. That's what I saw in their clinging bodies. Shortcuts. Friendship could be such a fast thing when it wanted to be.

I knocked on the doorjamb because they didn't notice me watching. "You two look cozy."

"What the hell are these pipe things?" Becky said.

"You're inside an old organ."

"No way!"

"Yes way. This chapel used to be off property, but when the Methodist church relocated closer to town in the seventies, Gran sold the back acreage of the Hive to buy the place.

She wanted to keep the structural integrity. I wanted to live inside the music."

"It's damn magnificent."

"I'm sure that's what the Methodists said about it too."

"Jennings, are you going to stand in the doorway all night?"

I was still clinging to the hall. My behavior at dinner felt like a stain they might hold against me. I shoved my toe into the carpet. "Look, I'm sorry about dinner. I didn't mean to—"

Becky lifted a corner of the covers and smacked the mattress. "Get your scrawny ass over here right now."

"Are we seriously going to all sleep in—?"

She smacked the bed again. I crawled in. Caroline tugged another beanie from the post and passed it over. Mom had been practicing Gran's pattern so Chan and I ended up with three or four of the suckers. We lay in my childhood bed, beanies pulled to our ears, listening to the Becky and Go Go playlist. Neither girl mentioned my leaving with Chan and returning with Rudy. Instead, Becky took to calling the final leg of our quest the Vadering of New York.

"Vadering isn't a word," I pointed out.

"Are you kidding? It's the perfect *Star Wars* metaphor. You are Luke Skystalker. This *Accelerant* thing is Vader." She attempted a Vader-worthy breath, and I resisted the urge to correct Skystalker to Skywalker. "And therefore, we're going Vadering. Redemption. Revenge. All that good shizz."

"Have you even seen *Star Wars*?" I asked.

"I've seen all the—"

"Gifs," we said at the same time.

She clicked the side of her mouth and cocked her hand like a pistol.

The three of us cracked up.

Caroline said, "I don't remember the last time I laughed."

"Me either."

Becky scrubbed our heads, filling my hair with static. "Laugh you will, no choice give I."

"Oh, stop," Caroline and I said together.

I loved the hell out of her terrible Yoda, and Caroline did too. We lay there talking and laughing until it was very late. We would have continued all night if I hadn't said we had a long drive the next day and we should sleep. I think we tried for a little while. But then Becky said, "Go?"

"Yeah?"

"You don't have to talk if you don't want to, but you can tell us about Chan."

Everything I'd held back with Rudy broke. Becky pulled my head onto her chest and I sighed. "He . . . ended things." Becky's throat gurgled air. Her heart pounded against my ear. "I probably made a mistake with Rudy. Let's leave it at that. Sorry I forced you guys to sit through hell at dinner."

Becky finger-combed the ends of my hair. "Oh, honey, come eat with my family sometimes. You'll feel better."

Caroline said, "You didn't have to protect me when you told the story."

"Not my piece to share."

"Dinner tonight brought back a million arguments," Caroline said.

"He was cruel to you all the time. Wasn't he?"

Caroline tilted her head away from us and drummed her fingers on her chest. "He told me once I was his remote control car. I didn't get to decide where I went; he did, and he'd run me into the wall if I tried anything."

I wasn't surprised. There were hundreds of other ways he'd kept her speck-size and scared.

"The whole thing with Jim—that was me attempting a new tactic. If I slept with someone else, maybe he wouldn't want me anymore."

I stared at the organ pipes so I wouldn't come unglued.

"I got Jim killed. Jim and eighteen other people." Caroline started alphabetically. "Anthony Alvarez, Mason Armstrong, Riley Best, Jim Conner, Evelyn Farrow, Sara Hillstead, Neil Johnson, Tim Kraggen, Brandy Marshall, Risha Novell, Johnny Popplewell, Roger Pritchet, Wesley 'Dozer' Reston, Oscar Reyes, Tomas Sanchez, William Tackett, Alicia Voyse, Ethan Watchmaker—" She skipped over Simon's name.

"Thomas Wiggington," we finished the list together.

She said, "They're dead because of me."

"Caroline."

Becky sat up, staring intently at Caroline's face.

Caroline waved her off. "I have two therapists who say what you're about to say. *It's not my fault. I didn't make that vest. I didn't choose his actions.* And I know, I know, I know. Except . . .

I had a front-row seat to his crazy."

I let Becky handle this.

"That doesn't mean you're to blame. I mean, hell, the investigation cleared you."

"You don't understand."

"Try us," Becky said.

"And have you hate me?"

Becky threaded her fingers into the beanie on Caroline's head. "I'll never hate you. I think you're desperately brave."

"Yeah, well, I was with him when he bought the dynamite. I drove."

"So? It's not like it was your idea."

"That's where you're wrong. Simon wanted C-Four and I told him he couldn't get C-Four; he should go after dynamite instead. It's not like I knew what he'd do. I didn't. But, oh, fuck . . . I knew what he did with a pipe so it's not like a Sherlockian leap."

Oh. I understood what she'd been carrying. Her part in this.

Caroline didn't cry; she did something worse. She gave a sharp inhale of so much air she couldn't breathe, lungs fully expanded until they literally creaked—then released the air through her mouth. First, a groan. Then a squeal. Like a puppy being kicked in the head.

Becky mothered Caroline after that—hushing and loving— and I lay still, our chests rising and falling together. I held my elbow over my wet eyes so they wouldn't know I was crying.

In an alternate universe, Chan and I sneaked toward the rear of the bus and Simon never saw Chan's arm around my shoulder or me planting a kiss on his lips; never called us out as a couple; never used us an example. And in that universe, Caroline Ascott lay in someone else's bed saying *twenty-two* people died because of her.

She wasn't totally wrong.

CAROLINE

Secrets are termites. They eat and eat and eat. I hear their buggish stomachs yapping and screaming that they are still hungry. "Shhhhh," I try to whisper. "We are almost through. They do not need to know." But there is Becky, and there is Go, giggling next to me in bed. When the room quiets, I think about the organ blaring suddenly and waking us—because we are inside an instrument—but it doesn't. The only music is the secret termites chewing me apart. Their spit is on my chest.

The mood was so light before . . .

Go waited until it was perfectly quiet and our breathing was in rhythm and then she said in a singsong voice, "Three little monkeys, sleeping in the bed. One rolled over and the other one said, 'Hey, you peed in my warm spot,'" and the love inside me was hot and melting all over my heart.

I wanted the conversation to continue.

I wanted them to tell me everything, so I could tell them everything about Simon and Z, Elizabeth and Althea. So I did.

They said they understand.

They said I am not to blame.

They said I am a victim.

But that is what people say when they are with someone in person; it is not what people think in their head when they are alone with their thoughts. Their quiet judgment slams into me harder than any of Simon's pipes.

Becky, who coiled around me at the previous hotel, who told me she loved me hours before, spooned her body around Go's last night. Even in sleep, I wasn't safe. And Go is so twisted by Rudy and Chan and her loving family that she spins like a never-ending barbershop pole—she doesn't have the emotional energy to deal with me.

My plan hurts only me.

I will do the *Accelerant Orange* thing that is so important to them. And then when we go to Ellis Island, I will wait until the ferry is near to leaving and tell them I'm walking around alone for a minute to clear my head. They'll listen, because that is who they are. Then, before I climb into the water, I'll text them a lie: *I am on the ferry. I am going home to Keuka Lake.*

I will think of Becky saying she loves me and swallow water until I drown.

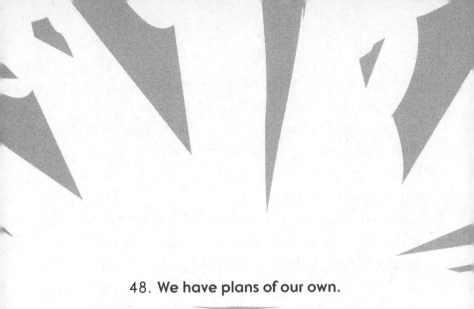

48. We have plans of our own.

$92,110.00

The kitchen was brimming with bodies when the three of us tromped downstairs freshly showered and packed for another day of Vadering. (I gave up on curbing Becky's use of the word; plus, it always eked out the slightest smile from Caroline.) The room smelled of butter, flour, and bacon, and was a flurry of activity. Dad had the newspaper open at the breakfast nook. Gran poured coffee into her favorite mug and winked at me. Mom zipped homemade biscuits into a bag. Rudy stowed them in a grocery bag.

"There they are," Mom said warmly. She pointed toward three juice glasses on the counter. "Milk or OJ?"

"Milk."

Rudy accepted the glass jug from Mom and filled the glasses overfull. "You eating?" I asked him.

Mom slung an arm over his shoulders. "Are you kidding? This strapping young man"—his back straightening with her praise—"has already worked out in the garage and downed an entire plate of bacon."

"Sorry, we're late." None of us slept, and we wore the evidence. But, unless I was mistaken, Caroline hadn't shaved her head or eyebrows. Part of me hoped talking last night curbed the desire, but it was probably the time crunch. We'd dozed through three alarms.

The cooler we'd taken to Orlando sat on the floor by the fridge. Mom counted a list of items on her fingers, mumbling, "Sandwiches, drinks, pickles; Rudy said he can't eat cheese."

At the mention of Rudy's name, I said, "Mom, what's all this?"

"Rudy said y'all need protein."

"He did?" And better yet, *You're fixing it for him?* That sounded strangely supportive.

"Smarter than strawberry pie," he said.

"Rudy, pie always trumps sandwiches." Becky stole a biscuit from the platter on the counter. "And biscuits trump everything."

"I'm not arguing with that," Rudy said.

Mom disappeared into the pantry. She dug around like a herd of mice and addressed me with a tone I couldn't easily

place. "What are your plans, sweetie? Because we have plans of our own."

Oh no, they were about to eighty-six us or state their decision to come along. I assumed the latter. "Mom. I told you last night we're doing this. I wasn't asking."

"Yes, honey, you were very emphatic." Mom leaned out the pantry door and smiled cunningly at Dad.

I checked my watch again: 8:10. My father left our house every morning at 6:20, unless he was milking, and then, five o'clock sharp. "Why is Dad not in a field?"

"He has better plans."

He never had plans better than his cows. I side-eyed Mom and then Dad, scrutinizing their every action and finding no obvious conclusions. "Are you going to tell me what?"

Mom reached for three bags of chips and placed them in Rudy's outstretched grocery bag. Without turning around, she said, "Honey, head over there and sit by your father." I did as she asked and Dad folded the newspaper. In a familiar motion, he steepled his fingers over the sports section. "How exactly are you four getting to New York?"

"Becky's Mustang."

He stroked the corners of his mouth and swiveled a juice glass on its rim. "Unacceptable."

"Dad! We're doing this."

"I know." His smile broke wide and true. "You're taking my truck." I spit my milk on St. Louis Cardinals catcher Yadier

Molina. Dad swiped the liquid off the sports page, smudging the ink. His eyes were large and very pleased. "And . . . I talked to some friends in West Virginia."

"*The* West Virginia friends?" A couple of years ago, we had five to ten conservative military families bunk at the Hive for a few months while they finalized the purchased of an old summer camp. No one said the word *prepper* but that's what they were.

Dad winked. "One and the same. They're putting you up for the night."

Mom shook her head at this plan, not upset, but somewhat awestruck at Dad's idea of suitable lodging. She turned to Rudy. "They're batshit crazy about nuclear war and the zombie apocalypse, but you'll be safer there than most places." And then she added another bag of cookies to our grocery sack.

I was fine with the preppers. I was shocked by my father.

"While you're considering my greatness," he said, "here's two hundred dollars. Gas and food only, you turkey."

"I don't know what to say."

He tapped the dimple on his cheek. "Put one right here, kid, and we'll call it even."

I threw my arms around his neck, letting the scruff of his whiskers tickle my cheek. I dug my nose into his Old Spice skin. When I leaned away, I said, "I thought you didn't want me anywhere near New York ever again?"

He huffed. "I didn't want you to have sex until you were forty either. Can't always get what we want."

"Pete!" Mom said.

"What! It's true." He kissed my forehead. "I'm . . . well, I'm . . ." He was either sorry or proud or both, but I put my finger over his lips and said, "Thank you." A dismissive *pshaw* followed and he opened his newspaper as if he might read while we drove away. I gave him that moment to collect himself, and exchanged proper jaw drops and fist pumps with Rudy, Caroline, and Becky.

After breakfast, they walked us outside, Dad lifting the cooler into the back and Mom handing over all the snacks. My parents stood under the old chapel awning, arms around each other. They were proud of me for trying this, and I was proud of them for letting me.

If that surprise wasn't enough, Chan appeared from the opposite side of the truck, bag in his hand. "Got room in this rig for one more?"

49. Refrain from sucking.

$92,999.00

The Ford F-150 was a palace compared to Dolly, but there would be no place to hide in the cab. Guilt spidered along my spine. Rudy. The grain bin. Chan. My brain knotted at his change of heart—which was undeniably a good thing, and an awkward thing. If we weren't us, what were we? This was brand-new territory. Did we talk? Sit together? Were we angry or hurt or numb? He appeared passive enough, like he knew he didn't get to dictate the mood. There were Rudy's feelings to consider too. I'd been honest with him at every juncture, but if I meant more to him than a kiss in a grain bin, Chan's presence complicated things. Then again, what about this trip wasn't complicated? We were getting on a bus that

blew ten months ago.

Becky, who had donned Caroline's purple headband, nearly backed out. She argued the cab would be less comfortable with five people. I didn't care. "You're good for Caroline. You're good for me. We're Vadering," I said emphatically. and requested backup. "Caroline, what are we doing today?"

"Vadering." And then to Becky she added, "Please come. For me."

That was that.

"Y'all are nutty," Chan said. He was trying.

In a beat, Rudy flicked Chan's arm. "Oh, just you wait, man. *Vadering* is only level one on their crazy scale."

"What's level ten?" Chan asked.

"Shoney's," I said.

"Digger the mechanic from Hickville?" Becky said.

Caroline lowered her sunglasses and cut her eyes over the wide black frames. "Alligators."

"See what I mean, bro?"

We girls exchanged furtive glances at this friendly exchange between the guys.

Chan was laughing, and he shot me a *Tell me that story later* look. Perfectly normal. Status quo. If I didn't know better, I'd think we were in for a smooth trip. For now, I grinned happily at our silent conversation. *Don't touch his arm*, I told myself for the first of many times. We waved goodbye to my family, and Becky explained to Chan that if he wanted to remain in the driver's seat he must do three things: refrain from sucking

(sucking occurred at speeds lower than eighty), never call this a road trip, and above all else, refer to our quest as Vadering. Chan huffed on the lens of his glasses, cleaned away the clouds, and looked ever serious about these tasks. I punched the radio button for NPR, which made Chan smile. He turned the vents in his direction so the air-conditioning wouldn't blow on me. Maybe we could do this.

We hit the interstate in fifteen minutes, and he hit ninety by the first mile marker.

"I've always liked you, Clayton," said Becky.

She liked him less when he got a warning from a state trooper near Bowling Green and reset the cruise to seventy-seven.

Somewhere between Louisville and Cincinnati, Rudy's phone rang. Caroline asked, "Is that Ms. Jay?" as Rudy leaned forward and showed me the New York area code. He jammed a finger in his ear and pivoted toward the window. Caroline, still under the assumption the caller was Ms. Jay, said to Becky, "Ms. Jay looks out for him and Victor. His mom is in and out of psych wards and his dad works on an oil rig. Seventeen days out. Ten days in. The state decided Vic and Ru could get in a lot of trouble during those days without supervision, especially after the bombing and Vic's gator injuries."

"Your aunt wouldn't take them?" Becky asked.

"She's had her hands full with me. But Ms. Jay stepped up and gave them a bit of structure. They love her like mad. Jane does too, but she's older."

I turned toward the back seat and whispered, "I don't think Ms. Jay's the one who called." We all listened closer.

"Okay. . . . No, Kentucky. Yes, the four of us. Right. Change of heart. . . . Sunday morning sometime. . . . Oh, I see." The color drained from Rudy's face. "No, of course, that makes sense. . . . It's good news. Great for *Accelerant Orange*. Well, sort of. I need to talk with Go and the gang. . . . Yep. Yep. We'll think about it, and I'll call you back."

We awaited the news. Rudy turned to me, eyes worried. "Here's the deal . . ."

Anticipating what he might say was impossible. Even if we'd known each other for years, that expression—half fear, half adrenaline—would have stumped me.

"Simon's parents are coming to the city. Not for the opening. They think that's too much for everyone, but . . . well . . ." A pause. Rudy swiveled toward me. "They would like to talk with you while they're there."

50. Think of the human-interest story.

$95,030.00

Becky asked the question first. "Why?"

Uh, yeah. I added another. "Also, why didn't Stock call me?"

"You know how Stock is. He didn't want to pressure you." Rudy mimicked Carter's Southern accent. "Hell, Rudy, if I put it to Go, it'll feel like an expectation. If you put it to her, she has a choice."

Caroline chewed the skin around her fingernails. She picked up her phone and began to text. Whoever she was texting didn't seem to have anything good to say.

"Stock didn't explain. He only said it was a good thing. The Westwoods have been grieving too, and something Go did helped them."

I checked in with Caroline, reassured her this was a fluke. Said, "I do not know the Westwoods." She didn't appear to care whether I did or didn't.

Where I was full of questions, Chandler was full of scorn, a cold demeanor rolling off him like breaking waves. He had his foot against the gas again, his hat as low as it would go. "How long have you known this guy, Carter? 'Cause it sounds like he's setting you up."

I explained eight months of *Accelerant Orange* videos, reaching out to Stock about the opening, how I trusted him. This information rested like a betrayal-shaped tumor in Chan's throat. Visible to me. Visible to everyone in the Ford. "Gran and I watched episodes together. He is not setting me up."

He started to say, *You could have watched them with me,* but I glared and he jammed his fist to his lips. We could watch movies but not *Accelerant Orange.* Not when he'd cut me off for using the words *skyscraper* or *taxi.* We'd gone another thirty miles when Chan reached a conclusion he chose to share. "You're out of your brain if you're thinking about going through with that meeting. I don't want you anywhere near them."

"I agree with him," Becky said. The words had spine and grit and love.

I said, "I'm not wild about it either, but if Stock says it's good—"

"You trust him over me? A stranger over your—"

"My what, Chan?"

"Someone who loves you."

"Carter Stockton loves us. If you'd watched the videos—"

"If you'd told me about them—"

"I left you five hundred dollars for a plane ticket—"

"I'm driving the truck, Go. I'm trying, okay?"

Becky butted in. "Children. I'll have you pull this vehicle over if you can't behave yourselves."

Chan took that literally, darted into the emergency lane and braked. Hard. Everyone except Rudy and me swapped positions. That put Becky behind the wheel and left Caroline and Chan sulking in the back seat next to Rudy. Chan rolled down his window and leaned toward the buffeting air.

Resetting the seating arrangement hadn't reset the conversation. Chan wasn't quite finished. He posed a question to Rudy. "I guess you agree with her?"

No hesitation. "Yep."

"Of course you do."

I heard Chan's anger. Understood its origin. He felt boxed in by this invite, deceived by me, and furious at Rudy for taking my side. Deception played by its own rules. I didn't feel I'd deceived Chan about *Accelerant Orange* when he'd clearly asked to be excluded. Rudy was a different story. I'd never told Chan what happened in the bathroom at Down Yonder, rationalizing that there was nothing to tell. But here, in a cab with Chan and Rudy, I couldn't avoid the truth: Rudy had always been my secret.

I tried to ease Chan's hurt. "Look, Chan, you don't have to have anything to do with the Westwoods. Attending *Accelerant*

Orange is enough. More than enough. I'm proud of you."

Chan melded his body to the window. I met Rudy's eyes in the side mirror. He leaned forward, rested his forehead against my headrest, blocked Chan's view of my body, and stretched his hand between the seat and the door. I brushed the tips of Rudy's fingers. There was an abridged narrative in that brief exchange. It read: *Thank you for always caring.*

Maybe Chan saw. Maybe he didn't. But he said, "I'm not going to the installation."

To which Caroline said, "Same."

From there, Chan and Caroline poured concrete around their decision. The fresh pavement set all through West Virginia until everything in the cab was hardened and fixed. Rudy argued they could stand in the back or visit *Accelerant Orange* after hours. Carter would work with us. No one had to know they were there. The Westwoods' desire to speak with me had nothing to do with the task at hand. Chan and Caroline simply said no to every suggestion Rudy made.

I thought of Carter Stockton. Of how the pieces of this puzzle came together and fell apart. Over the last ten months I'd watched the medic reassemble Charter Bus #21, as if working with a child's modeling kit. He'd spent hours on the burned hull, removing the ash and brushing away splintered glass. He'd welded and buffed the scarred metal into something smooth, and while I was watching, he'd attempted something similar with my pain. Maybe he'd done the same for the Westwoods. I could not imagine being them. How hated they must

feel. Maybe they'd raised a bomber and this was also their fault, but I wouldn't know if I didn't listen.

A drop of blood fell from my nose to my jeans.

I jammed my sleeve against my nose. "I want to hear them out."

"Of course you do," Chan said.

"Good luck with that," Caroline commented.

Rudy said, "Care, the event will be big enough you won't have to see them. If that's even where they meet us."

"Maybe so, but trust me, no one wants the girlfriend of a bomber at the party." Caroline slid her hand right to left like a headline as she turned on Rudy. *"Victim in wheelchair can't climb steps to art installation.* Do you want be that guy, Cuz? Because, Mr. Journalist, you know that's who you'll be to the media. Think of the human-interest story. It almost writes itself."

"Screw you, Cuz," Rudy said. "I've climbed a million steps since the bombing."

Caroline shrugged as if Rudy could not hurt her and she regretted nothing, but then her tears began to fall. Becky patted the console between us and Caroline climbed from the back to the front, buckling herself in next to Becky. Caroline's head rested on Becky's shoulder. We heard her sniffling until she finally fell asleep.

"See," Chan said. "Cities break people."

I said, "I'm not sure you can blame the city this time."

Chan moved the war to one of far-off stares and clenched

fists. Quietly, he rapped his knuckles against the window in time to the music. We exited at Morgantown, West Virginia, at 6:00 p.m. without exchanging so much as a sigh.

Becky bypassed all the restaurants and swung into a gravel lot on two wheels and announced, "We're going in or else we're driving home right now." She parked among a sea of cars. Spring breakers, from the looks of the overloaded minivans and SUVs. The vehicles to our right and left had scribbled glass chalk phrases about baseball and softball.

"Where are we?" Rudy asked, because he'd been napping when we exited and missed all the banners staked along the highway.

Becky opened the driver's door and said, "Welcome to the West Virginia Spring Break Fair. Best funnel cakes in the state."

Caroline plucked her purse from the floorboard behind the passenger seat, counted several hundred dollars from a Louis Vuitton knockoff wallet, or maybe it was the real thing, and located the red beanie she'd stolen from my bedpost. "I'll pay," Caroline told Becky, and jammed the cap to her ears. She'd already flipped the switch that was her face.

In the astonishing silence that followed, carnival music whirled and spun and amplified. Bloodcurdling screams. Heavy machines on rattling tracks. Air lapping itself as the Flying Carousel and Spider and Gravitron slung participants in stomach-lurching circles. The fair was a drum kit; I hardly believed I hadn't heard its clanging cymbals and snare from

the exit ramp, much less while Caroline collected her cash and Becky painted her lips.

"Fun is nonnegotiable," Becky said. "We're riding rides until one of you assholes blows chunks. And if anyone uses the word *bus* or *bomber* in the next two hours, I'm selling you to a carnie."

CAROLINE

I text my mother: What is going on with the Westwoods?

My mother texts back: We don't know.

Me: What do you mean you don't know?

Mother: We dissolved.

Me: Dissolved what?

Mother: The business.

Me: You dissolved THE WINERY and didn't tell me?

Mother: Linda thought it would be best to wait.

Me: What the hell is going on, Mom?

Mother: You knew this would happen.

I hadn't known any of this would happen.

I hadn't known . . .

Maybe I had.

Me: Are we moving?

Mother: Yes.

Me: Should I come back now?

Mother: I don't think that would be best for us.

I threw my phone on the floorboard. If Mom said anything else, she could wait a very long time for my response. They'd sold my history and my future without so much as a phone call. I was no closer to answers about the Westwoods, but I was solid on my answer for Caroline Ascott.

I was finished.

51. The lady picks her prize.

$96,450.00

Armed with my camera, I accepted a yellow ALL-PASS wristband to enter the east gate of the West Virginia Spring Break Fair.

There were so many photo opportunities I forgot my frayed nerves. A junior higher sharing a chocolate ice cream with her brace-face boyfriend. A mom handing money to her triplet sons. A couple paying five dollars a shot to launch basketballs. The rides themselves. An intercom system crackled to life. "Attention, ladies and gentlemen, the demolition derby will begin in the Westerly Arena in ten minutes. Come on over for a smashingly good time." There was a glorious timelessness amid the sounds and sights.

We marched on "streets" lined with barkers, clowns, and rigged carnival games. Every smell imaginable taunted our empty stomachs. Hot dogs, cotton candy, deep-fried Twinkies and Oreos, chicken on a stick, funnel cakes. Every surface was the brightest of bright colors.

"Can we wait and eat real food?" Rudy asked.

Becky kicked her head back and framed the Rock It Ride between her thumbs and index fingers. "Good idea. This isn't the sort of food you want to savor twice. Come on. Follow me, my flock of sheep." And then she took Caroline's hand and surged forward.

I followed, my senses enamored. I'd never been to a state fair or a large theme park, and Chan hadn't either. We magnetized, the way we normally would in new situations, our hips so close you couldn't put tissue paper or anger between them. He leaned toward me. "I'm glad we stopped."

Fighting or the truck?

"Me too," I said.

"Will you like riding stuff?"

"No idea."

Becky sat across Rudy's legs and pulled Caroline along with her. He tried to spin the girls in circles but they were too heavy and he booted them to the curb, laughing. They yapped over details, comparing the jankety pop-up rides to their experiences at Disney World. A man with an overlarge hammer baited Rudy. "Ah, strong guy. You want to show the ladies your

million-dollar arms?" Caroline handed the man five dollars and said, "He absolutely does." Rudy worked out the best way to swing the hammer and brought the tool crashing down. Lights raced up the machine and rang the bell. The man celebrated with us. "Winner. Winner. The lady picks her prize." Caroline chose a large Pink Panther. She rode the stuffed animal on her shoulders and made loops hooting and hollering. A whooping delight. I shot dozen of photos. Of Caroline smiling. Of her fingers cupping the sky. Of her skipping. The show was for Becky, and it was the happiest I'd seen Caroline. Through the viewfinder, I recognized the girl who closed the bathroom door at Down Yonder and sauntered away in style. And in my mental picture, her long, red ringlets stood on ends as she spun.

I fell into step with her and showed her one of the photos. "This is you happy."

She tapped the screen. "That's me relieved."

"The fair?"

"The end. This is nearly over."

I was thinking, *This is nearly the beginning*, but I kept the thought to myself.

We were heroes of the fair. Rudy won another animal. Becky busted up the ring toss. Caroline forced us to ride nearly every "thrill ride" in the park. And because joy is joy is joy, each time we queued, Chan checked our height requirements on those goofy wooden signs. "You shall pass," he said, and bridged his arms like a tunnel.

I recorded grins, smiles, giggles, squeals, groans, laughs. Love. Fear. Wonder.

"You look enchanted, Jennings," Becky said.

I nodded.

I balked on one ride: Mach1. Becky grabbed a fistful of my sweatshirt, swore in a way that made a nearby mom cover her daughter's ears, and said, "You're riding that beast before we leave." I hoped everyone would get hungry and we'd leave before we looped back to that section of the fair. During our second trip through the haunted house, which was laughable horror, Chan tucked me into the dark corner—he kicked two middle school kids out first, which made us hee-haw, because we would have been those kids a few years back. "Go, we are those kids right now," he said.

"No, because we aren't here to kiss."

"I'm sorry," he said.

"For what?"

"I don't know exactly. For the space between us," he said.

I wasn't nearly as interested in Chan being sorry as I was in his being honest. Which was hysterically ironic and terrible of me. I'd lingered in that bathroom talking to Rudy and never told Chan. When you altered someone's life in a forever way, every new admission added weight to an already heavy scale. To admit I'd wanted to spend that day in June with Rudy instead of Chan, and that day, that decision, had done irrevocable damage to his life, squeezed my chest to breathlessness.

Telling him now seemed cruel. *Yeah, I know we're not together and you're severely wounded, but no biggie, I chose him over you a long time ago.*

Secrets didn't change love. They affect it, sure. But I still wanted Chan to tell me about the sketchbook under his bed and his terror of the unknown. That he had nightmares about the explosion. That he'd gotten the bus in the barn for himself. Because he had. I'd seen it in his eyes. What did he see in my eyes?

"I dug up the fourth geocache," I said.

"Are you going to tell me where it is?" he asked.

"No, I don't think I will."

"Good. Now, come on," he said, squeezing my arm, but making sure not to linger. "We've got more fair out there."

"No one has hurled yet," Caroline complained when we arrived at the end of the haunted house. "Becky won't be satisfied until someone throws up. I'm taking volunteers." She clenched the front of Chan's shirt. "What I mean by that is I've chosen you."

He raised his T-shirt to show his abs, which were in fine form. "I've got a stomach like the Rock of Gibraltar."

"Challenge accepted, Clayton."

"Where?" he asked Caroline.

She picked the Gravitron, which advertised g-forces that sucked participants to the walls. She beckoned us too, and we declined. "That's all, y'all," Rudy said.

"What are you up for?" Rudy asked Becky, when it was just the three of us.

"Sitting down! My Rock of Gibraltar crumbled. Does your cousin never tire?"

Rudy laughed. "Vadering is good for her."

"The price we all pay."

Having a premonition of what Rudy would say next, I piled our treasures and bobbles with Becky on the bench. "Mach One?" he said.

I melted under the pressure.

On our way, Rudy said, "Tell me why this one scared you. Mach One's no higher than Freak Out."

"Oh, I was scared of Freak Out too."

"And you rode anyway?"

"Yeah."

"So how can you face one fear and not the other?"

"That's adorable. You want fear to be rational."

"Get in front of it, Jennings."

I had no idea what that meant. "*Guthrie*, they put this thing on a semitruck and move it from city to city. I am in front of it."

He shrugged gleefully. "At least you know the bolts are probably tight if they assembled it this week."

There wasn't a long line at Mach1. Half the fair was watching the demolition derby, and the other half were farm kids making out in the darkened halls of the haunted house. We waited two revolutions for our turn.

"Do they ever hassle you about riding?"

"Every now and then someone will be an asshat, but for the most part, accessibility isn't a problem. Disney even has a special pass for all sorts of disabilities. To be honest, I try not to think about it."

"I'm trying not to think about dying."

"Stellar plan," he said.

We buckled in. The worker stowed Rudy's wheelchair by the control booth where it would be safe. In the hubbub, he forgot to check my belt. Rudy jerked the straps and they were tight.

"You okay?" he asked.

"Dandy."

"The scholarship money is almost at a hundred thousand. Think about that," he said.

"We have to be alive to attend college."

"We're more alive than most."

Oh, how I hoped that was true. The ride functioned like a pinwheel, if you replaced the center spinner with a long ruler that had a basket on one end. Rudy and I were in that basket. When the ride started, our basket would spin as the entire lever spun in a circle. A circle that at its highest point was sixty feet.

"This is hard," I said to Rudy.

He took my hand. "Yes."

"You're scared?"

"Terrified."

Rudy tightened his grip on my fingers. "Don't look now, but you're in front of it."

It didn't feel like we were talking about the ride.

I closed my eyes and let Rudy be the anchor.

"You two ready?" the operator called.

And that was when I learned the West Virginia Spring Break Fair's greatest truth: sometimes, there was no such thing as "ready."

52. Mach One's a humdinger.

$97,450.00

Up was down was up. My chest imploded. My brain raced at thoroughbred speed, galloping through endorphins and dopamine. My lungs lodged in my ears. The music volume lowered from screech to roar. The dying was nearly done. Our metal cage rocketed skyward, but lost momentum. We slowed to a near stop—the ride giving one final violent jolt—then, blissful stillness.

"You were a banshee in another life, Go."

I didn't remember screaming.

I tried to say, "I nearly became a banshee in *this* life," but was too hoarse.

The operator presented Rudy his wheelchair. As soon I was

unbuckled, I punched Rudy in the arm, hard. The operator laughed. "Dude," he said. "Nearly every lady punches her man when they're back on the ground. Mach One's a humdinger."

"Oh, we're not—"

But the kid had already turned to his next victims. I checked to see who might have heard, but no one we knew was in sight.

Rudy tried to brush the comment off. "He says that to everyone."

"Yeah, I'm sure he does."

We wobbled our way around temporary fencing, through the ride exit, and down the aisle where we left Becky. The ground was uneven, pockmarked with trash. There was Rudy, handling every small challenge, nothing fazing him, and I couldn't stop obsessing over the operator's errant comment. "You want to talk about the kissing?" he asked.

"No."

"Me either."

"Good. Maybe I would if things were different, but neither of us is going to make life different during a four-day road trip. For now, let's say I liked it, you liked it, and Chan would hate it."

"Agree."

Despite my frustration at Chan's behavior and being dumped, Chan was the carry-on bag I'd packed many years ago. You didn't drop your luggage in Morgantown, West Virginia, because a thrill-ride operator made an assumption. But maybe you dropped it because he dropped you. I'd never been

dropped before and didn't know the rules.

"You clearly loved Mach One," Rudy said, segueing.

He ducked and evaded my swat with a quick spin that I recognized as a signature Rudy maneuver. "So awful." Still awful. My body hadn't stopped pulsing since we landed. The immediate threat of death had diminished, but all systems weren't back online yet. "Tell me you're queasy."

"My stomach has moved"—he gripped his windpipe—"permanently."

"Good," I said. "I hope it stays there."

I nearly tripped over my feet, and he said, "That's what you get for being mean to me."

It probably was.

We reached home-base Becky. Chan and Caroline were already there. Caroline's face was pressed to Becky's shoulder, and Becky stroked her like a stray she wanted to take home and feed. Chan leaned against an electric pole and had his head on another planet. His *Hey! How was Mach One?* was frosting sweet, but the real message was loud and clear: *Don't ask me what's wrong.*

Chan came out of the womb reticent. His first words were probably *I'm fine.* There were generations of Clayton men who'd been taught to nod, frown, or flex in case of rapture or natural disaster. Clayton men saved people with the unwritten caveat that no one was allowed to save *them.* He'd met his match in me, because I could game that shit step for step when I wanted to.

"I asked about Mach One?" he repeated.

Rudy and I recounted the experience. I didn't use words to ask if Chan was okay. I opted for a furrowed brow and my own *You'll tell me if you want to* look. Our first moment alone, he said, as predicted, "I'm as fine as you are."

"Yes, I know. Now, what's wrong?"

"Tit for tat. Have you considered that you have to give to get?"

That silenced me. The first chance I had, I looped my arm through Caroline's and asked, "What happened on the Gravitron?"

"As advertised; the bottom drops out."

"Of the ride?"

Her hesitation: an untold story. Her answer: "Yeah. You bet."

But she was back inside herself, and even Becky and Rudy couldn't tease her out.

53. Things shrink when I wash them.

$97,930.00

Something foul permeated the Ford. I squirmed with negative energy. Eager for food or escape, Chan steered the truck to a restaurant lodge called the Fin and Feather.

"There's a perfectly good Shoney's right there," Becky said.

Unfortunately, no one laughed. Everyone was starved. Things would be better after we ate. Chan pocketed the keys. "They have good reviews on Yelp."

"*They* aren't on Yelp," Caroline said.

Something deeper than irritation zipped along between them. When they noted us watching, each turned a head in the opposite direction. Chan softened. "You gave me permission to choose."

Caroline dug through her purse, paused, said, "I say a lot of things I don't mean." There were more than words to that exchange, but she rushed from her seat and busily retrieved Rudy's wheelchair. Chan sauntered ahead, hands in his pockets. "This'll do," he yelled from the menu board posted at the entrance, and then disappeared inside. The air smelled overwhelmingly of grilled steaks and fry oil.

"What the hell happened on the Gravitron?" Rudy asked no one in particular.

Nonchalant, Caroline slipped a ditty bag under her arm and walked fast to the door. Becky asked, "Do I follow?" and I lifted my hands. I wasn't even pretending I understood their behavior.

Rudy took out his phone. "Good luck. I'll be inside in a minute."

"You calling Stock?"

He nodded wearily. "To tell him Chan and Caroline are out. And that you'll meet the Westwoods."

I shifted my gaze toward the restaurant. I didn't know whether I envied Rudy his phone call or not. Talking to Stock sounded better than being the clueless barrier between Chan and Caroline. Rudy squeezed my forearm. "Don't stew on those two. It'll come out in the wash."

"Things shrink when I wash them."

I left him to his phone call. The restaurant's interior matched its exterior. Unadulterated log cabin. I had a feeling this restaurant epitomized Morgantown. Everything was

brown, and I had to hand it to management, they didn't repeat a single shade. Brown walls and floor. Brown miniblinds, closed. Brown ceilings. Brown round tables and chairs. Framed photos of smiling hunters wearing orange vests over camo were the only splashes of color. A mounted fourteen-point buck with hollow black eyes stalked me on the way to our table.

Chan ordered a round of waters and ducked behind his menu. Becky's eyebrows shot skyward, nonplussed at whatever the hell was going on. Caroline was in the bathroom shaving her damn head *again*. The way I saw it, we had two choices: force a leveling or ignore the tension. Through a series of hand gestures and eyebrow raises, Becky and I chose the latter. My current plan included ordering a Coke and the biggest, fattiest, juiciest hamburger I could afford.

Rudy arrived, and not long afterward, Caroline emerged from the bathroom lip-locked and freshly shaven. I smelled the menthol rolling off in waves. Despite her silence, she appeared wildly refreshed. Rudy nodded that the deed was done, and I tried flashing him some happiness but couldn't muster the strength. Wendy, our waitress, materialized from the kitchen with a tray of waters. She doled out extra menus and napkins, but nothing softened the mood.

Rudy said, "My dear Wendy, the finest screwdriver her credit card can buy." He tapped Caroline's menu. "Hold the vodka."

Wendy laughed generously. She was older than us, but young enough to be flattered by Rudy's attention. When she

smiled, she looked like someone who might get out of this town. Around the table, everyone took a breath. We soon discovered everything was funny to Wendy. Chan's rimless glasses. The skateboarding stickers on Rudy's wheelchair. Caroline's bald head. "Are you like an eagle or Natalie Portman?" she asked with admiration. "I wish I had the head shape for it."

The food arrived without incident, we ate without incident, and we might have escaped the rest of the night clean as a whistle if Wendy the waitress *held the vodka* from Rudy's orange juice. No such luck. Rudy drank three screwdrivers. He killed the first in a gulp, and the bartender at the Fin and Feather had been a bartender for thirty years and knew how to make a decent screwdriver. "I'm from Florida and this is *very* delicious orange juice," Rudy said several times. I can only assume Wendy and the bartender miscommunicated. The mistake would have been caught faster if we hadn't been so committed to silence and the consumption of calories.

"Wendy the Waitress," Rudy said, as she removed his empty plate. "Did you always want to be a waitress?" Becky jerked my shirtsleeve in a *You know he's drunk, right?* motion. People three counties over knew Rudy was drunk, as he sang every song that came on the radio, those he knew and those he didn't.

Expertly, Wendy stacked our dishes on her little round tray. "I'm taking paramedic classes."

"*Hey!* A paramedic saved our lives. Give it to me up here, Wendy the Medic." Rudy gave Wendy a high elbow because

her hands were full. The dishes shifted dangerously to the edge. We all held our breath as she rebalanced. Rudy didn't notice. He chattered on. "Wendy the Medic doesn't sound as good as Wendy the Waitress, but you'll make more money there than here. My mom's a waitress. Well, sometimes. Sometimes, she's a convict."

Caroline slid the orange juice glass to the table beside ours.

"Tell me about your medic," Wendy said. "The one who saved your life."

"Well, it's probably a secret, but you see these three"—he thumbed toward Chan, Caroline, and me—"we were all on Bus Twenty-One. Not that one with the smokin'-hot hair"—he pointed this time at Becky—"she wasn't there, but she's with us, you know? In our souls. Like family." Because he was drunk and patting his heart as he spoke about Becky, she admonished him, "Next time, mention my superhot lipstick."

"Too bright," Rudy said. "You don't even need it."

Becky whipped around to me. "Is that true?"

I didn't answer, but it totally was. Rudy and Wendy the waitress had already moved to the topic at hand. "What happened on Bus Twenty-One?" she wanted to know.

"You know that explosion in New York last summer?"

"Rudy!" I intended to stop this. "Let Wendy do her job."

"Oh, shoot, I've got time."

"Wendy's not going to tell. Are you, Wendy?" He patted her wrist in a patronizing way. The dishes slid sideways again.

"You're drunk, Guthrie. Zip it and zip it hard," Caroline told her cousin.

"No need to *shhhhh*, you guys." Rudy wheeled away from the table, spun three or four circles, and raised his voice to the restaurant. "Tomorrow. Green-Conwell. *Accelerant Orange* by the amazing artist medic, Carter Stockton. High *noooooooon*"— he howled—"that brave cowgirl and I are getting on a bus that blew last summer. You should check out the project online."

Mostly, the patrons ignored him. But to the overly interested, I waved my hand for them to return to their dinners. Without asking permission, I found purchase on Rudy's wheelchair—there were no handles—pushed him forward, and declared, "You're coming with me." I was aware this was perhaps insulting, but I was also aware he was moments away from barfing.

"Are we going to the bathroom together?" he asked, letting me steer. I heard his stomach. "I like it when we go to the bathroom together, Go. Get it? *Go?*"

Oh, I got it all right.

54. No longer a box

$97,935.00

I locked the door behind us, my shoulders pressed against the cool metal while I tried to figure out what in the hell to do now that I had him here. To make matters worse, the cramped restroom smelled of Caroline's shaving cream. Rudy performed an arduous study of his hands. His chin volleyed right to left, right to left. "I think my right hand is stronger than my left. I'm not sure," he slurred. His lips turned downward when his eyes eventually found mine.

"You look upset, Golden. Hey, does anyone ever call you Golden Gate Bridge?"

"No."

"You're upset. Did Chan hurt you?"

I crouched against the floor and put my face in my hands.

"I'll tell him to stop."

"I know you will."

His face tinted green with coming sick. There were nightmares in his eyes. "Wait. Are you mad I tricked you into Mach One?"

"You didn't trick me."

"Is it the bus?"

"Not right now."

His head fell forward and his chin smacked his sternum. When he popped upright, he asked, "Hey, why are we in the bathroom? Hey! Why are you crying, Go?"

Was I? I did feel the heat of tears forming in the corners. Lucky for me, Rudy believed me when I claimed I was sweating. "I'm hot too," he agreed, and shimmied out of his shirt. I caught the ball of fabric he launched into the air. "Why do they have two toilets in this stall?"

"There aren't two toilets. You're drunk."

"On orange juice?" he said, unbelieving.

"On vodka."

"Hey, Golden Gate Bridge, my stomach is here again." He grabbed his windpipe the way he had after Mach1.

"I'm sure it is."

"And I . . . I'm going to . . . throw up."

Yep.

"You need to leave." He reached for the doorknob and

missed. "I don't want you to see me on the floor."

"Rudy, look at me. Your wheelchair is a nonissue."

"We're . . . in a . . . bathroom."

"Yes."

"And you're leaving?"

"Nope. You know why? Because I wouldn't leave Becky under these circumstances, and that's our rule."

He lurched and covered his mouth. The transition to the floor wasn't graceful. He slammed the toilet seat against the lid and held on.

"Go!" Chan pounded the bathroom door. "Let me in. I'll help." I turned my head as the contents of Rudy's stomach splashed into the bowl. Vomit always made me dry heave. "GO! Let me help!" Chan said again.

Rudy lifted his head and bellowed, "Leave her alone, Cowboy. You broke Go's heart!" and hurled again.

"She broke mine first," Chandler said. "Go, let me in."

"Did you?" Rudy asked.

I shook my head. "No. He's just frustrated that he can't rescue me." To Chan, I said, "Chan, it's okay, I promise. We'll be out soon."

His footsteps retreated, and I flushed the vomit.

Rudy collapsed against the porcelain lid. "You know," he said, "she threw up all over me too."

"Who?"

"Car-o-line. On the day of the bus."

His cheeks, already streaked, reddened with heat and

memory. When he lifted his face from the toilet rim, he said, "I hit her so hard."

"What do you mean?"

I'd been crouching around him, holding his hair and balancing us, but I dropped fully to the floor and scooted closer so I braced his weight. Rudy tilted his chin upward, staring at me, and like a child, ran his palm down my face. "Simon made Jim go to the back of the bus."

"Because he wanted to blow everyone up."

Rudy buckled, threw his head toward the toilet, and retched again. Less came up this time; his stomach was nearly empty. He sagged, and I was there. His back was slick with sweat. His face was ashen. When he spoke, he slurred fewer words. "Simon and Caroline came to Aunt Linda's for the Fourth of July the summer before and we bought fireworks at a roadside stand. Simon caught four or five baby alligators that morning. They were no bigger than the palm of my hand. That night he taped M-Sixties around two and put them all in a box. Then, he waited to light the wicks until the alligators crawled to opposite ends. He killed them. And said the teeth were too small to put on a necklace. Simon sent Jim to the other end of the bus. Go, we were those alligators and the bus was our box."

I imagined the three of them in the orange grove.

The M60s reporting. *Bang. Bang.* A mouselike screech from the animals. Alligator guts littering the ground, the tree, a smudge on Rudy's knee. The cardboard is blackened in some places and

obliterated in others. No longer a box. A single Valencia tree in bloom, fragrant, but unable to cover the sulfur. There's Rudy. He's horrified. His hands are laced behind his head, his back straight, his head cocked toward Caroline, hoping for some display of rage. She's too numb. She drops to a squat and stares at the tree. Did she try to leave Simon after that? When the danger was still smoking and oozing? Simon bounding like a spring, swatting branches. *"Did you see those suckers explode? I wish I had a thousand alligators."*

"When he told you and Chan to leave, I slid to the edge of my seat. You tossed me your beanie. The second you cleared the steps, I hit Caroline with everything I had. We practically landed on you."

I'd forgotten. The memory had been completely wiped until he said it, which was mildly terrifying. What else had I erased? "You got her out, Rudy. That's all that matters."

"She was in the aisle." He closed his eyes. "I still see her. She had little blue stud earrings. Her hair was parted on the left."

Gosh, he was right. I remembered the details as he said them.

"I thought I'd cover those five feet and we'd roll down the steps. Which is what happened, except I hit Caroline so hard we slammed into the front dash and window first. She threw up. Impact and nerves. I pushed her down the well, tumbling behind her onto you and Chan. And then I was flying."

Rudy fell sideways, his head a weight on my knee. Then he turned and coiled around me, let himself sob.

"Simon was always going to blow the alligators, right?"

His hair was damp. I parted it left, then right. "Yes."

He lifted the dead weight of his legs and moved them closer to his chest, and then he swiveled and touched my heart, felt the muscle straining and pounding against my chest. "I didn't make this happen, did I?"

I smoothed Rudy's hair again and again. "No."

There was more pounding at the door. Caroline's voice. "Hey, you two. When Becky said we weren't leaving until someone puked, *she was joking*."

"See?" I said. "You saved her life."

Rudy touched his forehead to my knee. His voice was small. "I'm not sure I did. She gave Becky her purple headband."

"Yeah, I think they're . . . a thing."

"I don't think she'd give it away if she . . ." Rudy pulled me into a fierce hug. He was shaking when he said, "Caroline told me once she wanted to die at Ellis Island. What if we're just her ride?"

55. Those who save the things they should lose and those who lose the things they should save

$97,935.00

The bathroom reeked of puke. I held Rudy, who also reeked. His sweaty body was pressed against mine and the dichotomy surged to life, the torso and shoulders of a rottweiler, the thighs of an elderly man. He wasn't steady enough to transfer to his chair, and I wasn't strong enough to help him. We all wish to be stronger than we are.

The end. This is nearly over. That's what Caroline told me at the fair. *This is me relieved*, she'd said. Rudy could be right.

"Did you ever imagine this?" he asked.

"Us in a bathroom stall?"

"I guess."

So many twisted paths led us to a bathroom stall in

Morgantown, West Virginia. A third-generation photo. The black-and-whites framed on Gran's magnificent wall of history. Could I blame my involvement with Bus #21 on a man dressed in a smart wool overcoat and the serious woman pressed against his rib cage, the diamond on her hand mirroring the diamond I wore for three days?

If the journey here were a road, that photo represented the driveway.

Sure, I'd longed to see Ellis Island and re-create a cool family photo, but what I wanted last June was security, stability. Something steady and safe like the Hive that wasn't a place. I'd pinned that security to Chan, thinking if he and I took a family photo, we were family. God, from here, the notion seemed juvenile. Gran used to say, "Chickadee, unfortunately, there are two types of people in the world. Those who save the things they should lose and those who lose the things they should save. Don't be either." I'd asked, "What are you?" She'd kissed my forehead and replied, "Oh, darling, I've been both. And you will too."

I'd been both. And now, Rudy was drunk, Chan was antagonistic, Caroline was . . . whatever Caroline was, and then, there was me; trying to hold everyone and everything together with waning willpower and false bravado. I was tired. And I didn't think that was allowed.

Beside me, Rudy shifted. "What do we do about Caroline?" He sounded sober.

"For now, we watch her. We talk to her. Survive the day.

Forget Ellis Island and *Accelerant Orange* if that's what it takes. Then, we get her help."

"Agreed." He nodded toward the toilet and flushed the bowl again. "If Caroline came here to die, and I came here to prove Simon didn't destroy me, and Chan came because he's jealous, what about you, Go? What are you leaving here with that no one can take? Chan? Me? Hope? Money for college? The ability to get on a bus again? A photo for your gran?"

Every answer sounded saccharine. Like some too-perfect rosy line in a book. "I don't know yet."

"Well, you have a few more miles to figure it out."

56. Hazzard's the better choice.

$98,320.00

The tension at the table hadn't decreased during our absence. If anything, strings were tugged tighter. No one had the energy left to be civil, much less kind. When Rudy returned moments later, pale and splotchy from splashing water on his face and neck, everyone stood to leave.

Rudy donned a sheepish expression. "You guys want me to drive?" Chan dug his fists into his pockets and said, "That's an awful joke, man," which made Caroline rip the keys from the table. "I got you," she told Rudy, and dropped a hundred-dollar bill between the salt and pepper shakers.

We left, but we couldn't escape each other.

Dad's call to the preppers in West Virginia led us off the

beaten path, as I knew it would. A feeling started in the pit of my stomach that tonight would continue to be less Twisted Teacups and more Mach1. I didn't share the theory with the others, but Rudy, Becky, and Caroline indicated mild discomfort when we passed the third hand-painted No Trespassing sign. Chan shot a knowing glance in my direction. We'd toured a few semi-local places like this as kids, and they were always frenetic experiments complete with basement stocks and munitions. If I was correct, passing the entry point would be telling.

"Remind me again why preppers are prepping," Becky said.

"Disease plague. Nuclear war. Climate trauma—"

"So . . . the collapse of the free world."

"Basically," I said.

"We should all be so wise," she teased.

I wondered how long she'd keep that opinion.

For the last three miles, the trees caved around the Ford and gave the impression we were spelunking through moss-green tunnels. We bobbed silently along the rutted roads, no one daring to speak. Then came the flat, winter wheat fields, that were probably perfectly lovely in bright sunlight. We were, beyond a shadow of a doubt, in the crosshairs of a rifle.

"What the ever-loving eff . . . !" Becky was staring at the entrance to Eight Echoes *Summer Camp*. Twelve-foot wooden fences topped with icing—an additional three feet of barbed wire and solar lamps—surrounded the property.

"Jennings!" Caroline said, sitting forward in her seat. "Where did your dad send us?"

"Chill, New York. I've met these people. They're very kind. A little over the top, but kind. And they know we're coming," I said, but I had that itchy feeling.

"Do they think we're an army?" Becky asked, her voice reaching for humor and missing.

"As long as we're not the government, we're fine," Chan said.

"Or aliens," I added.

Chan nodded. It's not that all communes know each other's goings on, but drifters of the world drift. And some of them stay in touch. Mom and Dad wouldn't have sent us here if they were even slightly worried. Then again, they hadn't seen the two wooden fifteen-foot deer stands serving as sentries. We eased to a stop and Caroline put the truck in park and left it running. I opened the door.

"Jennings!" This time Caroline sounded afraid for me.

Rudy still hadn't spoken, but he tensed. I slid from the seat and raised my arms, palms open, at the stand. A spotlight, like the ones used by our favorite rednecks from home, hit my shoes and probed me like an alien life-form. I couldn't see anything, and they saw everything. "Pete Jennings is my father," I yelled toward the light. "He said you had a place for us to stay."

"I'll be right down," a young voice called from the tower.

The boy who tromped down the steps in his military-issue boots was a *boy*. Thirteen? Fourteen? Young in a way Chan

never was and old in a way I never had to be. Every gray, green, and black thread on him was military issue or military knockoff. He didn't have a visible gun, but from Dad's training, I logged the bulge at his ankle, and I suspected if he turned around there was another weapon tucked in the small of his back.

"Two?" Chan said discreetly from the truck, concurring with my initial analysis.

But the boy had another pistol, an appendix-carry. That's the only reason for the loose-fitting T-shirt he wore. I held three fingers behind my back, and Chan said, "Agree."

"We've been waiting on you all evening," the boy said jovially. "I need to check your license. Dad'll skin me if I don't. He'd be here to greet you, but he's teaching a session on the uses of paracord in the next town over and it ran late."

I handed over my license. He shone a flashlight on the plastic and then near my face before shoving his hand at mine. "I'm Flynn," he said as we shook.

"Golden Jennings."

"I remember you from Kentucky. You're the one with the grain bin."

"Sorry we're so late. We were at the fair," I explained.

"Went last weekend. Did you ride the Mach1?"

"I did."

His smile crested wide and large. He gave me a fist bump. "I can hop in the back or drive you to Hazzard. Whatever makes you happy."

"Hazzard?" Becky mouthed, but I shook her off.

"You drive," I told him, which made him like me more than he already did. Small boys liked driving a big truck. Flynn drove around several smaller homes and took a road that was less of a road than the one we'd come in on. We wound over a rise and into a valley of waist-high grass. I heard a pond or lake chirping and gulping, smelled it living, well before moonlight hit the calm black waters and winked with her sparkling eyes.

"That's Echo Lake," Flynn said proudly. "And that's Miss Hazzard."

Miss Hazzard was a houseboat.

Under other circumstances, this would have been a luxury. A funny story to tell about an unusual accommodation. Instead, Rudy shifted nervously. Our brains played leapfrog, eyes darting ahead to the dock, measuring distances and dividing danger. Neither of us sure of getting him onto the boat or through the sliding glass.

I smelled Flynn's sweat-soaked clothes—probably the result of waiting in an airless stand for us to appear—as he settled the truck into a spot, headlights pointed in the direction of the water. He dusted a hand over brown-blond curls at the nape of his neck. They were of near-mullet proportion. "Daddy said to tell you not to use the bedroom on the left. The one on the right isn't bad, isn't good. The couches fold down so you should have plenty of space. We were putting you in C Cabin, but mice pilfered the supplies, and trust me, Hazzard's

the better choice. I aired her out all day so it should smell nice for you." Better than he smelled for sure.

"What's in the bedroom on the left?" Chan asked.

"Guns, I'm sure."

Caroline wheeled around. "Are they loaded?"

Flynn's eyes pinched together, like he didn't trust Caroline's intelligence one bit. "They can be in a moment's notice. Just the way God intended."

57. A heap of shadows

$98,390.00

We were spending the night with loaded weapons. Some of them were guns.

Flynn trekked off up the hill, and I sent Becky and Chan on a walk-through of Hazzard. Chan came back and gave Rudy the lay of the land. "Bad news. The threshold between the dock and the boat is too wide. I'll have to carry you. Good news. After that, the entryways are wide."

There was a prickly moment wherein I was torn between being upset for Rudy, who clearly hated this news, and delighted by Chan. He might not like Rudy but he wouldn't emasculate him; he had far too much empathy for that to be the way he wounded an enemy.

"I'll sleep in the truck," Rudy said.

"That's crazy," Chan said.

"Would you want me to carry you?" Rudy asked.

"Hell no, but we're all doing things we don't want to do on this trip."

In the end, Chan carried Rudy over the gap and the guys retreated to their corners. A good idea since they probably had to share a bed later.

Chan commandeered the table, burying himself in his sketchbook. I sat nearby, watching the weightless way his pencil glided over the paper. Granddad's barn appeared with the door skidded sideways and the cavernous bus in shadows. On the corner, he roughed in his own face. He flipped the page over quickly and started another sketch. Caroline's eyes. He flipped again. His hand was heavy now, pressing lead to the page.

I watched for an hour, and that was my limit. I went out to the deck, passing Becky on her way in. Her head was bowed, her posture sagging. I caught her arm. "What's wrong?"

"Nothing," she said, but she meant *everything*. Her eyes were on Caroline.

"I'm here," I said, the words just popping out.

"I know you are." She paused long enough for me to rest my forehead against hers. Becky Cable didn't need me—she never had, but she appreciated my stilted attempt at comfort. There were many ways to be strong, and Becky was all of them, even as she was walking away from a situation she didn't know how

to solve. "See if you can help her." Caroline was a heap of shadows perched on the edge of the boat. "I've tried all my tricks."

That was the problem with tricks. Tricks could make a sad person laugh, but they couldn't keep them laughing after everyone went home. I sat near Caroline and listened to the frogs and the stars and the water striders doing their breaststrokes. Liquid pooled around Caroline's clothes, ran down her outstretched hand and returned to the lake, ran sideways on the aluminum deck and wet my shorts. She watched droplets fall like they were each a favorite television show. Her flesh was goose pimpled, and I heard the clatter of her teeth, but she didn't complain. April in West Virginia was many things, but it wasn't pleasant for swimming. A dip in this lake bordered on dangerous. No wonder Becky was upset.

It was a long time before I spoke. "What happened on the Gravitron?"

"Nothing. Everything. I flipped around upside down."

I pictured this.

The Gravitron was an enclosed spinning ride that generated g-forces. At maximum speed, you looked like a shrink-wrapped human. Clothing tightened. Bodies pressed against the wall. The floor dropped three or four feet and you were suspended. You felt like you were dying when you turned your head to see the person next to you. If Caroline was inverted when the ride slowed . . . I saw why Chan had been furious. She might have broken her neck.

"Why would you do that?"

Her heels bounced against the hull of Miss Hazzard. "That's what Becky asked."

"It's a decent question."

"Come on. Tell me you haven't thought about it."

"Turning myself upside down on the Gravitron? Because no, I haven't. I feel like we have wildly differently ideas of what makes a ride fun."

"We have wildly different ideas."

"I think that's fine."

"Jennings, I wasn't asking for your permission."

"You're wet as a fish. You're sitting on the back deck alone. You're asking for something, honeypie." I had to take the risk. To ask the real question I hadn't stopped asking since Rudy brought it up in the bathroom. "Caroline, did you come on this trip to kill yourself?"

"Yes," she said.

"Did you tell Chan?"

"I didn't have to, but he knew. He's not mad at me. He's scared. Maybe you forgot the difference. Or maybe you don't get scared anymore."

I was scared right then. "Do you have a plan?"

"Yes."

And we sat there weighted down with her admission, unsure of what came next. Could I say, *I'm not going to let you,* when a person was not a thing you could carry in your pocket like a wallet or a phone? There were so many words in the English language, and maybe doctors and psychologists had

ones that fit this situation, but I didn't. I felt small and afraid and inadequate.

I moved closer. Our thighs touched. I slung my arm around her back, not caring that my side was damp and then wet. Not caring about anything except keeping her connected to me. "I wish you wouldn't." I turned sideways to say this, and in my peripheral vision, I caught a glint of moonlight in her lap.

Metal.

She had a gun.

58. The gentle rocking of the boat

$98,590.00

Boarding Miss Hazzard with a Walther PPQ in hand was not how I pictured our evening, but like it or not, that's how the evening had decided to go. I disarmed Caroline and marched her inside on a diet of gentle words and calm suggestions. That wasn't how we looked to the others.

"Golden Jennings, what the hell are you doing?" Becky didn't sound scared of me, only alarmed at the situation. Things were spiraling and she was the first to spot the evidence.

"Chan," I said calmly, still holding the gun and keeping contact with Caroline. I was mildly afraid she might bolt past me through the door and jump into the dark cavity of Echo Lake.

He didn't budge from his sketchbook.

"CHAN!"

His head whipped up. He took in me, the gun, Caroline's crumpled Gollum shape. "I need your help," I said. "Please take care of this for us." I held the gun out, barrel down, grip facing him. She had given it over when I'd asked, but she stared longingly at the pistol like a child who has given up a pacifier.

Chan was beside me. In a swift, comfortable move, he released the magazine and reversed the slide. A bullet sprung from the chamber, hit the wooden paneling, and rolled under the galley fridge. We all watched the gold cylinder disappear and then reappear again with the gentle rocking of the boat.

"Disarmed," he said.

"Find a way to lock the bedroom on the left."

There was no lock. Chan asked Becky to kindly remove herself from the couch, which she did, but she was less Becky in those movements than I'd ever seen her be. She stood in the corner, arms folded over her chest, head bowed. This was the way Gran sometimes looked when she prayed, and if that was the case here, I supported the decision. The manufactured couch scraped the panel walls and scuffed the thin blue tiles as Chan dragged the beast through the hallway. He blockaded the bedroom door so efficiently he had to exit the boat at the stern. All eyes tilted toward the short ceilings as he crossed the top and returned through the door nearest the group. Removing the gun and barricading the door took three, maybe four minutes; each second felt like waiting on news from a doctor. I was full of thoughts, wishing I was full of wisdom instead.

"Thank you," I said, still managing to be calm.

Rudy rolled closer to his cousin, and I nodded that he should move her to his lap. It was all hands on deck, quite literally. Neither cousin argued when his arms caged around her wispy body. He tucked her head under his chin like a child. She was sobbing, and every sniffle and sob was amplified by the small galley.

I wanted to scream, but you can't scream at someone in that condition. I made a measured decision to be civil. "It's time to talk," I said. But I still didn't know what to say.

Life had us all by the throat. It was easy to blame Caroline for the thick, swampy feelings, but she wasn't the only carrier of the fear disease. We weren't just scared for her. Deep down, we were scared of becoming her. Sure, I'd gotten rid of the gun today, but what if there was another gun tomorrow? What if I failed at boarding Bus #21? What if I couldn't go to college? What if I woke one day and remembered I was supposed to die on June 15? That's what I felt when I saw Caroline under the orange grove and the fear hadn't changed a lick. Her trembling, weeping body reminded me I knew more about hurting than healing. Even when I tried to be *the strong one.*

Rudy spoke first. "I hope you guys know I'm sorry about earlier. I never meant to get drunk." This was an odd entry point when we'd just removed a handgun from a suicidal girl.

"We know," Becky said, slightly annoyed.

"I had to get that off my chest. Anyone else need to do the same?" Rudy asked.

Except for Becky scooting closer to Rudy's wheelchair, the room had no response.

Finally, Chan pointed at Caroline. "*This* is what happened on the Gravitron."

"Don't make family meeting all about me. He's just as tripped." Caroline didn't look up, but she was pointing at Chan. It was peculiar to hear such a substantial statement from such an unsubstantial life-form. Her body looked like clothes left in a laundry basket.

"I'm fine," Chan said, also in a measured voice.

He had a point there, as he was the one removing bullets from chambers, not loading guns.

"Come get eyeball to eyeball, Clayton, and tell me *you're fine*," Caroline said.

"This family meeting is about you and your death wish, not mine." That's what Chan said, but Chan performed a tell I recognized. He leaned against the door, stretched lazily, focused on his fingers splayed on the ceiling. He often made his physical body bigger when he felt smaller.

"What's she talking about, Chan?" I asked.

Caroline's tone was sharper than Chan's chain saws. "Hurt recognizes hurt, Jennings. Your boy here's in a wringer. Guilt's a real bitch, huh?" she said to Chan.

He frowned, tried to speak, and then couldn't.

I didn't know what was going on, but I moved closer. He definitely had something unsaid gathering in his chest. "Just talk, Chan. Maybe it'll give Caroline courage."

All of a sudden, Chan was eleven again. Huge eyes surrounded by a sagging jawline. So unsure. He twisted his arms into a pretzel shape, guarding his chest. "I'm not sabotaging your bus trip, if that's what you think," he said. *I hadn't thought that at all.* "And I didn't come along to hurt myself like she's suggesting, or anyone else."

"We stood in Granddad's barn and I begged you to come. And you were adamant that you wouldn't. Something must have changed your mind. What was it?"

Chan studied Rudy, and I anticipated for a split second what this was about.

"You." Chan's eyes darted between Rudy and me. "Him."

I made a dismissive noise in my throat.

"I saw you giving him a tour of the farm. The way you fawned. You gave him your beanie on Bus Twenty-One." Heavy sigh. "Something happened between you back then and this was my chance to see if you broke up with me for him. If all this fallout was his fault. It's shallow, but it's true."

"Chan, you broke up with me."

"Not last June I didn't."

"I didn't break up with you last June."

Caroline's head snapped up. "Yeah, you did," she said to me. She looked more awake than she had since the fair.

"No, I didn't," I said.

There was pity in her smile. "You two were in each other's faces on the sidewalk outside the Green-Conwell. Chan told you if you got on the bus, you two were over. And you said,

then consider us *over*. I'll never forget it because I thought, *Now, Caroline, that's how people end relationships.* But then Chan followed you on, fuming, still arguing, and I felt a teeny bit better. It's not easy to get rid of someone who doesn't want to leave."

"That. Did. Not. Happen."

But there was Chan's face, Chan's honest, earnest face. The face that planned for everything except me changing my mind. "It did," he said.

I pressed my brain through the sieve of June 15. I didn't even remember boarding the bus, much less arguing with Chan. I suspected I never would, but my lack of memory didn't make the story untrue. There was no reason to lie. Not about this. So every time Chan acted like I ruined us, he hadn't been acting. I had.

"But then you forgot," Chan said. "You came out of the hospital with this memory erased. Gone. Which was a relief, in a way, because *forgetting* meant you still wanted to be with me. But every day felt like the day you'd remember. Like the day I'd lose you. We argued last week and strangely enough, that argument made me believe the memory was never coming back. You said I *had an agenda*, and that was the exact phrase you used in June. If you were ever going to remember . . . those words should have been the trigger. I decided we were safe. I wanted to strike while the iron was hot."

Everything clicked at once. "You didn't want to talk about New York because you were afraid I'd remember?"

"Would you risk the person you loved most in the world

remembering that they didn't want you anymore?"

"What if I was being flippant that day?" I said, but I didn't believe that and neither did he. The truth sat uncomfortably in the center of the room. It was this: I'd spent several years keeping a promise that looked grand in framed photos. And our love story—the parts of us that kept growing and desiring each other—had expired when I started to long for a wider world and Chan hadn't. Only loyalty was left. It was a beautiful, marvelous loyalty, but it wasn't enough by itself. "Chan, I'm so incredibly sorry. For everything."

"You're telling me."

Chan set his sketchbook on the table and then hesitantly pushed the book toward me. He swayed as if he intended to leave, but I blocked the route to the sliding door. "Please don't leave. We still need you."

He flipped through the sketchbook until he found a particular drawing. "This is me, eyeball to eyeball. You see this, and you'll point the gun at me instead of you," he said to Caroline.

Chan had opened to a drawing of Simon, not from the bus. The bomber stood slack-jawed and chinless, beside our bar table at Down Yonder, one hand splayed on a cardboard coaster, the other fisting a clump of dark hair. A spot-on likeness.

Rudy reached from his chair and traced Chan's pencil line as if Simon might be alive.

"Simon never came to our table," I said.

"Wrong again, Golden," Chan said.

Chan, who never cried, had tears cresting. His voice shook as he faced not me, but Caroline. "Simon came to our table while Go was at the jukebox. And I told him . . . I told him that you had sex with that guy Jim Conner in the bathroom. I told him I thought he should know."

59. Nod if you understand.

$98,800.00

Chandler Clayton was 220 pounds of man. His favorite tool was a chain saw. He could deadlift me like a child or toss me effortlessly when we swam at the blue hole. He'd been Hulk-size at fifteen. Strength is the mantra of the huge, and strength often comes with a tagline: *Vulnerability is not allowed.* I don't know when adults started looking at Chan like he was already grown or when I came to believe Chan was the wall nothing penetrated, but I now knew we were all wrong. Last June, life pierced the wall of Chandler Clayton, and the blow had been devastating.

We all sat spellbound, thoughts buzzing like swarms of bees around our heads. No one was visibly angry; they were

all shocked, same as me.

"Chan," I said.

"There's nothing you can say, Golden."

"Chan," I said again.

Chan cut me off, speaking specifically to Caroline. "This isn't on you," he said. "I did this. To all of us. To every person attending the memorial." Chan did not scream or lash out. He didn't curl into a ball like Rudy had in the bathroom. He rose to full height and said to me what he'd been unable to say for months. "I didn't tell you sooner because I didn't want you to hate me. Not when I hated me enough for both of us." The words were long ghastly gasps, like he'd been underwater too long and had just crested the surface.

What did you say to a boy who believed he'd killed nineteen people?

"What did I promise when we were eleven?" I asked, trying to tell him in advance that I would not hurt him more than he was already hurting.

"I don't know."

"Yes, you do."

He whispered, "Chandler and Golden versus the world."

"Chan, do you really think we have to be a couple for that to be true?"

"I guess I did. I wanted to be perfect."

"Jesus Christ, Chan. You don't have to be anything but honest." His hand was sweaty when I took it.

Something intangible passed across the room, a calm exhale. Out of the corner of my eye, I caught Rudy gauging my response. I let him know that my guts felt like they'd reached the end of a marathon, everything knotted and tired, but accomplished. I noted Becky was also inching her fingers toward Caroline's bare knee, offering comfort where she thought comfort was needed. Chan stared at me, still waiting, waiting, waiting for the other shoe to drop.

"We're the same," I told him.

"No," Chan started to argue.

"You didn't know. You couldn't have known."

He replied, "It doesn't matter. I started this."

I trailed my hands along his arms and gripped his shoulders. "Caroline says it was her fault because she dated him. Rudy thought he set off Simon when he tackled Caroline. And now, you think it's yours for telling Simon something I told you. I've always, *always* known we would never have been on Bus Twenty-One if I hadn't been trying to get back at you that morning. Can't you see? This belongs to all of us."

"Go, he only gave us a head start off the bus because I told him. What does that make me? A coward and a monster—"

"Someone who wanted to survive," I supplied.

"You weren't a coward though. You wouldn't have left those people if I hadn't made you."

"Thank God you did, Chan. I'm not brave because I was frozen. And you're not a coward for wanting to live."

"But we're liars. He made us make those promises and we weren't even together. We didn't deserve—"

"Chan, Simon Westwood was a lunatic. So crazy we blocked out facts."

"We can't block out the effect. I can't swallow it whole. I choke on Simon Westwood. I choke on the moment I told him what Caroline did. I choke on *Accelerant Orange*. I choke on people supporting us. I choke on college funds and futures. I choke on watching Rudy roll through life when I know he was an athlete. He was going somewhere—"

"I'm still an athlete," Rudy said, hand raised like he was answering a question in class. "And I'm still going where I want to go. You should too, man."

Chan finally looked at Rudy with a true Chan expression instead of jealousy. "I'm glad you're great. I really am. But I can't stomach this . . . I can't stomach knowing . . ." The color drained completely from his face. "Caroline, you can't kill yourself. I can't be responsible for another death. I just can't."

Without warning, Becky, who had been mostly silent, stood in the middle of the room and locked her arms against the ceiling. "HELL NO!" she roared in a primal way, in a way that stopped all other emotions. She was the lioness of Hazzard. "Every one of you hookers look at me *now*."

I'd never been called a hooker, but I looked at Becky Cable, and the others did too. Even Chan.

"NONE OF YOU DID THIS. So good God, stop lobbying

for who gets to wear the *Blame Me More* badge."

"But—" Chan protested.

"Chandler. You. Did. Not. Do. This. Nod if you understand."

Chan didn't nod.

"Caroline. You. Did. Not. Do. This. Do I need to say your names too?" she asked Rudy and me.

No one nodded because deep down we thought we were right. Becky was outside of this. She didn't know. How could she know?

Becky spun a full three-sixty. "Oh, for fuck's sake. Raise your hand if you brought a bomb on Bus Twenty-One. Look around; no hands. You know how you become a runner? You run. Runners run. Singers sing. Players play. And bombers bomb. None of you bombed *anything*."

My heart thudded, abusing my chest.

I wanted Becky's words to be true. To put my head against a pillow and dream of hayfields and beautiful photos and kisses on silo floors. Instead, I was steel wool attached to a coat hanger; and last June I caught fire and started spinning, and everything burned.

"It's not that simple," Rudy said, trying not to patronize her.

Becky sank to the houseboat floor, her convictions framed in the set of her jaw. "It is. The parts that you've accused your-selves of playing in this tragedy are nominal. If this were a fucking movie, they'd be unnamed credits. Bathroom Girl Number One. Bathroom Girl Number Two—"

Caroline interrupted. "My role will always be Bomber's Girlfriend."

"Your role will always be . . . the role you tell yourself. So, please, dear God, tell yourself a better story, Caroline. All of you."

"Even if it's not true?" Caroline asked, and it sounded as if she was asking rather than arguing.

"This is a truth factory, sweetheart. You make tomorrow's truth on today's decision. I mean, look at Go over there. She's been telling herself one hell of a story since last June." Becky paused. "You guys, this will always be hard until you forgive yourselves."

I didn't know how to forgive myself. People said that expression—*Forgive yourself!*—as if it was a choice no harder than choosing bacon or sausage. A task that could be checked off a list. *Do my homework. Buy fresh cream for Gran. Upload a photo. Forgive myself.*

When I thought about the people I'd forgiven—Mom, Dad, Chan, even Gran for silly things—forgiveness was frequently my solution for loneliness. And that didn't feel applicable when I was the one I needed to forgive. With others, I faced the fact that someone I loved hurt me and lived with it or I dealt with the incredible displeasure of doing life apart from them. I never had the patience to wait very long before I was "It's no big deal," and "I still love you," all over the place. With myself, I'd compartmentalized.

"I think," I whispered, "I've been telling the wrong story for a long time."

Becky got in my face, placed a wayward curl behind my ear. "Jennings, tell me the right one."

"I don't know what it is."

"You do."

She wasn't yelling the way Simon had. She was love in a voice.

"I don't."

"You do."

I sighed. "I can't."

"There's the lie." Becky tapped the lobe of her ear. "Whisper it to me."

I leaned back on my heels and searched Becky's face. She was a skyscraper. Strong and gleaming. My inner voice said, *Tell her,* and my warring inner voice said, *Telling will change everything.* And that was usually when I shoved the voices into my toes. I had so many voices shoved in my toes—*Tell your mom you love her; Gran will love you without the photo; tell Chan you want to leave the Hive*—they didn't fit inside me anymore. I placed my cheek against Becky's and my lips to her ears. "I'm tired of being strong."

She put her hand around the back of my head, wove her fingers into my hair, and pressed me to her chest like I was a child. "Say more."

"If I fall apart, no one will be okay."

"I'll be okay," she said. Her heart was steady. "I've got room for your sloppy hurt."

"You do?"

"I've got mansions of rooms. Jennings, you're so strong everyone says, 'She's Luke fucking Skystalker,' and then you hand-select the people and places where you choose to fall apart. That's the secret. You get to be both strong and weak with the right people."

You can be vain about the way you look on the outside. I'd been vain about the way I looked on the inside. I didn't know if there was a term for that. Pride? Arrogance? Whatever it was, I needed somewhere my naked broken heart was worthy without dressing it in pretty bobbles and fancy clothes.

"I choose here," I said.

And for the first time since the explosion, I started to cry. Hard. I didn't hide my face. I didn't act like this was a passing event in my life. I let myself hurt everywhere.

It was an ugly, ugly hurt.

And I let them all see me.

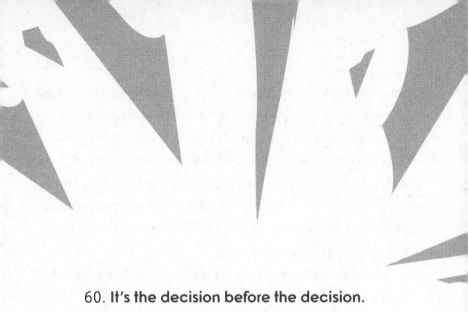

60. It's the decision before the decision.

$99,000.00

I was a puddle on the galley floor. Everyone had moved closer. I grabbed pant legs and ankles as I cried. They bent over me, their auras like a dome. I felt selfish for being in the middle, for having this moment when I was worried about Caroline and Chan, but it was magical too. Like I'd taken a cold shower after mowing the yard all day.

When I was upright and less of a fountain, Rudy asked me a question. "Were you able to forgive yourself?"

"I don't know. I was able to just be me in this moment. Is that the same thing?"

No one had an answer. Rudy said, "I think we should forgive each other—that would go a long way to helping us all

face tomorrow's story. If you guys can't, that's okay. But, you know, I think I need to say the words." He straightened his back and took a deep breath. "Chandler, I don't think you did this, and I forgive you for telling Simon. And Caroline," he said, "I forgive you and I love you. I wish I had a million legs so you could see me lose them over and over again to save you. That's how much you're worth. That and so much more. I need you to never pick up a gun again."

Tears spilled down Caroline's cheeks. "Will you forgive me for staying with Simon?"

"Of course," he said.

Caroline squeezed Becky's hand. "I'm sorry I scared you. I know I need help."

"You'll get it," said Becky, as she kissed the top of Caroline's head and then Rudy's.

It felt like my turn. "Chan, I forgive you for telling Simon. Will you forgive me for accepting Rudy's invitation to see the city? For treating our relationship without reverence? For not telling you my real thoughts because I didn't think you were strong enough to hear them?"

Chan wrapped his arms around me. The blood in his heart rushed against my temple. He squeezed me tighter than he had in months. And only then could I tell the gap between us had been filled with our hidden shame.

"You're my best friend. I should have told you everything," he said. "And Caroline, your relationship was your business. I

had no right to interfere. Rudy, man, I've been a dick because the girl I love loves you, but what you did, what Caroline said you did, makes you a hero."

Rudy held his fist out to Chan. They bumped knuckles.

I snatched the closest hands—Becky's and Chan's—which felt warm and safe. Sacred even. I remembered Gran telling me once, "Go, sometimes it's not the decision itself that changes you. It's the decision before the decision. The scaffolding you assemble to build the building." Maybe forgiveness was the scaffolding of wholeness, and from here, we'd build something real.

Most photographers took photos of runners at the end of marathons. We all wanted to capture the grit of the finish, the sweat of true accomplishment, the collapse of a body pushed to the edge, the medal hung around the neck that has strained against odds. But that philosophy lacked vision.

The beginning, the decision to train, was the mettle and steel of a soul who finished a race.

And there, on that houseboat, we began.

CAROLINE

I carry my shaving kit into the tiny houseboat bathroom. I plug the razor in the outlet as Becky turns the door handle and slips inside. Her arms come around my waist; her chin rests on my shoulder. I watch us in the mirror. There are three loves in the room when there should be four. I love Becky and Becky loves me, and Becky also loves herself. I don't hate myself today the way I hated myself yesterday, but I lift the razor closer to my widow's peak and turn the dial that controls the speed.

She holds my wrist so gently. "Why do you do that?"

"You know why," I say.

"I know why it was done to you. I don't know why you do it to yourself."

"It's a reminder of who I am."

"You don't know who you are yet."

I turn off the razor. The absence of sound makes the room hollow. We have to be on the road very soon, but Becky seems unconcerned with time.

"Tell me what you wish you could have more than anything in the world," she says.

There is no pause. I say, "I want to feel"—and then the pause comes and I fill it with a single word—"clean."

Becky turns on the shower and I protest. But when the water is warm, Becky steps over the lip in her socks and clothes and perfectly shaped eyeliner and ultra-long mascara that makes her eyes big as a giraffe's. She says, "This is your chance." The water pounds and splashes off her back and rolls onto her arm and into my hand because she is touching me. "Come on. All of life is one step at a time."

We are in the shower. I cry and we drink the shower when we kiss. Her mouth is warm, like Aunt Linda's sunroom in the early morning. In that kiss, I smell the orange groves coming alive in April and feel the slow rolling of the earth toward another day. In that kiss, I imagine throwing a piece of freshly popped popcorn into the air and Becky Cable catching it on her tongue. And for the first time, I am living a day I want to live.

"Can I ask you something?" I say, when we are drenched to the roots and all kissed out.

"Anything."

"No matter what. Don't let go of my hand on Ellis Island."

61. This doesn't have a title yet.

$99,321.00

There were only four hours between falling asleep and our alarms. I heard Rudy and Chan scribbling—one words, one images—long after I turned out the light.

I probably would have busted my ass in the shower if not for Becky. She was peeing on the other side of the curtain, and said, "You almost done in there?" That's when I realized I was napping on my feet with a bar of soap in my hand.

When I was more awake and packed, Chan, Rudy, and I left the girls on Hazzard. The still-dark morning of West Virginia greeted us with brisk, northern air. Chan carried Rudy over the gap, and we fixed a camp breakfast on the tailgate. Flynn

and his dad, Mr. Grimes, stopped by on their way to church.

"Y'all make it through the night okay?" Mr. Grimes asked.

I glanced sideways at the guys. Their eyes were wide. "Yes, sir," I said, like we'd had the most normal night in the world.

Mr. Grimes toed the ground. "My apologies if the armory made you uncomfortable. I told Flynn last night we probably should've moved 'em for you."

"We put a couch in front of the door," I told him.

"Your dad told me you could handle yourself. I see he was right." He and Flynn climbed back into their Jeep. "You're welcome anytime at Eight Echoes," he said. Flynn waved goodbye and they drove off.

"Sometimes weird people are more normal than you'd think," Rudy said.

"You can say that again," Chan said.

The girls appeared, still wet from a shower, and we offered them Mom's biscuits. Everyone listened to Miss Hazzard lap gently against the dock.

"It's going to be a nice day," Rudy said, stretching in his chair.

Whether that was optimism or prediction, I didn't know, but I smiled. And I hoped.

Without ceremony, we tossed everything into the back of the truck and rock-paper-scissored for driver. Becky took the wheel, even though paper covered rock and driving technically fell to me. She had the cab toasty and our playlist music

cranked and it would have been a fine time if we weren't so tightly wound.

Before we'd fallen asleep last night, Becky had taken a vote for *Accelerant Orange*. Unanimous to attend. That was the only thing on our minds today, and there was very little to say that hadn't already been said.

We crossed into Pennsylvania in no time. Sunrise exploded pink and orange along I-81, and I thought of Carter. Was he unloading last-minute artifacts, driving toward the Green-Conwell with the bus in a trailer? Or was everything set up already? Were the Westwoods there somewhere, waiting in a sequestered room for me to arrive? Hoping no one identified who they were on the way in? Was today the day I disappointed the people who had given nearly a hundred thousand dollars by fainting in front of the bus?

Around Allentown, Rudy dialed the radio to a hum and asked if he could read what he'd written during the night. There was a chorus of nods. "This doesn't have a title yet."

He cleared his throat and read.

"Terrorism isn't a bomb; terrorism is being afraid there will always be a bomb.

"I know terror.

"I do not know the white-hot rage of revenge that lines a vest with dynamite and screws and nails. I cannot imagine standing in front of a man, any man, and zipping a death shirt from waist to Adam's apple like a mother puts a coat on a child in the morning before school. I will never know the explosions

that occur in a bomber's brain before he acts. I cannot fathom pressing a trigger to cause the end of the world.

"For these things, I am thankful. I would rather die thousands of times than be one who kills senselessly.

"Pain isn't a bomb; pain is being afraid no one understands your pain.

"I know pain. I'm intimately acquainted with the loneliness of believing I am the only one who understands pain like mine.

"Blame isn't a bomb; blame is a single arrow I shoot at myself.

"I know blame.

"Fear isn't a bomb; fear is a friend I greet every morning like a spouse on the other side of my bed.

"I know fear. Fear reminds me that the world takes what it wants, and it probably wants me. Fear whispers, *Today could be your last day.* Fear is my tattoo, the one on my face, the one strangers see at first glance and think, *My God, boy, what happened to you?*

"There were days I wanted to be done with terror, pain, blame, and fear. I planned to kill the bad emotions like they were monsters. But it's hard to kill the monster that lives inside you.

"Today, I'm exorcising the monster.

"There is no way to know in advance if I have the strength. I won't know until I touch Bus Twenty-One and look at my friends and say, 'I'm ready.' I won't know until I allow them to

lift my chair onto the very bus that stole my legs. But if a man can be ready to be ready, I am that man."

He dropped the laptop into his backpack and laughed a little, the way honest people often do when delivering truth.

"You're going to be a journalist," I said.

"I'm going to be a journalist," he repeated.

62. Two hands on the wheel

$99,800.00

From Interstate 78 we took the New Jersey Turnpike and figured out we were near the Statue of Liberty and Ellis Island. According to the signs, the two islands were on our right, beyond Liberty State Park.

"I'm not looking," I told them, and shut my eyes like it was the day before Christmas and I didn't want to see my gifts yet. No one else looked either. Becky informed the group there was nothing to see except concrete and trees and power lines. We were close, not that close. Sunday traffic ran heavy. I was in the front passenger seat, noting the easy way Becky wove through multiple lanes. I pictured her living in a big city like New York, using her MetroCard and talking on her phone,

getting groceries from a market and running in Central Park.

"Could you live here?" I asked as we entered the Lincoln Tunnel.

"Couldn't you?" she said. "*Roomies*. We could do our own Kentucky version of *Girls*. HBO would pick up that series for sure. Can't you see it? Golden Jennings, struggling photographer. And Becky Cable, struggling . . . tennis player."

"More like advice columnist Becky Cable becomes next Oprah. Rudy will run your magazine for you."

"If you guys move here, I'm coming too," Caroline said from the back.

I was relieved to hear her mention the future in a positive light.

"For sure. Rent-split, baby."

I laughed at this fantasy future. "Gosh, what would your mom say if she knew you were driving into New York City today?"

"*Becky*, two hands on the wheel. You're in traffic, for God's sake."

Everyone laughed, because Becky was capable of many things, but driving with two hands wasn't one of them. Her route took us around Times Square and into the heart of Midtown. We approached the final turns to the Green-Conwell and everything slowed except Becky's voice. "I'll let you all out and then look for somewhere to park the tank."

The Green-Conwell, now in sight, hadn't changed. Two flags flew above the awning. The concrete was the color of

wet sand. The gold lettering sparkled in the noon sun. People crowded the sidewalks, and everywhere there was a buzz. My heart started its somersaults. Becky eased to the curb and put on her hazard lights.

A doorman lumbered forward and opened my door. Chan grabbed Rudy's wheelchair before the smartly dressed man could properly assist us. "Here for the art show?" he asked. We were no one to him.

"Yes," Caroline said.

"Cross all the way through the lobby. It's on the opposite street. Cops have got everything blocked off. You'll see the setup. Can't miss it. Oh, yeah, there's a bank of iPads by the front desk if you need tickets or want to donate to the scholarship fund."

I hesitated, finding it strange to hear about the scholarship fund from someone else. What would this man say if he knew we were the recipients? Would he ask me where I was going to college? Would I smirk and say, "Emerson?" And what if I did? Would this dapper New Yorker watch me standing before the bus, knees knocking, and think, *Don't give that kid another cent*? Is that what the lady in the red hat under the flag or the man in the black sweater with the newspaper tucked under his arm or the kid carrying the teacup poodle or the woman using a cane and balancing a bag of fruit would think? I didn't want to fail, but I also wasn't sure I could try. *You're already trying*, my inner voice said. My inner voice now sounded a lot like Becky Cable.

Chan briefly put his fingers on the small of my back. "Come on, Go."

Caroline pressed a few folded dollars into the doorman's hand, and we entered the rotating door one at a time. It was 11:24. Thirty-six minutes to connect with Carter and the Westwoods, or change our minds. Chan asked the concierge where we might find something that had been left for us, and we were directed to the front desk. I did my best to stay on Chan's six, but the lobby was packed and spilling over. People stepped on my toes and bumped my shoulders. They were all moving in a wave toward the opposite doors. I felt like a child in the mall at Christmastime.

Beside me, Rudy stopped and texted Carter.

"We're supposed to meet him"—Rudy searched for some unknown marker and finally pointed at the wall opposite the concierge—"over there. Near that fireplace. He's going to introduce Go to the Westwoods and then escort us outside."

Chan curled his fist as if he wanted to squeeze something to death. He touched an orange in a glass bowl—I assumed to see if it were real or fake—and then said, "Golden, I have a confession." I braced for Chan to say he wasn't getting on the bus. That he'd come this far, and yes, we'd had a moment on the boat last night, but he'd meet us at Ellis Island. Or he was forbidding me to see the Westwoods. Instead, he said, "I left your dad that money you gave me. I told them to use it toward buying tickets."

That was the only warning I had before I heard my mother's voice behind me. "Oh, there they are, Pete."

I turned slowly to face them. There they were: Pete and Beth Jennings. And . . . there was my gran, bent but spry, guided by the strong arm of my father and her sturdy cane.

"You're here," I said, aware it was an idiotic proclamation because I was already holding her hand and kissing her cheek. She drummed two fingers against a small gold pin clinging to the fabric of her cardigan. Brass wings.

"God wanted me to fly," she said with a wink.

I kissed her again, hardly believing that we were all in New York together. And that Chan had worked to get my family here. They didn't even like driving to Nashville, and yet they'd traveled to the city that never sleeps.

"But the money?" I said.

"The Hive covered the rest. Everyone understands."

Chan shook my father's hand and asked, "How was your flight?"

"Probably better than your drive," Dad answered. "How were the Grimeses?"

"They were *the Grimeses*," I said in a way that meant I'd tell them the full story later.

"This was a much better trip because we weren't heading to a hospital," my mother remarked, eyes tilted to the ornate ceiling, wonder shining. They looked out of place and perfectly in place, like tadpoles in a pond after they've sprung legs.

"Thank you for coming," I said, and I put my whole self into the words. Then, just for my mother, I said, "I love you, Mom."

"I love you too, baby."

That *baby* was a balm.

I was about to say as much when Rudy squeezed my arm. A tall woman in a very lovely black dress set a course for us.

"Go, that's Ms. Jay."

I'd always figured Ms. Jay would be old. This woman was athletic and in her thirties. A bombshell. Every line of her body suggested she wasn't to be messed with, but her eyes were kind and warm, and I liked her on sight.

They greeted each other with affection. "Victor and Jane wanted to be here, but flights, and Deuce," she said.

Rudy introduced us and we shook hands like strangers.

"It's very nice to meet you," I said to Ms. Jay.

She was fed up with shaking. She swept me against her side with no warning. "The pleasure is all mine. I've been trying to convince Rudy for months that when this show opened he ought to be here. He was resistant, as you can imagine. But it's better to see him here with all of you. What triumphs you are."

"I hope so," I said.

"Bus or no bus, you are triumphs."

Rudy nodded in Ms. Jay's direction. "See why I love her?"

I did. Meeting the people of someone you cared about was like meeting a new part of that person. Feeling that way gave

me a sliver of clarity about Rudy. Chan wasn't wrong in what he'd said last night. I felt love for Rudy. Improbably. Ironically. Love doesn't adhere to neat timetables or fairness. It comes into the world of its own accord and makes up its mind like a stubborn toddler.

I wasn't sure I could ever love anyone the way I loved Chan. He owned what would probably amount to a fifth of my life, and not just any fifth—the first fifth. I couldn't unlove him, and I didn't ever, ever want to. And . . . I'd never been more proud of who Chan was than last night. After all this time, he still surprised me.

The Chan of the coming year would be different from the Chan of last year, and I would love that Chan even more. I had no idea what would happen to us long-term—there was Rudy to consider—and I was not ready to predetermine my whole life. Life on the Hive was the definition of predetermination. If I stayed there, I could tell you precisely what I'd be doing twenty-five years from now on a Tuesday because Tuesdays were garbage days. And Saturdays were chores. And on Friday nights we made popcorn after homemade pizza. All the photos had already been taken. Chan and I had outgrown what we could become there, and I could no more ask him to leave than he could ask me to stay.

After Ellis Island, I would tell Chan and my family I wanted to apply to Emerson. And after that, I would traipse out into the great, wide world and then look to my left and right and see

who was beside me. I had a feeling there'd be a bandit nearby. And maybe a cowboy.

Whirling back to Rudy, I said, "I can't believe we're all in New York."

"I see Stock," he said in return.

It was eleven forty-five.

63. You'll be surprised by the things that survived.

$105,230.00

Carter Stockton hadn't changed. The man who put me on the gurney, who I'd watched in videos, didn't move like an artist. Artists had man-bun topknots or dreads and hippie clothes. The newest thing on Stock was a pair of boots he'd had for twenty years. He was sweating at the temples and through the armpits of his plain blue T-shirt. People greeted him as they passed. When he caught Rudy's eyes, he gave us a shy wave. Beside me, Gran cooed.

"That's the Westwoods," Caroline said. "Short, dumpy man in an overcoat and ball cap. Short woman in a beige pant-suit. Under the big clock."

They were near Carter, but not next to him where they

might be noticed. The man stared at his toes. The woman dug through her purse.

"You sure about this?" she asked.

"No," I said. "But I'm going anyway."

Rudy went first, like a buffer. Chan and me behind. Caroline lagged back with my family and Ms. Jay. The tempo of the room beat harder, faster. We walked straight to Carter.

There was a moment where we didn't know how to greet each other and the actions that followed didn't make sense. Hands went into pockets as other hands stretched out. *Hi* and *hello* and *nice to, uh, yeah*. Nothing worked until Stock said, "Thanks for coming all this way. I know it wasn't easy." The Westwoods inched closer to our circle. Stock added, "For any of you."

They kept their heads down. Mrs. Westwood had black mascara tear trails down her cheeks. Mr. Westwood held one hand over his mouth, like he was trying to keep his emotions where he could control them.

There was no response except a million unasked questions.

I tried to eyeball Mrs. Westwood. "I'm Golden Jennings," I said, hoping she might take it from there.

"Carter?" she said, helplessly.

"Just give her the envelope. Start there," Stock said.

Mrs. Westwood removed a white, business-size, unsealed envelope from her purse and handed it to me. I shook a black-and-white photo from inside. I recognized the unique grain—a No. 3 Kodak—and then the subject. I gasped. I snapped this

photo on June 14 at Down Yonder. I'd taken three or four shots, pleased with the lighting and shadows made by the neon signs behind the bar. In my hand was the third photo from that night: a young man holding a chicken leg in each hand, grinning as he decided which to eat first. Simon Westwood.

"Where did you get this?"

Mrs. Westwood tilted her head at Carter.

"But . . . how?" I meant the question for Stock, but Mr. Westwood spoke first.

"We wanted . . . we wanted to apologize to you." He spoke through his clenched and trembling fist, each word labored. "This boy in the photograph. Our son. He hurt so many people. We should've seen, but we were too busy. Too selfish to notice." He gasped; the words crumbled like limestone. "Stock gave us this photo you took—"

"I don't under—"

"And the photo was a wake-up call. Far too late to stop Simon and change Bus Twenty-One, but early enough to help others. We're doubling the scholarship fund, whatever it is, and we're going to help other troubled young men. Because"—he touched the photo—"what if he'd been this? Instead of a boy with a bomb. An apology is worth shit if you can't back it up, but change, well, someday it might save lives."

I could do little more than nod. I hoped they understood why. They walked away holding on to each other, and I wished them well. I didn't know if their plan would help others, but I thought it might help them.

Carter touched my shoulder. "That was brave of you to meet them."

"Where did you get the photo?"

"I've got your camera on the bus. I had it repaired months ago. Hope you don't mind."

"The Kodak survived?"

"You'll be surprised by the things that survived. The Kodak took a real beating. I didn't know it was yours until the other day when Rudy mentioned it. You'll recognize your photos out there. I would have gotten permission if I'd known."

"You have it."

The crowds were pressing in tighter around us. Carter checked his watch, which made everyone check his or her phone: 11:57. "We should go," he said.

Chan extended his hand, stopped Carter with a touch. That's when I realized he had his sketchbook out. "You might want these. For the display."

Stock opened the book, flipped through the tabbed pages with awe. Nearly every person on the bus, captured by his memories.

"You can do whatever you want with them," Chan said. "The other families donated stuff. This is from our family. The survivors." He nodded at the circle of us.

64. I didn't expect flowers.

$137,993.00

I expected the bus to blind me. I expected Becky to come running, yelling, "Gird your loins, hookers." I expected my parents to squirm and shift and to feel their discomfort from three yards away. I expected my nose to bleed.

I expected flashbulbs, extended microphones, clipboards, recorders in outstretched hands. I expected "Tell us how it feels to be back in the city," from the reporters and camera crews and boom mics. I expected to feel the pressure of nearly $138,000 dollars of support.

I didn't expect flowers.

Carter Stockton's progress on Bus #21 ended a month ago on the video series. I understood why. He'd turned every

exterior surface of the bus into planters. Tiny orange flowers covered the burned hull and remade it into something recognizable yet new. It was afire again, this time with life.

"Can you describe what you're feeling?" a reporter asked. He'd clearly been briefed on who we were. His attention generated more attention. Slowly, the media became aware of the four survivors standing on the sidewalk and flocked toward us.

The gathered mass was in the way of Rudy's wheelchair. He waved them off without speaking. Someone thrust a mic in his face. "What do you call yourselves? How do you feel? What will you do with the scholarship money?"

My dad bellowed, "Back up! Give these kids some room," as a policewoman blew her whistle. "You heard what he said. Back up!" he yelled.

The crowd parted. Silence rippled away, from those closest to us to the back of the crowd. I shielded my eyes from the camera flashes and slunk closer to Chan. There must have been five thousand people on the blocked-off street, all cheering at the sight of us. I felt their reverence. A little girl with a Pokémon backpack and bright yellow wellies raised her hand and grinned. I slapped her five. She looked at her mom with delight.

Rudy stopped rolling.

The four of us stood side by side, Charter Bus #21 directly ahead. Police officers flanked each side, making a perimeter of blue. The flashes increased. Someone in the middle of the crowd began to clap. The horde gathered themselves into a

perfect rhythm, their hands a steady heartbeat. The shadow of the bus fell on the sidewalk. We stood in the light, and I didn't know what would happen when we took the first step toward darkness.

Not far away, Carter raised a hand to silence the crowd, and even the horns and whistles and traffic on adjacent streets seemed to obey his command for a second. He tapped the microphone, sharing the small platform space with the mayor of New York City. Their voices were hollow, like they'd been the day of the bombing. From a long way away, I heard him talking, thanking people for attending, thanking them for giving so generously of their time and money.

"We're going to read the names of those we lost on June fifteenth and offer sixty seconds of silence to remember them."

Caroline took my hand. Together, with Carter Stockton, we said the names.

"Anthony Alvarez, Mason Armstrong, Riley Best, Jim Conner, Evelyn Farrow, Sara Hillstead, Neil Johnson, Tim Kraggen, Brandy Marshall, Risha Novell, Johnny Popplewell, Roger Pritchet, Wesley 'Dozer' Reston, Oscar Reyes, Tomas Sanchez, William Tackett, Alicia Voyse, Ethan Watchmaker, and Thomas Wiggington."

The crowd hardly blinked. Sixty seconds passed on the street.

Carter spoke again. "There are four other names we honor today. Four teens whose lives were touched by violence on June fifteenth. Caroline Ascott. Chandler Clayton. Rudy Guthrie.

Golden Jennings. Today is a brand-new day for Bus Twenty-One, and we pray it's a brand-new day for you."

The applause was extraordinary. I couldn't hear anything but the pounding of hands until Chan's lips found my ears. "You were right. We were supposed to be here."

Carter wrapped with an explanation. He would escort us on first and then the exhibit would open. A trickle of blood rolled onto my lip. Chan wiped it away with his thumb. "Thank you for coming with me," I said.

I pulled two beanies from my shoulder bag and shoved one over my head. "These things have enough lives to survive the apocalypse." I handed the other to Chan.

With false bluster, Rudy smacked Chan's arm and said, "Suit up, Clayton," and tapped his beanie.

I wiped my nose again.

Chan took off his hat, handed it to my dad, donned a beanie. We were all wearing them then.

Rudy said to Chan, "I'll go first if you'll help."

From the crowd we heard, "Get out of my way. Hey, excuse me. I need to be with them."

"Becky!" Caroline said as Becky bumped a reporter.

"I'll get this side. You get the other," she told Chan, and gripped the wheels of Rudy's chair. Becky wasn't a muscleman, but I heard her adrenaline pumping three feet away.

Chan did what she asked, and in a blink Rudy was on the bus. He'd done it, his face sheet-white and victorious. "You're coming with me," he said. The crowd would have thought he

said it to them, but he looked at me and mouthed, "Bandit."

"Okay, Care, your turn," Becky coaxed.

Caroline climbed the first step, and then the second and third. Success. She disappeared behind the glass after kissing Becky on the cheek, very near the lips.

There were four of us. There were three of us. There were two of us. I was the only one left on the sidewalk.

Chan stood at the top step, waiting. I looked beyond him. What if I'd come all this way and couldn't move?

Becky buzzed around Chan and said, "Vader your frickin' heart out, Jennings."

Becky. Always being Becky. "I'm ready to be ready," I told her, but I didn't move.

Chan said, "I know the way home." He pointed toward the inside of *Accelerant Orange*. "You can do this."

Becky and Chan put their hands out to me at the same time.

I checked over my shoulder. My parents stood with Gran. My mother cried. My father beamed. If I wanted, I could fall into their arms and they'd whisk me away saying, "Nothing will ever hurt you." That was a beautiful lie. My gran mouthed, "Ellis Island, baby," and I stretched out my arms and took Chan's and Becky's hands.

CAROLINE

Becky held my hand all day. The only time she let go was when I asked if I could have my purple headband back. She laughed and put it around my neck.

"That thing will clash with red hair," she told me.

I told her, "We'll have to see about that."

Golden Jennings
Mr. Cullivan
ENG 1001
September 14, 2020

From Here to There

John William Jennings came through Ellis Island on June 16, 1907. His great-great-great granddaughter, Golden, followed in his footsteps on April 15, 2018.

It was a glorious spring Sunday in New York City, a great day for sightseeing with family and friends. Golden was fortunate enough to have both at her side.

People who witnessed Go that day said she held a No. 3 Kodak and captured freedom through an antique lens. But Go said she'd captured freedom earlier that day. At high noon. On a curb. Outside the Green-Conwell Hotel. With the world watching.

Maybe you were there too. Maybe you cheered. Maybe you donated. Maybe you loved. But if you didn't, you should know this: Her name was Golden Alistair Jennings, but everyone called her Go. She came not from England or Ireland, nor by ship.

She came by bus.

ACKNOWLEDGMENTS

To my publishing trifecta: Kelly Sonnack, Rosemary Brosnan, and Alyssa Miele, my deepest thanks for listening, loving, and growing me as an author and human. And to the entire team at HarperTeen, I'm incredibly grateful. Hats off to Yuschav Arly for cover art and Erin Fitzsimmons for design.

Patricia Riley, Erica Rodgers, Kristin Tubb, Mary Weber—from the kitchen table to Voxer to countless emails and phone calls, this one came together bird by bird and love by love. You held up my arms. Exodus 17:12.

Maggie Stiefvater, Sarah Batista-Pereira, Brenna Yovanoff—you gave hours and hours of brainstorming, reading, and encouragement. Maggie, you set up the rhythm for page one and gave me a title. Both made a huge difference. There aren't enough thanks for how you all have shaped me.

David Arnold and Ruta Sepetys—I can't navigate this world without you. Thank you for reading and always offering insight.

Thanks should also be extended to this marvelous lot of folks: Shaun and Bridget Chambers; Ed Stiefvater; my whole Nashville Taco crew (Lauren, Ashley, Alisha, etc.) for the constant queso, love, and support; Gwenda Bond, Megan Shepherd, Carrie Ryan; Batcave 2015; S. R. Johannes; J. T. Ellison; Paige Crutcher; Myra McEntire; Katie Cotugno; Kim Liggitt; Kate Dopirak, Stephanie Appell, Niki Coffman, Parnassus Books; Andrew Hummel; Home Church Nashville; Maura Buckley; and Katie Corbin.

Mom, Dad, Matt, Carla, Christa, and my whole wonderful family—I love you so much.

To the readers, you will always be my better half.